Soft Feather

by

Richard James Dussart Regnier

Cover Design by

Chris Hieb

**Authors' Publishing House
Midland, Texas**

Copyright (©) 2008 by Richard James Dussart Regnier. All rights reserved. Printed in the United States of America. No part of this book may be used or reproduced in any manner, whatsoever, without written permission from the author or publisher, except in the case of brief quotations embodied in critical articles and reviews.

ISBN: 0-9799297-6-8   (ISBN – 10)
ISBN: 978-0-9799297-6-2   (ISBN – 13)

For more information, contact:

> Authors' Publishing House
> 2908 Shanks Drive
> Midland, Texas 79705

Or visit our website at:

www.authorspublishinghouse.com

to contact the author, please visit his website at:

dussartworkshop.com

Dedication

This book is dedicated in loving memory

Of my mother, Iris Ruby

and

My mother-in-law, Norabel Mercer

About The Author

Richard James Dussart Regnier, a coal miner's son, was raised in a small town in Colorado. He is a veteran of World War II and Vietnam, with fifteen years of military service.

He has a bachelor's degree from Southwest Texas State University, and a master's degree from Sul Ross State University, both in education.

Mr. Regnier is a retired schoolteacher and probation officer. He spends his retirement time as an author, artist and a poet.

Soft Feather

CHAPTER 1

Jimmy stood in a vacant lot in downtown Mercer, Colorado waiting for Joe Crow. Joe started a fight earlier with him on the school grounds during recess and challenged him to meet him downtown after school to finish the fight.

Joe didn't show and Jimmy was about to leave when he heard a lot of yelling. It was Joe and his buddies. They saw Jimmy and yelled and laughed as they ran towards him. Joe stopped in front of him and took off his shirt. He threw it to his buddy, Elmer, and flexed his muscles.

Jimmy unbuttoned his top button then stopped. He wasn't going to do what Joe did.

Joe stepped up, grabbed the front of his shirt with both hands and tore it open. Two buttons flew off. It surprised Jimmy and made him mad. He took his shirt off and threw it to one side.

Joe laughed as he danced around Jimmy and said, "Where's your muscles skinny boy? I've seen girls with more muscles." Then, without warning he ran at him, swinging both fists.

Jimmy put his hands up to protect himself from the blows. Joe stopped and kicked him in the shin.

Jimmy dropped his guard and Joe hit him in the mouth splitting his lower lip. It bled a little.

"That's the way, Joe!" his buddies yelled.

Jimmy sized Joe up as he limped around him. Joe smiled as they slowly circled.

Again Joe ran at Jimmy, but Jimmy sidestepped to the left. A left-hand punch found its mark and Joe's nose bled.

Joe yelled and ran at him again, but Jimmy stepped to the right and swung at him, hitting him in the nose. Blood now ran from their noses and dripped off their chins.

Soft Feather

Jimmy pulled out his handkerchief and held it up to his nose and the blood stopped.

Joe didn't have one and looked over at his buddies. Earnest pulled out his handkerchief and gave it to him.

Mr. Armstead was the only barber in town. He sat in his barber chair looking out his side window, watching the fight for some time. "Just like two fighting roosters strutting their stuff," he thought. No one got hurt much and he knew that when the boys tired they would quit and say they won. So, he just sat and smiled at the boxing match that turned into a waltz now and then.

He laughed as he watched the two boys circle round and round each other then go at it. Suddenly, they were going at it and both of them had bloody noses. "I guess they could use a little help," he thought. He got up and went over and opened a drawer. He got some cotton balls and hurried out the door. He handed Jimmy two cotton balls, then went over and gave two to Joe. "Anything to keep the fight going," he thought. This was the most excitement around his shop since the carnival came to town the 4th of July. Besides, the boys were just working off some bad energy.

He hurried off as each boy stuffed the cotton balls up the side of their noses.

They began the circle dance again, with a lot of swinging, and this time Jimmy punched Joe and he struck him back. They exchanged blows several times. Then, Jimmy hit him on the side of his head, knocking him to the ground.

"I'll get you for that!" Joe yelled at Jimmy, getting up and brushing off his clothes.

Jimmy waited until Joe was ready then round and round they went, glaring at each other.

Jimmy's thoughts turned to the morning at school when Joe said that his dad was a drunk and his mother

Soft Feather

didn't want him. It still burned inside of him and he got madder and madder. Finally he let out a whoop and ran at Joe, fists flying.

Mr. Armstead sat straight up. He could see that the taller boy got mad. He felt it from where he sat. He jumped up and headed out the door on the run.

Joe was surprised and went down under the blows. Jimmy jumped on top of him and pounded him with both fists.

He tried to protect himself but couldn't. Blow after blow found its mark. One smashed into Joe's right eye and he fell to the ground again. He rolled over and put his arm up to protect his face. This was not the way he planned for it to end.

"Get up kid and beat him up," someone yelled.

Joe was about ready to give up and tell Jimmy he won.

Mr. Armstead ran up beside them. One at a time he grabbed them by their hair and pulled them up.

"Fun is fun, but this has gone too far," he said, holding them apart.

"Why are you fighting?" he asked, as he turned them loose. They didn't answer.

Joe swung at Jimmy, but missed. He took a couple steps backwards then stopped. He wanted to make sure Jimmy couldn't hit him again.

The crowd broke up and walked off. "That turned out to be a good fight," someone said, and others agreed. There were a couple that grumbled as they walked off. "The last five minutes were the best."

Others talked about different things that happened and they agreed it was a good fight.

Mr. Armstead walked back to his shop, sat down again and watched the crowd leave.

Soft Feather

Joe walked over to where his friends waited and Elmer handed him his shirt. They gathered around him and patted him on the back telling him he won. He thought about what they said, then smiled. "Yeah," he said, squinting out of his swelling right eye. "Yeah, I did."

He swaggered down the street with all of his friends, laughing and bragging about how he took care of the troublemaker.

He glanced back at Jimmy, making sure he didn't follow him.

Jimmy pulled the cotton balls out of his nose. It didn't bleed, so he threw them in the ash pit behind the barbershop.

He picked up his shirt and put it on. Turning, he searched the ground for his shirt buttons. He found them and put them in his pocket. He buttoned up his shirt with the remaining buttons, as he walked by himself. He didn't have many friends his age in the small town of Mercer, Colorado.

There was Mary Wilson, who trained hawks with him. She was a close friend. So was Don Nix, but that was it.

Then he remembered he made friends with Ted Simmons and Henry Bramlett a couple days ago. But their friendship just started. He spotted Henry and Ted standing on the sidewalk. They gave him a 'thumbs up' and a grin. They turned and headed across the street and went into the drug store.

Jimmy looked longingly as he saw them sit down at the soda fountain for a soft drink. He could almost taste their cold drinks.

He looked down at the ground and thought about what happened. He kicked a small rock out into the street and walked towards home. Sad thoughts filled his mind. He

Soft Feather

shook his head as he walked along. "Most of the kids in town didn't act like they cared about him," he thought.

Sure, some of the older people told him how proud they were of him and his hawks, but that was before he had to give his hawks away.

He didn't come up through the grades with the other kids; so, no one at school knew much about him, not even the teachers. He stopped and looked at the stores across the street. Maybe Joe and his crowd were right. No one wanted Indians around here.

Mr. Armstead shook his head as he realized that those who watched the fight now ignored Jimmy.

He walked over to Jimmy and stuck out his hand. "I'm Bob Armstead. I own the barber shop right behind you," he said. "How would you like to come inside and let me take care of those cuts and bruises on your face?"

Jimmy turned and looked at him for a moment. "Thank you," he replied. "I'm Jimmy Warrior. My grandpa is Tom Warrior."

"Oh, yes," Mr. Armstead said, smiling. "I know your grandpa real well. So you're Tom's grandson. Glad to meet you, Jimmy. How come I never see you in my barber shop?"

He opened the door to his shop, and they walked inside. He closed the door and motioned for Jimmy to sit in the first chair. Jimmy got into the chair and sat and looked at him.

"I don't have enough money to pay for a haircut, Mr. Armstead," he said. "My grandma cuts my hair. She's real good at it. I like the way she cuts it. I wouldn't let...." He stopped and looked at Mr. Armstead.

"I agree, Jimmy," he said. "It looks like your grandma does a real good job cutting your hair. I couldn't do any better myself." He stopped and looked at Jimmy's

Soft Feather

face for a second. He turned the chair one way, then the other.

He turned around and grabbed a bottle off the shelf in front of him. He reached down and picked up one of the clean towels.

"This might burn a little, Jimmy," he said, "but the way you handled yourself out there, I think you can take it."

He poured some of the liquid onto the towel and wiped Jimmy's face. If Mr. Armstead hadn't said what he did, Jimmy would have yelled. But instead, he gritted his teeth and moaned a little.

Mr. Armstead grinned, knowing it hurt. "This young Indian boy is more of a man than a lot of people around here," he thought.

It took some work, but finally Jimmy was cleaned up. He looked much better, but there was no way he could make it look like he hadn't been in a fight. "There you are, Jimmy," his new friend said at last. "You can go home now."

"Thank you, Mr. Armstead. I don't have any money to pay you, but I can sweep out your shop for you."

"Well, Jimmy, I appreciate your offer, but I don't want any money. Just do some good deed for someone else when you get the opportunity," he said, smiling.

Jimmy got down from the barber chair. "I'll do that, sir."

Mr. Armstead opened the door and watched as Jimmy walked out into the street.

"That's a good boy," he thought to himself, as he closed the door. "We need a lot more like him around here."

He looked up and down Main Street. There was no one in sight. "What will these kids around here do next?" he thought, as he closed the door and sat down in his first

Soft Feather

barber chair. He smiled. Whatever it was, he had a front row seat.

Memories filled Jimmy Warrior's mind as he walked home. He thought of all the things his grandma and grandpa told him about his mom and dad, and of things that happened since he came to live with them.

His mom, Mabel, was born in Taos, New Mexico, and was a full-blooded Taos Indian. Alice and Tom Warrior, also, Taos Indians, moved to Mercer, Colorado where Jimmy's dad, Tommy, was born. Tommy and Mabel met when Tom and Alice visited relatives and friends in Taos one summer. They fell in love and ran away and got married. A year later, Jimmy was born in Denver.

WWII just started, and Tommy was deferred. He lost his job, so he joined the army and was sent to Hawaii. On Midway Island he was wounded and sent back to Hawaii for recuperation. He suffered from severe shell shock and was sent home on leave.

The doctors at the Denver VA Hospital decided he should he discharged from the army.

Tommy tried to put all of the things that happened to him out of his mind, but he still had horrible dreams. He wound up in Newark, New Jersey, where he spent some time in a VA hospital.

After the hospital released him, he had a hard time holding a job and started drinking. He left home and wound up in a ward for alcoholics in a VA hospital in Big Spring, Texas.

Mabel stayed in Newark, where she worked nights at a café and nightclub. She slept during the day, and Jimmy ran loose. At the age of 13, he was arrested for stealing two apples.

Soft Feather

He was placed in a damp cell under the police station with hardened criminals. It was there that he had his first dream of flying like a big bird. High above everyone, he looked down at the beautiful sights below.

The policeman in charge liked to help young boys. He got Jimmy' grandparents' address and called them. They agreed to take him and would send the money for him to come.

Off to Mercer, Colorado, Jimmy went on a bus. He tried to run away three times but failed. He tried to run away from his grandparents two times. The second time he hopped a freight train. He was locked inside a boxcar and was trapped for three days. That stopped his attempts to run away.

One day he caught a wounded female hawk. She had three babies. He told his new friend, Mary, and they got two of the babies. The two trained the hawks to hunt. They not only became great hunters, but champions at the hawk shows. The birds changed his life. He loved something that depended on him for everything.

Then a game warden told them it was against the law to hunt with hawks, and they gave them to the Air Force Academy.

Because he felt so low about losing his beautiful hawks, a friend took him deer hunting. They went up in the Rocky Mountains near the gold mining town of Ward. He shot a 12-point buck, but lost his way back to the cabin. A large manhunt ensued, and Mary's dog was taken along to help. A hunting trip that turned awry, ended happily.

With no hawks to care for, he again wanted to run away. The more he thought about it, the more he liked the idea. Maybe he'd go down to Texas and see his dad.

Soft Feather

As Jimmy walked home, he shook his head to clear it, and felt better. No one would know he'd been in a fight. Of course, his grandma would. She'd get all over him when she found out that he fought someone.

He turned the last corner and saw his grandma coming down the road toward him.

He pulled his shoulders back and made himself look as tall as possible. He walked along, as if nothing happened.

Alice walked up and smiled at him. "I was coming to see where you were, Jimmy," she said. "You should have been home..." she stopped and took a closer look at Jimmy's face and the torn shirt with the missing buttons. "Oh, my," she murmured.

Jimmy's eyes filled with tears. She put her arm around him, as a tear slowly ran down his cheek. All of the hurt from the fight, the hurt from mean words and the hurt from the medication that Mr. Armstead put on his face, came out. He looked into his grandma's compassionate eyes and told her what happened.

She pulled him close to her and let him tell her the whole story. She felt the hurt deep inside her grandson as tears filled her eyes. When he quit talking she put her arm around him and they slowly walked home.

"It is good for a person to cry now and then. It gets the tension and hate out of one's insides," she thought. She knew how he felt. Jimmy did well that day, and she was proud of him. He, like others in their family, stood up for the Warrior name.

She couldn't have asked him to do more. She told him how proud she was of him as they walked along.

There was silence when they reached the house. The quietness filled both of them as they made their way up the steps of the porch and into the house. She knew he needed to be alone for a while.

Soft Feather

She removed her arm from around him, and watched him walk on down the hall to his room. He went inside and closed the door.

He pulled the chair out from under his desk and sat down. He looked out the window but didn't see a thing. He felt so alone. The old feeling that used to invade his thoughts returned. The things Joe said about his parents stung him deeply. He struggled in his mind to prove Joe wrong, while deep inside he knew he was right.

Jimmy sighed, as he recalled again the day he was arrested and put in jail in Newark for taking two apples.

His mother came to the police station the next day and told Officer Bob to send him to a reform school. She was angry and told him she didn't ever want to see him again. It broke his heart.

Officer Bob called his grandparents, and they agreed for him to stay with them in Colorado. They spent all of their savings for him to ride a bus. He was sure the only reason they did that was because they felt obligated to take him in.

While on the trip to Colorado, he got off the bus and tried to hitchhike to Big Spring, Texas, to visit his dad in the veteran's hospital.

But a highway patrolman picked him up and took him to the next town, where the bus waited for him.

With his elbows on the table, he put his head in his hands and sat there shaking his head.

Jimmy knew that his grandparents liked him a lot, but he knew he was a burden to them. They didn't have any money. At least, his hawk caught food for them to eat. "But now that's gone," he thought. "It's back to no meat for grandpa." He remembered how thin he was when he got there.

Soft Feather

He sat back in his chair, closed his eyes and buried his head in his hands. "I've got to do something, but what?"

There was a knock on his door, and it opened. Alice stuck her head in. "Come into the kitchen, Jimmy. I want to talk to you."

"Yes, ma'am," he said, without turning around.

She closed the door, went back to the kitchen and sat down at the table.

Jimmy's door opened, and she waited. He slowly made his way into the kitchen. Looking up, she gasped.

Jimmy stood a few feet from her. His eyes and face began to swell from the fight and from crying. She got up and put her arms around him.

She didn't say anything as she led him over to her chair and sat down. She took his hands and pulled him downward until he knelt in front of her.

"Oh, Jimmy," she said, looking at her grandson. "Tell me all about it."

"I feel so alone, Grandma. My mother doesn't ever want to see me again. I tried to run off and go live with my dad a couple of times. But he can't even take care of himself.

"The truth is he doesn't want me either.

"Joe hit me in the back with a big rock the first day I arrived in Mercer. He and his friend, Brad, yelled at me and told me to get out of town and never come back.

"You and Grandpa are stuck with me, because my parents don't want me.

"The game warden took away my hawk, the only thing I really loved.

"You and Grandpa spent all of your savings for me to come live with you, because you felt obligated."

"S-h-h-h", Alice said. They said nothing for some time, as she sat with her eyes closed.

Soft Feather

She bit her lip as memories of her own life filled her mind. Memories of when her parents disowned her caused her to shiver all over. It was because she did not follow the tribal Indian law and tradition and marry the boy they chose for her when she was a young girl. Her parents were part of the tribal council and were required to do this to keep the bloodlines pure.

The young lad's parents were also members of the tribal council, and when he was young, they chose the girl he would marry.

The only problem was that Little Dove didn't care for the one they chose for her. During her teenage years she fell in love with the tall, quiet, Indian lad named Still Water.

Still Water liked the girl they chose for him but when he was around Little Dove, he didn't think about the other girl. Their parents discovered their attraction for each other and scolded them. They were both told again that they would marry the ones they chose for them.

Being rebellious teenagers every chance they got, they sneaked around to be together. Restrictions were placed on them, which made it impossible to see each other. Then Still Water was sent to another part of the reservation.

One night Little Dove woke up from a noise outside. She got up and opened the door. There stood Still Water. She got dressed and quietly made her way outside. He told her he wanted to marry her, but that they would have to leave the tribe to do that.

She agreed with him, and the next night they left with what little they managed to put in deerskin bags that they hid outside the camp. They hitchhiked and caught a ride with a couple going to the small coal-mining town of Aguilar, Colorado. They changed their names to Tom and

Soft Feather

Alice Warrior. He got a job in the coal mine, and they started their married life there.

They found out later that their parents disowned them and never wanted to see them again. Just the thought of their not ever seeing the parents they loved was a hurt that still tore at Little Dove's insides. "Even now it is hard to deal with," she thought.

They went back and visited them a couple of times, but it was hard on both families.

Now her grandson's heart was broken like hers. Their situation was different, but the feeling that comes when your parents don't want you is the same.

"You know what, Jimmy? I love your daddy, very much. I know he's doing the best he can after what happened to him in the war. That's all anyone can ask of anybody.

"The time is not right for you to be with him. He has a lot of problems that he alone has to work out before he can handle a normal family life.

"I also know that you are doing the best you can. That's all anyone can ask of you."

She gently put her hands on his face, raised his head up and looked him in the eye.

"Every time I see you, I see my son, Tommy. I love him, but you know what, you're my grandson. That means you are grand to me. There's a different love a grandma has for grandchildren than she has for her children. It's a deep love, because it is the love you have for them, plus the love you have for your own children.

"Your father loves you and is so proud of you. What your mother said was said in a moment of anger. She didn't mean it. The game warden is so proud of you that he tells everyone around here what you did when you gave your hawks to the Air Force Academy as mascots.

Soft Feather

"There will always be those in your life who don't like you. Just treat them with respect, letting them know that you don't dislike them. It's hard to do at times, but the more you do it, the easier it becomes."

She pushed him back and looked at him. "I made some oatmeal cookies for you today," she said, smiling.

Jimmy's eyes lit up as he got up off of his knees. "Thanks, Grandma," he said. "Thank you for everything."

Alice watched his face slowly change until there was a large smile on it. That was what she wanted to see. In days to follow he thought of all he said to her, but along with that he thought about what she said to him. The truth is always the truth, and when he was through thinking about it, she knew he would choose the right course.

Getting some of his grandma's oatmeal cookies was like a refreshing breeze caressing Jimmy's mind. It was exactly what he needed right then.

Alice got up and soon had a large glass of milk in front of him as he ate the cookies. She looked out the kitchen window and was surprised to see that the sky started to get dark.

It grew dark earlier in the winter, but tonight it looked like there would probably be snow on the ground in the morning. It was the time of year some dreaded and others loved.

A snowflake drifted by the window. "It's starting to snow, Jimmy," she said. "Look at how dark the clouds are. There's lots of snow up there just waiting to come down."

Jimmy got up from the table and walked over to the window. He watched the snowflakes pass by faster and faster. Soon the ground turned white. "I'd better fill up the wood box," he said, and turned and headed for the back door.

"That's a good idea. We sure don't want to run out of firewood on a night like this."

Soft Feather

It wasn't long until Jimmy had the wood box filled and running over. When he finished, he sat down at the table. He ate a few more cookies and drank his milk.

"That heavy quilt with the birds on it…the one that you made and embroidered pigeons on it for dad…it sure is going to feel good tonight, Grandma," Jimmy said.

Alice smiled. "It sure will, Jimmy," she replied, as she recalled the winter she made the quilt and how she lovingly put each stitch in it for Tommy.

A soft moan came from outside as the wind blew around the corners of the house. It was a good night to be inside next to a warm fire.

They heard footsteps on the porch, and the front door swung open. Tom Warrior came in and closed the door behind him.

"Hello, you two," he said, as he walked into the kitchen and looked at the wood box. "Sure glad to see that wood box filled, Jimmy. Thanks."

"You're welcome, Grandpa."

Tom looked at Jimmy and didn't move. He saw his son, Tommy, standing before him when the town bully just beat him up. It was a sad day in the Warrior house.

Now his grandson stood before him, and someone beat him up. His jaw and nose swelled and a small trickle of blood dried under his nose. At work he heard someone say that two boys got into a fight, and one of them was Joe Crow, but they didn't know the other boy. Tom now knew who that other boy was.

Tears filled his eyes as he looked at Alice and she nodded and turned away. He knew what the fight was about. He stretched out his arms and beckoned to Jimmy.

Jimmy ran into his grandpa's arms and threw his arms around him and hugged him tight. Two strong arms wrapped around him and he had a feeling he never had

Soft Feather

before- - security with love, the kind of love that binds a grandfather and grandson together forever.

Alice pulled up her apron and dried her eyes. She smiled at the sight before her.

Nothing was said for a long time. Jimmy looked up and saw tears running down his grandpa's face. His head was turned upwards, eyes closed, as his head slowly moved from side to side.

He stopped and looked down at his grandson and slowly nodded his head. "I'm proud of you, Jimmy. Yes sir, I'm proud of you."

Jimmy did not know what to say.

"And I love you very much. You've been a blessing to me and your grandma." Smiling he hugged him again.

Jimmy returned the hug as hard as he could. He'd take all of the loving he could get from his grandpa.

Tom released him, and stepped back and looked at Alice. "I've got to go wash up." He turned and hurried down the hall to the bathroom. Soon, Jimmy heard water run and his grandpa sang some kind of song he didn't understand.

Alice nodded her head, understanding each word.

Tom returned. Alice waited for him. She gave him a hug, then looked up at him and smiled.

"You two start the fire in the front room heater, and I'll fix supper," Alice said. "We'll be nice and cozy tonight."

Alice and Jimmy got up and got busy, as Tom just watched.

Alice hurried over to the wood box and grabbed a large stick. She turned and looked at Tom.

"Yes, dear," he grinned, as he rushed into the front room. "I can take a hint."

The three of them laughed. It was going to be a night to remember.

Soft Feather

CHAPTER 2

Jimmy stood on the side of his favorite hill behind the Warrior house. Slowly, he turned and looked at the beauty that was all about him. Snow fell the night before and covered everything in sight.

He took a deep breath of the cold mountain air and let it out slowly. All of the drabness of winter was gone. The small creek at the bottom of the hill was frozen over. Even the wet ground beside the ice was frozen.

The dead weeds and grass between the creek and his grandparents' house was no longer a bunch of scattered lumps and bumps, but a white pristine area with a trail through it that he just made.

His thoughts recalled a time not long ago when he lived in Newark, New Jersey. There, the snow covered everything on the streets like it did here. After it snowed, the cars and sidewalks were soon cleaned off. The little that was left on the sidewalks became dirty slush. Even when it snowed so much that it stayed for a long time, it wasn't white.

The soot from all of the wood and coal-burning stoves soon turned the snow a dark gray.

Here in Mercer, the snow was a beautiful white that glistened when the sun shone on it. The air was clean, crisp and cold. His breath seemed to hang in the air when he breathed out very hard.

He looked down at his footprints in the snow. "How sad," he thought, as he looked at the trail from the house to where he stood.

They were marks in the snow, and marred the beauty. "How nice it would be if I could fly," he thought. "I could just land here where I am and not disturb the beauty."

His mind went back again to the time when he first came up this hill. He wished then that he could fly. It was

Soft Feather

warm, and the grasses were tall. He walked up to where he now was. But his trail disappeared as the grasses returned to hide his tracks.

He lay in the grass and watched a large bird circle high above. How he wished he could join that bird. It was a large falcon hawk, which he later captured. Strong Feather Lady Samson was the name he gave her.

As he thought about things that happened, he realized his nose was cold. He put his gloved hand over it. As he looked up into the sky, hoping to see another hawk, he got an idea.

He bent over and made a large snowball. It was good snow, and it packed hard in his hand.

He dropped it onto the ground and rolled it in the snow. It picked up more snow and became larger. He grinned and kept on rolling the snowball round and round on the ground.

It wasn't long until it was so large he had to pick it up and dump it over to make it bigger. When it was the size he wanted, he made another small snowball.

He rolled it round and round, and it, too, grew larger. Again, he decided it was the right size. He rolled it over to the other large snowball.

He grunted and groaned and finally placed it on top of the first ball. "There," he said out loud, and stepped back and looked at it.

"Not bad," he thought.

The next snowball was not quite as big. He picked it up and placed it on top of the other two. It didn't look like what he wanted.

"I'm going to have to do a lot of work on you before you're a good-looking snowman," he said, talking to the balls of snow in front of him. "Let's see what's wrong with you."

Soft Feather

He walked around the snowman, picked up some snow and patted it into the spaces where he placed the balls of snow on top of each other. He worked on trying to make it look just right.

Slowly, it looked more like a snowman. This was his first snowman, and he wanted it to be a good one.

After much work, he stepped back and took a good look at what he did. It looked much better.

"You need a face and arms now," he remarked, frowning. He ran down the hill to the creek, leaped across, and ran to the wood-and coal-shed. It took him some time to find the right-sized pieces of coal. He knew exactly what he wanted.

He put them in his jacket pocket and ran back to the creek. He broke off a couple of dead branches from one of the bushes. Jumping back across the creek, he hurried up the hill.

It was so cold that the snow made a crunching sound under his feet as he walked along. He breathed hard when he arrived in front of the snowman. He used two nice, round pieces of coal for the eyes, a three-sided one for its nose, six smaller ones for a smiling mouth, and three round ones for buttons on its chest.

One branch was placed in each side of the snowman for arms. That completed his snowman.

He stepped back again and laughed. "You're my first snowman. What shall I call you?" he said. "Let's see, I want you to stand out here for me. That way, if I miss something, you'll see it."

"You'll be all alone, just like I like to be alone out here. You will be my Lone Warrior. Now, I don't want you to let me down."

Jimmy walked up to the snowman and turned to look in the direction it faced. He put his arm around the snowman and stood silently for a few minutes.

Soft Feather

"It sure is beautiful out here, Lone Warrior," he said softly. "I envy you standing here."

"But you must realize, my friend, you, too, are now part of this beauty. That should make you feel good."

Jimmy removed his arm from around the snowman. "I've got to go now. But I'll be back the first chance I get." Jimmy walked off a few feet, then turned and waved good-bye to the snowman.

A gust of cold wind came over the hill and down past the snowman and Jimmy. Evening came on fast as the sun started to set behind the mountains.

Jimmy stayed on the hillside longer than he realized. It was time for him to head back to the house.

He took one last look at the snowman with branches for arms. A small gust of wind made it look like it was waving good-bye, and he waved back. He turned and hurried off down the hill towards the creek bank.

Again, he stopped and looked back. Lone Warrior stood there, smiling down at him.

With that sight filling him with pride, he turned and ran down one side of the creek bank, leaped across the small stream, and up the other bank. It felt good to run, so he continued running across the field to his grandparents' house.

At the top step of the back porch, he stopped and looked back toward his hill. There near the top of the hill, he saw his snowman, Lone Warrior.

He opened the back door and went inside and down the hall to his room. He closed the door, took off his coat and gloves and laid them on his bed. He pulled the chair out from under his desk, and sat down.

He quickly took off his rubber overshoes. The snow on them started to melt, so he got up and placed them by the door. He returned to his chair.

Soft Feather

His feet were cold, so he took his shoes off and rubbed his toes. They were colder than he thought. As they began to warm, there was a knock on his door, and it opened.

His grandma came in and gave him a long, hard look.

"You were outside quite a while, Jimmy," she said. "I started to worry about you. You don't need to stay outside so long at a time. Your face is still puffy from that fight."

"I'm feeling fine, Grandma. In fact, the cold and snow made me feel real good."

"I'm glad to hear that," Alice replied. She looked around the room and saw where Jimmy put his wet overshoes. She looked back at Jimmy and asked, "What have you been doing?"

"Come let me show you, Grandma." He took her hand and led her out of his room to the back door. He opened it and pointed toward the hill. She tried to see where Jimmy pointed.

Then she saw it. "It's a good-sized snowman, but it's kind of hard to tell much about it from here, Jimmy. I'm sure it's a nice one."

"It surely is, Grandma," Jimmy said, laughing. "I call him Lone Warrior. Since I can't be out there guarding us, he's taking my place."

Alice closed the door and put her arm around him. Together, they walked back into his room. She picked up his coat and hung it in his closet, as he put his gloves on top of his dresser. Jimmy sat down on the side of his bed, and Alice sat in the chair at his desk.

"You know something, Jimmy?" she said. "You named that snowman well. It stands alone out there on the side of that hill. In a way, so do we. We all stand alone as far as the direction we take in life.

Soft Feather

"Oh, we have friends, and when you get old enough, you'll have a mate that will stand with you. But no matter what happens to each of us, we must realize that we alone have to choose which road we take. The road that leads to the Lord, or the one that leads the other way.

"We are all 'Lone Warriors' as we pass from here to there. No one can stand in our place and do that which we have been given to do.

"Helping others is one of the best things we can do when someone is in need. But doing their job for them, when they are able to do it, causes them to lose the blessing.

"We must be careful how we help them complete their tasks in life and not do their tasks for them.

"You're learning how to do that, Jimmy. The chore list I first gave you when you came to live with us seemed to be a heavy weight for you to carry. You struggled with it and fought it until you decided on your own to do them.

"I now see you do the things you should without having to be asked. I'm proud of you."

"Thanks, Grandma," Jimmy replied.

"You get ready for supper," she said. "Clean up, and by the time you get to the kitchen, I should have it ready for you." She grinned at Jimmy.

"Your grandpa is sitting at the table waiting for us. I forgot all about him. You hurry up and get ready."

She got up and hurried out the door. Jimmy went across the hall to the bathroom and cleaned up. He quickly dried his hands and face, opened the door, and rushed down the hall to the kitchen.

As he entered the kitchen, his grandpa thumped his fingers on the table. He didn't say anything to him, just frowned. Jimmy ducked his head, pulled out his chair, and sat down.

Soft Feather

His grandma looked at him and broke the silence, "Your grandpa is a little put out with us, Jimmy. He thinks we have another secret and won't tell him. Do we have another secret, Jimmy?"

Jimmy started to shake his head 'no'; then, he remembered the snowman he'd shown his grandma. He stopped and smiled. His grandpa caught it and grunted. "I knew it," he said. "I knew it."

"That's all you two do is keep secrets from me. Now I want to know this one. Come on Jimmy, you can tell me. I want to know the secret you and your grandma have. Come on-- tell me."

Jimmy looked at his grandma for her approval. She didn't look at him at all. She just kept busy fixing supper. Then she walked over to the table and placed a dish of sliced turkey on it. "Go ahead, Jimmy," she said. "Tell him."

"Well, Grandpa," Jimmy began. "I don't know if you would call it a secret or not, but I went up on my favorite hill across the creek this afternoon. While I stood there and looked at the beauty around me, I decided to make something."

Jimmy stopped and looked at his grandpa, then went on. "I made a large snowman and put pieces of coal in it for its eyes, nose, and mouth. Then I put some round ones down the front for buttons."

His grandpa just sat and listened.

"I put some branches in the side of it for arms, and I named it Lone Warrior, as it stands out there all alone. Grandma said I named it well. All of us are 'lone warriors' in this life.

"She said that we each stand alone, and only we can do that which we've been sent here to do. She said we choose which way we will go in life. I agree, Grandpa. I don't think anyone else can do what I was given to do, and

Soft Feather

no one can choose for me. If I make a bad choice, it's my responsibility to correct that."

Tom just sat there with his mouth half open and stared at Jimmy. Was all of this wisdom coming out of his grandson?

After a couple of minutes, he found his speech. "That's the best secret anyone ever told me, Jimmy," he said.

He thought about it some more as his wife continued to set the table. When she finished and sat down, the three of them joined hands and bowed their heads. Tom looked at them with their heads bowed.

He lowered his head and said, "Thank you, Lord, for this day and this food. We are so grateful for all of thy bountiful blessings." He paused, then, continued.

"We thank you for being the 'lone warrior' that stands alone for all of mankind. We're grateful. Amen."

Jimmy smiled at his grandpa as he raised his head. They looked at each other. He surely was glad he built the snowman that day. He didn't know at the time that it would mean so much to him and his grandparents.

Tom picked up the plate of turkey and handed it to Jimmy. "Here, Jimmy," he said. "Have some turkey. You need a lot of food to build up your strength. Especially after getting into a fight, and now building a snowman."

Jimmy looked at his grandma. His grandpa reminded him of the fight. He forgot about it today. He smiled as he put some turkey on his plate. His grandpa was right. He needed all the strength he could get. His grandma's turkey was just the right thing.

After supper Tom and Jimmy helped Alice clear the table and did the dishes. Alice appreciated it and told them so. Jimmy walked into the front room and looked out the window at the snow.

Soft Feather

The sun disappeared behind the mountains, and darkness approached fast. The shadows of the trees danced upon the snow as they gently swayed back and forth in the front yard. A feeling of emptiness came over Jimmy. What would he do during the long, cold winter nights that lay ahead?

His hawks were gone, and he had nothing to turn to. He lay down on the couch and put his head on the armrest. He sighed as he lay still and looked out the window, watching the night slowly make its arrival.

Tom sat back down at the table in the kitchen. He watched his grandson and thought he understood his problem.

"Jimmy," he said, "come in here and give me a hand. I'd like to show you some things I used to do when I was your age. It kept my mind busy when the nights were long, and winter lay upon the land. Come on. I think you will find what I did was quite interesting."

Jimmy slowly got up and made his way into the kitchen. "What now?" he wondered to himself. He saw nothing on the table that would interest him.

Tom turned and looked at Alice, and she smiled at him.

"Do you have some bars of Ivory Soap, Alice?" he asked.

"Yes, Tom," she said. She walked over to the sink and opened the cupboard door below the sink. She got two bars of soap and closed the door. She walked back to the table and gave them to Tom, then winked at Jimmy.

"You're going to enjoy what your grandpa is about to show you. He's one of the best soap carvers around."

Tom gave her a loving look and grinned. "I'll need a couple of your empty thread spools. The large ones." Tom thought a minute. "What else?"

Soft Feather

"A couple of rubber bands and some wooden matches," Alice replied.

"That's right Alice," Tom said, smiling. He winked at her. "You sure know what I need, don't you? Do you want to show Jimmy how to use those items?"

Alice looked at Jimmy, smiling at each other. Jimmy's grandma seemed to always know what he thought. She'd done the same thing to Tom. "No, Tom. This is your time to let your grandson see you have many talents," she said.

"I have a lot of mending to do for you two men. Jimmy wears his new clothes to school, but I think he also needs some older ones to wear around here. He needs a couple of patches on some of his old trousers, and a shirt needs mending and buttons sewed back on. You two go on and let me get my work done."

Tom looked at Jimmy. "Your grandma brags a lot on me, Jimmy," he said. "I'm pretty good at carving soap, that's true, but being the best around, I don't know about that. Maybe next to the best."

Jimmy nodded, and some interest started to show in his face. He had never seen anyone carve anything, let alone a bar of soap. "Why would anyone want to cut up a bar of soap?" he thought. His eyes followed every move that his grandpa made.

Tom unwrapped one bar of soap and placed the wrapper out of the way on the side table. He took his knife out of his pocket and opened it to the thinnest blade, then picked up the soap.

The bar of soap had a place in the middle where it could be broken if you wanted to use only half a bar instead of a full bar. Tom broke it, then, took his knife and smoothed the rough edges of both pieces of soap.

"I'll carve this piece, and you can carve the other," he said, and handed Jimmy one piece of soap. Jimmy took

Soft Feather

the soap and looked at it. It was not heavy at all and felt smooth and soft.

Tom took his knife and slowly drew an outline on one side of the soap. He then held it up and looked at it. Just then Alice came back with two large, empty wooden thread spools, two small rubber bands and half a dozen wooden matches.

Smiling at Jimmy, she put everything in the middle of the table, then went back to her bedroom.

Tom worked fast with his knife and soon had an elephant carved out of the bar of soap. He turned it and carved a little here and a little there. When he thought it was just right, he handed it to Jimmy. It was beautiful.

"It's yours, Jimmy. I want you to try and carve one now." He handed Jimmy his knife. "The first thing you do is make an outline on the soap. Then follow the design like I did."

Jimmy took the knife and made an outline on the side of the bar of soap. Slowly, he cut the soap. He stopped now and then to see how it compared to his grandpa's elephant.

It didn't look too good. He finally finished it and set it down on the table next to the one his grandpa made. "It surely doesn't look like the one you made, Grandpa," he said.

Tom said nothing all the time Jimmy carved. He nodded his head, agreeing with him.

"That's true, Jimmy. But that was your first try and look at it," he said. "It would beat most people on their first try."

"You do have a talent, Jimmy. If you work at it, and enjoy doing it, you'll be carving better than I do."

Tom turned his head, "Alice, will you come here and look at what your grandson just did?"

Soft Feather

Alice walked out of the bedroom and over to the table. Tom pointed at the two elephants. "Who carved what, Alice?" he said.

Alice looked at the two pieces of soap. She picked up the one Tom carved and said, "That's very good, Jimmy. You have a talent."

Tom made a grab for her, and she laughed and stepped back. "I know this is yours, Tom, but the other one is very good.

"You know you shouldn't be surprised at his carving. He is a Warrior and you know that nearly all of the Warriors have the talent to carve. Jimmy's only problem is he doesn't know it yet."

Alice put the elephant down on the table and went back into the bedroom. Tom shook his head. "That's some woman there, Jimmy."

Tom reached over and picked up the other bar of soap. He unwrapped it and cut a couple of pieces off the end. He picked up one of the wooden spools and cut notches on the raised ends of the spool.

The raised part had a slit in it so that the thread could be hooked, and it wouldn't unwind when not being used. When both ends had notches in them, he stopped. He put it down and cut the small pieces of soap in two.

Taking the small blade of the knife he slowly bored a hole in the center of one of the small pieces of soap he cut off earlier. He was careful not to crack the soap.

He then took the rubber band and placed it through the hole in the spool. When the rubber band stuck out each end of the spool, he placed one end through the holes in the soap.

He picked up a match and scratched it under the table and it lit. He lit another match from the first one and then blew both of them out.

Soft Feather

With his knife, he cut the burned part off each match.

He broke one of the matches in half and placed one of the halves in the end of the rubber band on one end of the spool.

Taking his time, he slowly checked it out. He then placed the long match through the other end of the rubber band where the soap was.

When he finished, he put it down on the table and looked at it with a big smile.

Jimmy frowned as he sat there wondering what in the world his grandpa was making. He never saw anything like it.

Tom found a pencil in of one of the cabinet drawers. He came back and placed it on the table. He picked up the spool and started winding up the rubber band with the large matchstick while holding onto the half matchstick.

He kept winding up the rubber band that ran through the spool. It became tight and tighter, and then he stopped. He placed it on the table. When he released it, the spool moved across the table like a tank. It quickly climbed over the pencil like it wasn't there.

Jimmy's eyes got big as he watched the tank spool move across the table. It stopped when the rubber band unwound.

"How does it work, Grandpa?" Jimmy asked.

"The long match rests on the table," his grandpa replied, "which makes the spool turn, instead of the match stick. When the rubber bands unwind, the spool moves across the table. The notches in the spool help it to climb over small objects like a small tank would."

Tom handed it to Jimmy, who wound it up and placed it on the table. The spool moved off, fast at first, then slowed down and stopped.

Soft Feather

"That is great, Grandpa," Jimmy said. "Where did you learn to make it?"

"Well, Jimmy," he replied, "on long winter nights when I was much younger than you, my grandpa showed me how to make spool tanks."

"I showed my son how to make them, and now I'm having the same pleasure again. Everything comes full circle, Jimmy, if one lives long enough."

Alice came out of the bedroom. "It's time for bed, Jimmy," she said.

"Yes, Grandma," he replied.

Tom picked up the elephants and spool tank. "Here, Jimmy," he said. "These are yours. Take them to your room."

"Thanks, Grandpa," Jimmy said, and reached for them. "I've enjoyed this winter night."

Tom nodded at his grandson. He winked at his wife.

Jimmy got up and hurried off to his bedroom. He placed the two elephants and the spool tank on his dresser and got ready for bed.

As he lay in bed with the light off, he looked over toward the dresser. It was a nice clear night. The moonlight brightly shone through his bedroom window, falling on the top of his dresser.

He saw the two elephants and spool tank in the moonlight. He felt good inside. His grandpa showed him something he did as a child.

"Not every grandson has a grandfather like that," he thought. Grandpa cared for him and let him know it.

Then he remembered that Lone Warrior stood out on the side of the hill. "Please guard all of this for me, Lone Warrior. I don't want to ever lose it." Smiling, he turned over and went to sleep.

Soft Feather

CHAPTER 3

The sun just came up when Jimmy opened the front door and stepped onto the front porch. He closed the door and quickly made his way down the steps. He stopped at the bottom and listened. It surely was quiet. He took a deep breath, and the rush of cold air into his lungs quickly cleared his head. He opened his eyes wide.

Off in the distance he heard a dog bark. He wondered if it was Mary's dog, Goldie. He had a special place in his heart for her. She found him when he was lost in the mountains.

He decided to take a detour and walk down to Wilson's Garage before he went to school, to see if Goldie was there. Off he went over the snow-covered yard, listening to the squeaking of his shoes. The cold air seemed to make the snow squeak instead of crunch. He reached the street and stepped into the tracks a car made earlier.

He found it a lot easier to walk in the car tracks. When he reached the highway, it was covered with a thin layer of ice.

He stepped up onto it and found it very slippery. He tried to skate on it with short little steps. It wasn't long until he sat on the slippery highway, wondering what happened.

Getting up was no easy task. With both arms out to his sides, he made his way over to the edge of the road. He hurried along until he came to Wilson's Garage.

Mr. Wilson's pickup truck was parked out front. Goldie sat on the seat of the truck, looking at the garage. She heard Jimmy coming and turned and barked when she saw who it was.

He waved at her and said, "Hi, Goldie."

Slowly, he made his way over to the truck without falling. He opened the door, and reached in and patted her

Soft Feather

on the head. "Where's Mr. Wilson?" Goldie just sat there with her tongue hanging out, enjoying being patted.

"O.K., Goldie, it is good to see you, too, girl. I'll just go inside and see what Mr. Wilson is doing."

He closed the door and made his way over to the office. Through the office window he saw Mr. Wilson pick up some newspapers off a chair. He was busy making a fire in the potbellied stove.

He wadded them up and shoved them into the stove. A half dozen pieces of wood followed. He patted his pockets, trying to find a match. He didn't find one so he went over to his desk and got some. He struck one and lit some of the paper and closed the door.

There was a candy counter at one end of the office, and at the other end was the door that opened into the garage where he worked on cars. When the wood began to burn well, he put some coal in the stove.

He went over and opened the door into the garage. It needed to warm up some. He went back and stood by the stove.

Jimmy opened the door to the office and walked in. "Good morning, Mr. Wilson."

"Good morning, Jimmy. I saw you coming down the road back there. It looked like you tried to ice-skate down the highway until you sat down and rested. What happened? Did you get tired?" he asked with a brief smile.

Jimmy laughed. "Oh, I just wanted to see how hard the ice was on the highway. I can assure you it is nice and hard."

"When you land like you did, Jimmy, it seems harder than it really is," Mr. Wilson said.

The wood started crackling, and the heat slowly spread throughout the office. They both backed up close to the stove and enjoyed the warmth.

Soft Feather

It wasn't long until their backsides were warm, so they turned around and faced the stove. "I believe that these stoves are really the best you can buy. That's just my opinion, though," Mr. Wilson said.

"I'll keep that in mind when I get married and have my own home," Jimmy said.

"Well, I hope you don't plan on getting married any time soon," he answered. He smiled as he walked over behind the candy counter.

"No, sir, Mr. Wilson!" Jimmy said.

"Have you ever ice-skated, Jimmy?"

"No, sir," he answered. "I've never had a chance or a place to learn. Except for the short lesson I had on my way over here."

Mr. Wilson didn't say anything as he walked over to his desk and knelt down behind the candy counter. There was a good-sized wooden box back there. He opened the lid and dug around in the box and brought out a couple of wrenches. Another stirring, and he brought out a couple of funny-looking things Jimmy had never seen before.

He closed the lid and came out from behind the candy counter. He sat down in his chair next to the stove and held up the two objects. They swung back and forth.

"These are my old ice skates. They are the ice skates I used when I learned to skate. Of course, I was a little younger than you, Jimmy," he said, rubbing his chin.

Jimmy just looked at them.

"You're more than welcome to use them. I tell you what. When you come home from school this afternoon, you come by here and pick them up. Go over to the ditch that runs along the other side of town.

"It has plenty of thick ice. I checked it out yesterday, and it held me, so I know it will hold you."

He paused and watched Jimmy's face. Jimmy didn't know what to say. He didn't know how to ice-skate, and he

Soft Feather

sure didn't want to make a fool of himself in front of Mr. Wilson, or anybody else.

"You come by and take them over there by yourself, Jimmy. Try them out and see if you can skate with them. If you like ice-skating, you can use them all you want. All I ask is that you bring them back at the end of winter. They are kind of special to me."

"I'd like to try them, Mr. Wilson," he said, and walked over to the door. "I'll come by after school and get them."

"I think the ice on the ditch is as hard as it is out there on the highway, Jimmy. You might want to take a pillow along with you."

They laughed as he closed the door and walked over to the truck. Goldie still sat on the truck seat. He opened the door and patted her again. "What are you doing sitting in the truck, Goldie?" he asked. "It's a lot warmer inside."

Just then the door behind him opened and Mr. Wilson came out. "Come on, Goldie," he said, opening the truck door. "I've got the fire going for you and it's warmed up inside."

Goldie hopped out and ran inside the office. "That dog has me trained real well," he said. "My garage has to warm up some, or she won't come in. I don't blame her though, do you?"

"No, sir," Jimmy replied. "I think she's pretty smart."

"We do agree on that, don't we?" He turned and went back inside. He waved at Jimmy through the window.

Jimmy waved back and walked down Main Street. He heard the grade school bell ring. That let everyone know they have five minutes before classes start.

He walked a little faster, knowing he wouldn't be late. He kept shaking his head as he walked along.

Soft Feather

As he neared the grade school, someone yelled at him. He saw Mary running toward him. "Good morning, Jimmy," she said, stopping beside him. "It sure is cold this morning. I'm glad to see you're doing alright."

"Yes. I'm doing fine," he answered. "The salve Grandma put on me is causing all the swelling to go down. She has to look real close to see anything. I sure don't want to go through anything like that again."

He stopped and looked at her. "Grandma said she might teach me how to make the salves some day."

"That would be nice, Jimmy, My daddy told me that she would only pass on her knowledge to one she finds worthy of carrying on her work. He said she has helped just about everyone around town at one time or another. Of course, there are some who won't let her. They don't know what they're missing. She would be glad to help them, too, but they have to ask."

They walked toward school, each deep in their own thoughts. Mary stopped, and Jimmy walked on ahead a few steps.

When he realized she stopped, he looked back to see why.

"What were you shaking your head for back there when I called to you? It looked like you were having quite a conversation as you walked and shook your head from side to side."

He continued walking. Mary hurried up to him. He started shaking his head again.

"There you go again," she said, laughing at him. "What is it?"

"Oh, it's that dog of yours," he said.

Mary grabbed his coat and stopped him. "What about Goldie?" she asked. "What has she done?"

Soft Feather

Jimmy looked at Mary and saw that she didn't know whether to be mad, worried or what. "It's nothing to get upset about, Mary," he said, laughing.

Mary thought he was now laughing at her and started to get mad. She raised her voice. "What is it, then?"

Jimmy stopped laughing and said, "Well, Goldie sat out in your father's truck when I came up to his garage this morning. I went over and patted her, and she enjoyed it as much as I enjoyed doing it.

"I went inside and talked with Mr. Wilson. When I left, he came out and told Goldie the fire was lit, and it was now warm enough in his office for her to come in.

"She jumped out of the truck and ran inside the office. She got up in his chair by the stove and lay down as if to say, 'It's about time'." Your father said she has him trained very well."

The anger quickly disappeared from Mary's face, and she turned a little red. Soon she smiled, and then laughed.

"I'm sorry, Jimmy," she said. "I didn't know what you were thinking about. It made me a little mad to think that you would think anything bad about her, especially, after she found you when you were lost."

"I see that you were not laughing at her, but at what she does. I forgive you," she said. She walked toward the school, leaving Jimmy standing by himself.

"You what?" Jimmy said. Mary just kept on walking. He ran to catch up with her. "What's the matter with you? I didn't do anything to Goldie. I'm grateful for her and love her very much. I agree that I owe her a lot. But I didn't do anything to need forgiveness for."

Mary seemed to not hear him. He threw up his hands in exasperation. As they walked onto the school grounds, she ran to where some of her girlfriends were talking. She said something to them, and they laughed.

Soft Feather

He stopped and shook his head. "Girls!" he muttered out loud, as he turned and walked off.

The bell on the side of the building rang. It was time to go in. Classes would start in a few minutes. He hurried through the door and down the hall to his locker.

He got the book and notebook he needed for his first class, and slowly made his way through the crowd to his classroom and sat down at his desk. He looked around the room and saw a new student come in with the teacher. He looked over at him and said, "Hi."

It surprised the new student, and he said, "Hi," back to him.

Then he recalled seeing him somewhere before. Inside, he felt good about him and felt that he would be someone he would like. Somehow, he knew they would be friends.

The thought made him feel good. "To finally have a friend in Mercer would be great," he thought. No young kid around town tried to be his friend. But now there was another new person in town like himself.

Then he remembered who the new kid was. He told him about his hawks being stolen. They put them in a cave. He found them because of this guy.

When class started, Mrs. Davis introduced the new student. "This is Donald Nix. His parents have just moved into town from one of the coal mining camps between Longmont and Denver. We are glad that his parents chose to live in Mercer.

"I want everyone to welcome Donald to our class and show him around so he will feel at home." She stopped and looked around the classroom.

"Donald, you can sit over there near Jimmy Warrior. It hasn't been long since he, too, was a new boy in town."

Soft Feather

Don walked over and sat down next to Jimmy. They looked at each other and nodded. Class started, and Don didn't have any paper or pencil. Jimmy lent him a pencil and some of his paper.

Don thanked him and said to let him know how much he owed him, and he would pay him back the next day.

At lunchtime, Jimmy got to talk to Don for a couple of minutes in the hall, before they both ran home to eat.

After lunch, Jimmy ran back to school to see if Don returned. He saw that he was talking to a couple of girls. Jimmy was not one to talk to girls much, so he didn't bother him.

Sure, he could talk to Mary, but that was different. She was a year younger, and they had some of the same interests. Jimmy recalled a conversation he and Mary had a few weeks before that he still wondered about though.

He was surprised that day when she told him a little about her family and her own life. Her parents, Bill and Helen Wilson, married later in life than most of her friends' parents did. Her mom was married before, and her husband was killed in an accident where he worked, a year after they married. That left Helen a widow at 25.

Three years later, she met Bill Wilson. They began courting, and eleven months later, they married. Two years later, Mary was born. Helen was 30 and Bill, 32. Since Mary was an only child, they tried not to be over-protective and not to spoil her. But that was hard for them, and they often let her know that she was spoiled.

Mary wanted to try out for cheerleader when school started. At first they told her they didn't like the idea. But after talking to her teacher, they said she could try out.

The teacher assured her parents that Mary and all the other girls would be closely supervised. Bill and Helen

Soft Feather

told her they would go to all the basketball games they could if she became a cheerleader.

Jimmy liked her because she always had a kind word for everybody, and that meant a lot to many of the students in school. He found out that she was voted "Miss Personality" in the 6th grade.

Then she told him that someday, when they had more time, she would tell him a little about her grandfather and grandmother's lives. Since then, they hadn't had much time to get together and talk. School and other related activities took up most of their time. When they did have a little time, they seemed to be irritated about one thing or another.

Training their hawks brought them together. With them gone, there seemed to be a vacuum between them.

The bell rang, and the students filed into school. The noise of lockers opening and closing rang through the halls as students got their books and headed for their classes.

When school ended that day, Jimmy left on the run to pick up Mr. Wilson's ice-skates.

He ran all the way and hurried into the office. The ice skates lay on the chair beside the stove. Mr. Wilson was nowhere around. Then he heard a noise out in the garage. He picked up the skates and hurried out into the garage and looked around.

He saw a light move around under a car in the grease pit. Mr. Wilson was greasing the car.

He bent down near the side of the car so Mr. Wilson could see him. "I've got the ice skates."

"Fine, Jimmy," he said. "Have lots of fun with them. I did."

"I will," Jimmy answered. He stood up and hurried out of the garage. As he reached the street, he noticed that

Soft Feather

some of the ice melted off the highway, but only where the cars traveled.

The rest of the ice was still hard. He walked out to a dry place on the road and headed home.

Before he took two steps, he heard someone call his name, but he kept on walking. It was Mary. He didn't want to talk to her now. He wanted to go ice-skating. Anyway, she made him mad that morning.

She surprised him in the way she treated him. It not only surprised him, it made him mad the way she did it. He was not in the mood to talk to her.

He hurried on down the road towards the last road off the highway. His grandparents lived at the end of the road. When he reached the road, he followed the car tracks up to his yard. He was in a hurry, and he just waded through the snow up to the house, making another set of tracks.

In the kitchen, he proudly showed his grandma the ice skates Mr. Wilson lent him. When she saw them, she said, "Ice-skating brings back a lot of memories for me, Jimmy."

Jimmy placed the skates on the floor next to the wall.

"I'm glad Bill lent you his skates. He is a nice man, you know."

"He sure is," Jimmy said. He took his books to his room and changed into his warmest clothes. He was excited as he put on his stocking cap and gloves, and then hurried back down the hall to the kitchen.

"May I go ice-skating, Grandma?" he asked. "Mr. Wilson said there's a big ditch on the other side of town, and the ice is good and thick. He tried it yesterday, and it held him."

"I don't see why not, Jimmy," she replied, looking at him. "Just make sure you're home in plenty of time for

Soft Feather

supper. We're going to have some of that deer meat you brought home. You surely don't want to miss that, do you?"

"No, ma'am!" he exclaimed. "I'll be back in plenty of time for supper, Grandma." He started to the front door, then stopped to pick up the skates.

He opened the front door and went outside. He was a bundle of energy, and he was looking for a place to unleash it. "Look out, ice, here I come!" he thought.

Jimmy ran down a couple of back streets so that he wouldn't have to go by Mr. Wilson's garage. He didn't want to see Mary right now, maybe later, after he learned how to ice-skate.

He made his way back to the highway and walked along the road until he was out of town. "Where is that big ditch Mr. Wilson talked about?" he wondered.

He walked a couple of more blocks, then saw a bridge up ahead. He ran to the bridge and stopped in the middle of it. He walked over to the bridge railing and looked down. There was no water in the ditch. It was all ice - - frozen up to the banks on both sides.

The ice looked nice and smooth. There were spots of really rough places a short distance down the ditch. He sure didn't want to fall on one of those spots.

He shrugged his shoulders and walked over to the other side of the bridge. Slowly, he made his way through the weeds and rocks down the bank to the ice. He stepped out onto the ice with one foot to see if it would hold him. It did.

Gently, he stepped onto the ice with both feet. Then he hopped up and down a little to see if it would take that kind of punishment. The ice didn't crack anywhere. It was a solid block of ice up and down the ditch.

Soft Feather

With quick, small steps, he ran a little, then slid quite a ways. "This is all right," he thought as he walked over to a smooth rock on the bank and sat down.

He looked at the ice skates and then at his shoes, trying to figure it out. Holding one up, he decided that they were supposed to clamp on to his shoes. All he needed to know was, "How?"

He then saw a leather thong wrapped around one of the skates. Taking a closer look, he saw there was a key tied to one end.

He untied the key, took it off, and looked closely at it. Then he looked at the skates.

"Of course, the key adjusts the clamps," he said out loud. He tried the key, and it worked.

He placed his right foot on one of the skates, and soon had it clamped to his shoe. He quickly tied the straps around his ankle.

It wasn't long until he had the other one clamped to his shoe, and the straps tied around his ankle.

He then re-tightened them. The leather thong with the skate key went around his neck.

"Now to stand up," he thought. He pushed himself up and stood there, smiling. Then his feet went both ways, and he sat down hard on the ice.

Slowly, he stood up, but, again, his feet flew out from under him. The only difference was that he fell forward instead of backwards. His hands broke his fall.

He rolled over and sat up. He shook his head, knowing he would have to do better or give up ice-skating.

This time he carefully turned over and got up on his hands and knees. With great effort, he stood on the skates with both of his feet bent inward until his knees touched.

He slowly bent them outward until his ankles were almost touching the ice. They were weak, which caused him to have a hard time standing on top of the skates.

Soft Feather

Still standing, he decided that he would try to walk on the skates. That worked a lot better, so he walk-skated at first. The more he worked at it, the better he became.

The problem that he now faced was to watch out for the rough ice. Most of it was smooth as glass, but he soon discovered some was like sandpaper. When he skated into the rough ice, he would usually fall forward. Fortunately, his gloves protected his hands, and his pants, his knees.

He didn't go very far up the ditch that day. There was a large section of real good ice, and he skated on it. It wasn't long until his bent-over ankles bothered him.

He skated back to where he put the skates on, sat down and took them off. He took a shoe off and rubbed his foot. It felt good, so he put that shoe back on and did the same thing to the other foot. He stood up again. His feet felt so strange that he had a problem standing. It didn't last long.

He picked up the skates and made his way up the bank, heading back towards the side of the bridge.

He looked up and was surprised to see Don Nix sitting on the railing in the middle of the bridge. He had his skates in his hand and held them up. He smiled at Jimmy as he got down and walked toward him.

Jimmy made his way around the corner of the bridge and stopped. Don walked up to where he stood.

"Hi, Jimmy. I just found a new place to set my traps. I practiced ice-skating a little. Then, I saw you skating up the creek there," he said. "I see you skate like I do. I'm hoping with a little more practice, the two of us will be able to skate a lot better."

They both laughed. "This is my first time," Jimmy admitted. "It's a lot harder than it looks. My ankles were bent over all the time."

Soft Feather

"Mine, too," Don replied. "It's going to be a long winter, Jimmy. By the time it's over, I'm sure we will both be skating like professionals."

"That sounds good to me," Jimmy said, "but I don't know about skating like a professional. I just hope I can stand up without falling down so much."

Don laughed and agreed as they walked down the highway toward Mercer. As they came close to the edge of town, Don walked to the left at the first street. He stopped and pointed down the road.

"I live down this road two blocks," he said. "You see that two-story house on the other side of the railroad tracks? That's where I live. Come over and see me when you can. I'll be doing a lot of trapping now, since it turned cold."

"Trapping?" Jimmy asked.

"Yeah, Jimmy," he said. "Here in town and not far out of town in the creeks and ditches."

"Oh?" Jimmy said.

"Muskrat trapping. If you'd like to learn how to trap muskrats, I'll show you how. But I have to go out two or three times at night to check my traps."

"If you like to sleep a lot, you won't like muskrat trapping. I've gotten used to it, but it takes a lot of time."

"I don't know, Don," Jimmy said, slowly. "I'll ask my grandparents. My grandpa knows a lot about hunting. Being an Indian, I'm sure he knows something about muskrat trapping."

Don looked at Jimmy. "Your grandpa's an Indian?"

Jimmy could feel it coming, but he went on, anyway. "Yeah. Both of my grandparents are full-blooded Indian. That makes me an Indian," he replied. "What about it?"

"My mother's an Indian," Don said. "My dad is French, but my mother is Indian. That's what people say is

Soft Feather

a half-breed. Lots of people don't like me because of that, but I don't care."

Jimmy smiled. "I know the feeling, Don," he said. "Lots of people don't like Indians. My mother is Indian, and so is my dad. They both came from the same tribe, the Taos Indian tribe in New Mexico. There's even a town named after them. Taos, New Mexico."

"Hey, that's great," Don replied. "I don't know what tribe my mother came from, but I believe it's in New Mexico, too... maybe farther west. I heard her talking about living in the western part of New Mexico one time.

"She mentioned something about the Black Feet. I don't know if that's a tribe or not. I think she was talking about my feet. They surely get black now and then trapping and hunting."

Jimmy laughed. "We're almost blood brothers, Don," he said. "Wouldn't that be great if we were? That would be something, all right."

Don thought about that for a while. "I don't know, Jimmy," he said thoughtfully. "I've got three brothers already. I don't know if I could stand another one."

They both laughed. It felt good to have someone to laugh with. Jimmy needed it.

"You know, you said you didn't care if people like you," Jimmy said. "Well, I don't believe you. I know I care a lot. I like for people to like me, and when they don't, I feel bad. I'm like you, though; I cover up my feelings a lot and try to act like I don't care. "

"Yeah, I understand what you're saying, but I'm not going to let jerks that don't know anything about me make me feel like I'm not as good as they are, just because I'm part Indian," Don said, angrily. "I'll get even with them for treating me like that."

Jimmy wanted to tell him he didn't think that would do any good, but he decided to let it go for now.

Soft Feather

Changing the subject they talked about Mercer and school.

Then he remembered he promised his grandma to be home for supper. "I've got to run, Don," he said. "I promised my grandma that I'd be home for supper."

"I shot a deer a couple of weeks ago and we're going to have some of it for supper. I'm sure looking forward to it."

"You shot a deer?" Don said, smiling. "That's great. We'll go hunting, too. Both of us being Indian, we'll become the best hunters and trappers in the world."

They laughed as they parted. Jimmy ran down the highway as fast as he could.

As he passed Mr. Wilson's garage, Mr. Wilson waved at him. He waved back and yelled, "We're having venison for supper, and I have to hurry home. I'll see you in the morning and tell you if it's any good."

"It'll be good," Mr. Wilson shouted back. "Everything your grandma cooks is good. I envy you."

He ran on, heading for the last street again. He slowed down as he approached the street and turned the corner that led up to his house. He stopped and looked at the beautiful sight that lay before him.

The lights were on in his grandparents' house, and the glistening snow all around it brought a big smile to his face.

Behind the house rose the magnificent Rocky Mountains with their tops all covered with snow. Green pine trees with snow lacing their branches, stood tall, dotting the timberline and trailing on down into the valley.

It looked just like some of the Christmas cards he saw at the drug store. It made him feel good inside and he smiled.

Soft Feather

As he looked at his grandparents' house, a pleasant thought came to him, "Not everyone can live in a Christmas card."

His smile disappeared as he thought about his parents. One lived in New Jersey, the other in Texas, and here he was in Colorado. His eyes clouded, and a tear rolled down his cheek.

The idyllic picture in his mind slowly faded away, leaving only a blur.

"Another Christmas without my parents. It's not fair," he thought, as he wiped his eyes. "It is not fair."

Soft Feather

CHAPTER 4

Jimmy's school week went by slowly. His friendship with Don grew as the days and weeks passed. They were together everywhere they went during school hours. But after school hours, Don had other things to do.

Jimmy had no idea where he went or what he did. He asked a couple of times, but all he said was that he needed to work with his dad. His dad worked hard in the coal mine. When he came home, Don was expected to be there to work with him. They did a lot of hunting and trapping together. Jimmy wondered what was going on in Don's life. As the days got shorter, no one could work much after dark.

One day Jimmy asked his grandpa about muskrat trapping. Tom told him there were quite a few muskrats in some of the creeks and ditches around Mercer. He said if he was serious about catching muskrats, he would borrow a few traps for him from Mr. Miller.

"You will have to give them back when you make enough money to buy your own. You will also need a pair of rubber hip boots. I've got a pair you could use. They're old, but they didn't leak the last time I used them."

"I'll think about it, Grandpa," he said. He thought about it all week.

"It might be fun," he thought. Don warned him that anyone who traps muskrats loses a lot of sleep. That part bothered him. Jimmy liked his sleep, especially on the weekends.

Friday came, and when the last class was over, Don walked with Jimmy out of the school building. Before they parted, Don said, "Would you like to go out with me tonight on my trap run, Jimmy? I ran them this morning before I came to school and pulled all of the traps."

"Well," he hedged.

Soft Feather

"I've got to go put them out again tonight. Would you like to go and see how muskrats are caught?"

"Sure, I'd like to go," Jimmy said.

"You come over to my place about nine o'clock tonight," Don said. "Wear some high rubber boots. Do you have any?"

"My grandpa has a pair," he said. "I'll see you at nine tonight."

They each headed home. "Well, you did it again," he thought to himself as he walked along.

"You'll probably lose a whole night's sleep. Oh, well, I know it's going to be fun." He thought a moment, then shouted, "I know it!"

"You know what?" came a voice from behind him.

He knew the voice. It was Mary's. Jimmy kept on walking as Mary came up alongside him. "You know 'what', Jimmy?" she asked again.

"Come on, Jimmy. Speak to me. Are you still mad at me?"

She grabbed his arm and stopped him. "Can't you take a joke?"

"Was that what that was, Mary?" Jimmy asked, without looking at her.

"Yes, it was," she said, sheepishly. "Don't be mad at me, Jimmy. We're friends and I want to keep it that way. Don't you?"

Jimmy smiled. "Of course, I do," he replied. "But I didn't know how to take what you said." They walked, not saying anything.

"I'm going trapping tonight," he said.

She stopped, and so did he. "Who with?" Mary inquired, stepping back and looking at him.

"Don asked me to come over to his house tonight at nine, and he'll show me how to trap muskrats."

Soft Feather

Mary didn't say anything for some time. They walked up in front of her father's garage and stopped.

"I've noticed you and Don hanging around together a lot at school, Jimmy," she said, as she headed for the office door. "Hope you both have a good time tonight and trap a lot of muskrats."

Winking at him, she smiled. "They make wonderful, soft fur coats."

She opened the door and went inside. He walked home thinking about what she said. He'd never thought about muskrats making soft fur coats.

His nose smelled something good when he opened the door. It smelled so good he was pretty sure he knew what his grandma cooked. "What are you cooking, Grandma?" he asked.

"Nothing but a cherry pie, Jimmy," she said, smiling. "You don't like cherry pie, do you? No, I didn't think so. Well, I'll probably have to give it away to the first hungry person that comes along. If you see anyone like that around here, you tell them I've got a nice piece of cherry pie for them."

He beamed. Cherry pie was his favorite pie. "I'll go into my bedroom and see if there's anyone in there that would want some cherry pie."

He ran to his room and put his books on the dresser. He quickly changed clothes and went back to the kitchen. With his head bowed, he said, "That boy in the bedroom told me you had some cherry pie for a starving boy."

Alice put her hands on her hips.

"Grandma, I surely hope you have a lot, because I really am starving for cherry pie."

They laughed as she cut a large piece of pie, got the milk out and poured a large glass.

Now that was what she liked to see, her grandson sitting at her table, wanting some of her cooking. She

Soft Feather

placed the pie and the milk in front of Jimmy and watched him.

Memories filled her mind as she remembered how Jimmy's father, Tommy, sat in that very same chair eating her cherry pie.

She longed to see her boy so much that it hurt way down deep inside. She got up and walked around the table and stood behind Jimmy.

"Please, Lord," she prayed, "If it's your will, I'd surely like to see my boy one of these days." She straightened Jimmy's hair with her hands. "Thank you."

It was Friday, and Jimmy's grandpa had to work. Supper was a little later than usual, but when Tom came home, he found Jimmy waiting for him at the door. "What is it, Jimmy?" he asked, as he took off his coat and gloves. "Let's go into the kitchen and sit down. Then you can tell me."

"Don Nix, the boy I told you about asking me to go muskrat trapping with him - -, he wants me to go with him on his trap run tonight. I'd like to use your boots, if I may," Jimmy said.

"Sure," Tom replied. "I told you, you may use them whenever you need them. They're in my closet. I'll go get them for you."

Tom got up and went into his bedroom and soon returned with the boots. "You'll need to wear a couple of pairs of socks to keep your feet warm. Try not to let any water get inside the boots. If you do, the wet socks will cause your feet to get very cold in that freezing water."

Jimmy went to his room and came back with two pairs of heavy socks. He held them up so his grandpa could see. "Will these do?" he asked.

"Yep," his grandpa answered. "When are you going?"

Soft Feather

"I'm supposed to be over at his house at nine o'clock," Jimmy responded.

Tom pulled out his pocket watch and looked at it. "We'd better eat, then," he said. "You'll be late if we don't eat soon."

"After you two get cleaned up, supper will be ready," Alice said.

They looked at each other and headed for the bathroom. When they returned, it was on the table.

They sat down, and Tom asked the blessing.

"The day has been great, so far," he thought, "I wonder if tonight will be a great night."

It was after eight when they finished eating and Jimmy went to his room. He put on his long underwear, followed by two pairs of pants and the socks. He walked out to the kitchen, where the boots were.

"I'm glad to see you're all bundled up," Alice said. "It's cold out there. If you get too cold, Jimmy, you come home. Don't stay out there and freeze a hand or foot. There's nothing in this world that's worth one of your fingers or toes."

"Yes, ma'am," he said. He'd never thought about it being that cold outside. He went over to the hall closet and got his heavy coat. He picked up his grandpa's boots and headed towards the door.

He began to get too warm. "It wouldn't be good to start sweating before I get outside," he thought.

"I'll see you later," he said. "Don't worry, I'll be all right."

When outside, he made his way out of the yard and down the street. As he walked along the street, a car came around the corner and headed toward him. He jumped to the side of the road, not knowing who was in the car.

The car slid past him and came to a stop. Jimmy hurried over to the car and looked inside. It was Don.

Soft Feather

"Why are you driving your dad's car, Don?"

"Oh, I get his car all the time, Jimmy. It's the only way I can get around and check my traps. Come on, get in."

He ran around the car with his boots swinging back and forth, and got in.

Don turned the car around and headed back towards the highway. Turning left on the highway, he drove down the main street of Mercer.

Jimmy could hardly believe that Don got his dad's car. He watched as the stores quickly passed by. Soon they were driving outside of town. "I'm going to set my traps in a new place tonight, Jimmy," Don said.

"Remember the other day when I met up with you ice-skating? I told you I found a new ditch to trap. It's right up here."

Don slowed down as the two of them started looking for the ditch. He clicked a button on the floorboards, and the headlight high beam came on. A small bridge came in sight.

"There it is, Jimmy." Slowing down, he pulled off of the road and parked.

"Put your boots on while I open the trunk and start getting things out."

Off came his shoes, and on went his grandpa's boots. Then he rushed around to the back of the car.

The trunk was open, and Don had a flashlight in each hand. He handed one to Jimmy and turned on the other one. "Grab some of those traps," he said.

"Get a handful of those sticks, too. We'll need them to anchor the chains on the traps to the bank of the ditch."

Jimmy started to pick up the traps when he saw the shotgun. "What's that for, Don?" he asked.

"That's for anyone I catch running my traps," he said. "I don't mess around when I catch someone stealing from me, Jimmy."

53

Soft Feather

"Grab all of those traps right there, and we'll get them placed as quickly as we can."

Jimmy picked up the traps and sticks. Don closed the trunk lid, and they walked over to the bridge.

Don led the way with his flashlight as they made their way down the bank of the creek and into the water.

Jimmy was pleasantly surprised when he stepped into the water. "It wasn't as cold through the rubber boots as he thought it would be."

This trapping wasn't going to be as bad as he imagined. He turned on his flashlight and followed along after Don, shining it here and there.

Don moved his light back and forth, searching along the banks of the ditch. Then he stopped.

"There's one, Jimmy," he said, pointing.

Jimmy looked, expecting to see a muskrat. But it was only a hole halfway in the water. Don went over and placed his traps on the side of the bank. He took one and opened it and set the trigger that held it open.

He gently put it in the water inside the hole. He set it down carefully and slowly removed his hand. Wiping it off on his coat, he doubled it up and blew into his fist a couple of times to warm it up.

He took a stick and stuck one end through the large ring at the end of the chain attached to the trap. Using another stick, he pounded it into the side of the ditch next to the hole.

"That looks good, Jimmy. We should have a muskrat here when we come back at midnight. I hope."

They continued walking, looking for another hole. Jimmy got pretty good at spotting the muskrat holes. It wasn't long until all of the traps were in the holes in the ditch bank.

"Not all of the holes we have traps in are muskrat holes, Jimmy," Don said, as they splashed along, headed

Soft Feather

back to the road. "But those that are will give us a muskrat if we don't let it get away."

"How can they get away after they have been trapped?"

"Oh, they chew off their leg," Don replied. "They would rather lose a leg than be caught. So if they are left in the traps too long, they won't be there when we come back to get them."

"How about that," Jimmy said, shaking his head.

They walked along the banks, not saying anything. Jimmy broke the silence as he looked at the water and then at Don. "Why is it that this water doesn't freeze in this ditch, but it does in that other ditch?"

"The water is too shallow here, Jimmy. The water is still running under the ice you skated on the other day."

That made sense to him. When they reached the bridge, they climbed out of the ditch and got back in the car. Don turned around and headed back to town. He turned at the first street and drove up in front of his house.

Jimmy felt a little strange going into Don's house like this, but he invited him. Don opened the door, and they walked in.

He found himself in the kitchen. Don's mother sat at the table and waited for him to come in so she could go to bed.

She had long black hair like his mother. "She surely is Indian," Jimmy thought to himself.

He saw some of his mother's characteristics in her as she stood there looking at him. He didn't say a word as she came toward him.

"This is my mother, Jimmy," Don said.

"Hello, Mrs. Nix," he said, realizing he was daydreaming.

"Don tells me you're Indian," she said, as she neared Jimmy. "I'm Indian but not part of the Taos tribe. I'm from

Soft Feather

the western part of New Mexico. That's where the Apache tribe comes from, you know."

"Yes, ma'am," Jimmy said, even though he didn't know.

"Your dad is asleep, Donald. Don't make any noise out here to wake him. You know how mad he gets when he's disturbed late at night."

She walked toward the door leading to the other room. "Goodnight," she whispered, before she opened the door, then closed it.

Don pulled two chairs out from under the table. He turned them so they faced the coal stove in the middle of the room. He took off his coat and placed it on the back of one of the chairs.

He sat down and looked over at Jimmy. "You might as well sit down," he said. "We have a few hours to wait until midnight. Sit down and get warm. Take off your coat and boots. We'll need to be good and warm when we go back outside. It gets colder after midnight."

Jimmy took off his coat and put it on the back of the other chair. Taking his boots off, he wiggled his toes around to see if they still worked.

Don reached over and opened the oven door. He lowered it until it lay flat. "We can put our feet on it as soon as it cools down a little. Nothing like warming your feet on a nice warm oven door, Jimmy," he said.

It wasn't long before their stocking feet were toasting on the open oven door. They did a lot of whispering at first. Not being old friends, they didn't have much to talk about.

They waited for midnight to come. The two of them found it hard to stay awake.

It seemed to Jimmy he just closed his eyes when a strange noise brought him wide-awake. It was Mrs. Nix.

"It's midnight, Don," she said.

Soft Feather

Don was almost asleep, but his mother's gentle shaking brought him wide-awake. They got up and put their boots back on. Their coats were next as they headed out the door.

The cold air hit them in the face, and sleep vanished. With cleared minds, they were ready to go get some muskrats.

Don started the car and slowly backed out of the yard. He sped up as they drove back down the highway toward the ditch where they placed the traps. Nothing moved anywhere.

He parked the car and hurried around to the trunk and opened it. He got two sawed-off broom handles and two good-sized potato sacks. He handed one of each to Jimmy and closed the trunk lid.

"What do I do with these?" he asked, waving them around.

"We put the muskrats we catch in the sacks, and the broom handles are to hit them with." Don said. "It sure is a lot easier to carry them in a sack than by their tails. You have to be real careful that they don't bite you."

"I've had them bite me through my boot. It not only hurts, but it makes your boot leak, and your foot can freeze."

They made their way down the ditch bank and into the water. "It's really hard to stop a boot from leaking once it has a hole in it," Don said, shining his flashlight along the creek bank.

"Just watch me and you won't have any trouble with muskrats."

Slowly, they moved up the ditch. "Try to not make any noise," Don said. "If we do have any in the traps, noise will scare them, and they will frantically try to get loose."

They walked along as quietly as they could. Their lights moved back and forth on the banks ahead.

Soft Feather

"There's one over there, Jimmy," Don said, as he shined his light into the hole in the bank.

Jimmy couldn't see anything, at first, but then he saw the funny-looking rat under the water. Don walked over and pulled the stick out of the side of the bank. He lifted the chain up in front of him.

The muskrat came out of the water with its foot clamped in the trap. Don took his broom handle and hit the muskrat in the neck behind its head. It stopped moving, and Don laid it on the bank.

He opened the trap and placed it back in the hole very carefully. Again he drove the stick in the bank, only this time using the broom handle.

"That's one, Jimmy," Don said, as he lifted it up so he could see it.

It sure didn't look soft and furry to him. It looked like a wet rat.

With one muskrat in the sack, they walked on up the ditch. Don hoped to find a lot more.

Some of the traps were the same as when they left them. A few were sprung with nothing in them.

In one of the traps they found the leg of a muskrat. Don shook his head and reset the trap.

They set a dozen traps and caught four muskrats. Jimmy didn't think it was too good, but Don was overjoyed. When they started back to the car, they each carried two muskrats.

Nearing the highway, Don said, "Not a bad catch, Jimmy. We could have caught nothing. Many a night I've found nothing in my traps. That's when I get discouraged and want to quit. But these four muskrats will bring me over ten dollars. They pay me by how big they are."

"These will bring about three dollars each. If we catch a couple more tonight, we might make over fifteen dollars. That's a lot of money for one night's work."

Soft Feather

Jimmy hadn't looked at it that way. That would be more than his grandpa made sweeping out the beer joints on the weekends. They climbed out of the ditch and walked over to the car, and Don opened the trunk.

Don placed the four muskrats and the broom handles in the bottom of the trunk. He turned the flashlight on the muskrats. "Sure glad you came tonight, Jimmy. Now you can see how much fun trapping is."

"Yeah," Jimmy agreed, turning off his flashlight and placing it in the trunk. He hadn't thought of it as that much fun, though. He didn't like seeing Don kill the muskrats that way. Besides, it was cold and wet, and he could have been asleep in a nice warm bed.

But there were the four muskrats that could be sold for money. It did change his thinking a little.

Don drove back to his house, and again they sat in front of the warm stove. It wasn't long until they fell asleep. Mrs. Nix came in and woke them at three.

The next time they went out, they came back with two more muskrats in the traps. The third time Mrs. Nix called them, it was five in the morning. They heard Mr. Nix say something in the bedroom. He had to get up and go to work.

They got dressed quickly and left before he came into the kitchen. Don didn't say anything, but Jimmy felt like he didn't want him to meet his dad.

After he heard Mr. Nix's gruff voice, he followed Don out the door, not sure he wanted to meet him, anyway.

They made the trek back to the ditch and made a quick check of all the traps. There was nothing in the first one. Don pulled the trap and threw it over his shoulder, holding onto the large rings in the end of the chain.

He handed Jimmy the stick that secured the traps, and they continued walking. There were no muskrats. Don

Soft Feather

pulled the last trap and handed it to Jimmy. He then drove the stick back into the side of the bank.

"This stick will let me know how far we came this time," he said, "Tonight, when I come back, I'll know where to start."

As they started back toward the car, Jimmy's mind began to sort out what happened that night. He learned a lot from just this one night's work with Don. He was sure he could trap now by himself if he had to.

They talked and laughed as they walked, not caring how much noise they made. It started to get light in the east. It wouldn't be long until the sun would be up.

It had been a long time since Jimmy was up this early. He took a big deep breath and slowly let it out. It felt good.

"We didn't get all of the muskrats here tonight," Don said. "There are still a lot of them around here. But you never want to over-trap a place. They must have time to multiply and grow, and then you come back."

"We got six muskrats tonight from this little creek. Most of them were large adults, but two of them were young. The thing to do now is to leave them alone for a while and trap further up the ditch."

"I'll work this ditch as far as I can without getting in trouble with a farmer. You sure don't want that."

Jimmy nodded his head in agreement as they climbed out of the ditch and opened the trunk.

"I've had to sneak onto a lot of farmers' land to trap," Don said, as he put the traps and sticks in the trunk. He closed the trunk, and they got in the car.

Don looked at Jimmy. "The farmers think they own the ditch. They don't, but try telling them that. So I just walk down the center of the ditch so I don't leave any tracks. No farmer gets up in the middle of the night to check the ditch that runs through his farm.

Soft Feather

"When I get out here on my last trap run, it is close to the time most of the farmers around here get up. If he sees you, you've got trouble. I've only been caught one time."

"He told me, 'Never come on my property again'!"

Don laughed as he bragged, "I was there that night and caught ten muskrats. I made my last run an hour earlier, and he didn't even know I trapped his ditch before he got up. He still doesn't know, and it surely hasn't hurt him."

Jimmy agreed with a small laugh. Don was a sly one, but Jimmy felt a little uneasy about his bold attitude.

Don started the car and headed back to Mercer. It was six o'clock when they drove down Main Street that morning.

All of the stores were closed. The sun came up, and a soft orange glow settled on all of the buildings.

There was still a lot of snow that hadn't melted on the north side of the buildings.

Shadows from the trees and buildings on the east side of the road moved slowly down the buildings as the sun came up. They soon passed Mr. Wilson's filling station and garage.

They were the only two out in the sleepy little town that Saturday morning.

Then his eyes opened wide. "It's Saturday morning, and I'm still up. I'm going to miss all the fun I usually have on Saturdays." Sleeping in was one of the things he liked to do best, but he didn't want to sleep all day.

He looked towards the mountains and thought of something. He turned and looked towards the hills behind his house.

He remembered the snowman he built on the side of the hill behind his grandparents' house. It was over a week

Soft Feather

since he built it. Unfortunately, other things filled his mind. He would have to correct that.

Don turned off Main Street and drove to where Jimmy lived. He pulled up in front of his house. "Thanks a lot, Don, for showing me how to trap muskrats."

"Sure, Jimmy," he said. "I'm going home and get some sleep. See you later."

"OK. Me, too." He picked up his shoes and got out. He closed the door and waved, then went into the house.

He walked into the kitchen and found it was nice and warm. Alice stood by the stove. She smiled. "Well, how did you two trappers do last night?"

"We caught six muskrats, Grandma," he answered, as he took off his coat. "Don said he could get about fifteen dollars for them. Two of them were rather small."

Alice nodded her head in approval. "That's not bad for just one night's work, Jimmy."

"That's what I was thinking, Grandma," he said. He took off his boots and put his shoes on. "Grandpa said he would borrow a few traps for me if I want to try trapping. I believe I'll try it and see if I can make some money."

His grandma didn't say anything for a while. She began setting the table and was soon putting oatmeal in a bowl for Jimmy. As she put it on the table in front of him, she said, "That's a fine idea, Jimmy. But remember, school comes first. You can trap on Friday nights if you want, but not Saturday nights. You would have to sleep on Sunday, and Sunday is for church, school homework and rest."

"That's fine with me," he said, smiling up at her. "I don't think I could do it much more than that, Grandma. I like sleeping too much."

Alice didn't answer. He finished his oatmeal, and leaned back in the chair and closed his eyes. The nice warm room soon took its toll. His head nodded a couple of times, and he was asleep.

Soft Feather

Alice got up and shook him. When he opened his eyes, she helped him up and led him down the hall to his room. He undressed and got into bed under the heavy quilt with the birds on it. She picked up his clothes from the floor where he dropped them.

She opened the door and turned and looked fondly at Jimmy as he lay in bed, fast asleep. "Pleasant dreams, oh, great trapper of muskrats," she whispered, and closed the door.

Soft Feather

CHAPTER 5

It was late in the afternoon when Jimmy awoke. He thought about getting up but didn't. As he fought the idea, he remembered the snowman, Lone Warrior. He jumped out of bed and looked for his clothes. They were gone. "Grandma must have put them up," he thought.

He looked in his closet, but they were nowhere to be found. He had no choice but to get some clean clothes. He put them on, and after he washed and brushed his teeth, he hurried into the kitchen.

Tom started to the door to leave for work. He stopped and looked at Jimmy and smiled. "Heard you and your friend got six muskrats last night, Jimmy," he said. "That's not a bad night's work."

"Yes, sir."

Tom looked at Alice, then back at Jimmy. "Your friend, Don, came by earlier to see if you were up. He told us all about your trapping adventure last night. He left here on his way to Longmont to sell them.

"He came by to see if you wanted to go with him. But you were asleep, so he went by himself."

"Oh," Jimmy replied, kind of sad.

Tom shook his head and walked over to the front door. "You surely are a barrel full of excitement when you wake up," he said, laughing as he went out the front door.

Jimmy sat down at the table and looked out the window. "Grandma," he said slowly."

"Yes," she said.

"Don's the same age as I am. How come he gets to drive his dad's car and I don't get to drive?"

"His father lets him, Jimmy, that's why."

"Well, it just doesn't seem fair," he said.

"Don't go worrying about driving a car, Jimmy. You'll have more than your share of driving in your life."

Soft Feather

"Enjoy the time now that you don't have to. Your craving for driving a car will be fulfilled, wait and see."

She set his place at the table and put some turkey and trimmings on it. Jimmy ate two plates full and knew he couldn't eat any more. He was about to get up when his grandma cut a piece of cherry pie and gave it to him.

He didn't know what to do as he looked at it. He was full. But he loved cherry pie.

As he thought about it, he decided that he wasn't as full as he thought. He didn't eat it as fast, though, as he usually ate cherry pie.

"Grandma, I'm going out and see how Lone Warrior is doing. He may be melted away by now."

"Don't stay too long, Jimmy," Alice called after him.

"OK," he replied, opening the door. He stopped at the bottom of the porch steps.

He was surprised at what he saw. The sun was gone, and it was cloudy. It had even snowed some while he slept. "Sure is strange weather we're having around here," he thought.

Off he ran across the field behind the house. He jumped the creek and quickly climbed up the other side of the bank. He stopped and looked up the hill, glad to see his snowman was still there.

He made his way on up the hill. The sun melted a lot of Lone Warrior, but his eyes, nose, and smile were still there. One of the arm branches lay on the ground. He picked it up and laid it aside.

He gathered handfuls of fresh snow and began patting it onto the snowman. He repeated it over and over. He reshaped the belly, picked up the coal off the ground and put the buttons back on. He finished and stood back to admire his work.

Soft Feather

"There. You look like the old Lone Warrior!" he said.

"Well, almost, that is," he said, as he removed the branch arm and the coal from the face. It took some work to get it just right; then, he put the coal back on the face. He didn't put the branches back on this time.

"You've done a good job guarding our territory, Lone Warrior. I'm sorry that I didn't come sooner, but other things caused me to forget you were here. I'll try not to do that again."

He turned around and looked down the hill toward the house. His eyes took in everything, coming to rest on the creek below.

"I wonder if there are any muskrats in the creek," he thought to himself. "I'll go down and see."

He ran down the hill to the creek. Lone Warrior was left standing there all by himself again.

Down the embankment he went. The creek still trickled along, though there was ice here and there.

He walked along the creek bed, looking for a hole in the bank. "I know there's a muskrat hole around here somewhere," he thought. When he saw a hole, he assumed it was a muskrat hole. That's what Don did.

Jimmy stepped on some ice, and his foot went through and into the water. He now had one cold wet shoe and sock.

He kicked his foot a couple of times to get rid of some of the water before he continued along the creek. It wasn't long before he came to the highway bridge. He counted over a dozen holes in the creek bank.

He stopped, thinking about what he found. Why should he go far away to trap muskrats when they were right here close to home? By trapping here, he wouldn't need a car.

Soft Feather

He climbed up the bank onto the road and headed for home.

As he walked towards town he recalled his grandma telling him he could trap on Friday nights.

He turned off of the highway and hurried down the street that led to his house. He decided to ask his grandpa to borrow the traps. That way he would have enough time to get them ready to trap next Friday.

As he walked, his wet foot started to hurt. The cold hadn't bothered him while he walked along the creek. But when he walked on the frigid road, his foot got very cold and started to get numb.

There was a good six inches of snow covering the lane up to their house. As he walked through the snow, it began sticking to his wet shoe. He stayed in the tire tracks that Don's car made, but found it hard to walk straight.

He hurried along and quickly climbed up the porch steps and rushed into the house. He slammed the door. "Grandma!" he called.

Alice came out of the kitchen on the run. "What's wrong, Jimmy?" she asked.

"I stepped on some ice down at the creek, and my foot broke through. It's hurting."

"It didn't bother me until I walked down our lane. The snow stuck to my shoe, and my foot is getting numb now."

She helped him into the kitchen and sat him down at the table. She rushed to the bathroom and got a wash pan, filling it with cold water, and hurried back to the kitchen. "Take off your shoe and sock," she ordered.

He took them off and looked at his foot. It was pale with blue streaks through it. He felt it with his hand---it was icy. His grandma put the pan of cold water on the floor and started to put his foot in it.

Soft Feather

He hesitated about putting his foot in the frosty water. His grandma pushed it down into the water. To his amazement, it felt warm.

"How come it feels warm, Grandma?" he asked, as he looked up at her. "I know you put cold water in the pan."

Alice looked at his foot. "Your foot got a little frostbitten, Jimmy," she answered.

"Your foot is colder than the water, so the water feels warm to you. Just sit there for a few minutes, and it will gradually warm up. If we let it warm up slowly, you will never know it was frostbitten."

She went over to the wood stove, took the large teakettle off the back and filled it with water. She placed it on the front of the stove. Lifting one of the large lids on the front, she placed two large pieces of firewood in and put the lid back on the stove.

She opened the damper on the stovepipe, which let the air flow through the stove, helping the wood to burn faster.

When the wood started crackling, she placed the teakettle at the front of the stove where it was hotter. It didn't take long before the fire in the stove roared, and the water became warmer in the teakettle.

The bottom of the teakettle made a funny bubbling noise, as it got hotter and hotter. In a short time, a small amount of steam started coming out of the spout of the teakettle.

Alice reached up and closed the damper on the stovepipe, and the roaring in the stove stopped. Picking up the teakettle, she quickly moved it to the back of the stove.

She put her fingers in the water in the pan where his foot was, to check the temperature of the water. It was cool to her touch.

"How does your foot feel, Jimmy?" she asked.

Soft Feather

He took it out of the water and felt it. "It feels about the same, Grandma," he answered, as he eased it back into the water. "The water feels cold."

"I'm going to warm it up a little at a time," she said.

"Tell me when it starts feeling too hot for you to keep your foot in the pan. We'll do it slow and easy.

"Yes, ma'am."

Alice poured a small amount of hot water into the pan. Jimmy pulled his foot out fast. "It's too hot already," he said.

Alice laughed and shook her head. "No, Jimmy, it's not too hot. It just feels like that at first. Put your foot back into the water."

He dipped his big toe into the water and pulled it out quickly. He looked at his grandma, and she shook her head at him.

Slowly, he put his toe back in, then all of his toes, then all of his foot. The water soon felt cool.

"It's cold now, Grandma."

Alice poured some more hot water into the pan, but this time the water felt warm instead of hot. He liked that a lot better.

She poured a little more into the pan. It felt better and better.

She watched his face as she poured the water. When she saw him start biting his lip, she stopped pouring. She now realized that her grandson was not going to tell her it was too hot again.

She smiled, knowing that he felt like he hadn't acted like a man the first time; now he was going to be a man and take the heat.

She waited a while before she got the dipper out of the knife drawer, and a bucket from under the sink. She dipped some of the water out of the wash pan so it wouldn't run over.

Soft Feather

She felt the water again and found that it was just barely warm.

She repeated the process several times, going slowly each time. There was no reason to let Jimmy go through the pain he went through before. She looked at his foot in the pan now and then. It was now nice and pink.

"Everything is going to be all right," she thought.

Placing the teakettle on the back of the stove, she hurried down the hall to the bathroom. When she returned she had a large towel in her hand. She checked the water again. It was warm.

She handed the towel to him. "Here," she said. "You can dry your foot. It's all right now."

He took his foot out of the water and looked at it. It was a pinkish color. Alice took the pan to the bathroom sink and emptied it. She cleaned it and dried it with a towel, then put it back under the sink.

Next, she emptied the bucket into the sink and put it under the sink with the pan.

Jimmy sat and rubbed his foot with the towel. "It sure does feel a lot better. Thank you, Grandma, for all you did."

Alice came over to the table and sat down. "You are welcome. Always remember, you can't mess around with wet hands or feet in the winter temperatures that we have here. You had a mild case of frostbite.

"If you had been out in the cold a little longer, it could have been serious. When we tell you to be careful and watch what you do when you leave the house, this is one of the things we're talking about."

She stopped and looked at him. "Please don't take this as a scolding, Jimmy, but I have seen grown men lose a foot or a hand because they stayed out in the cold too long. When any part of you gets frozen, it's hard to save."

Soft Feather

The door opened and Tom came in from work. He saw the towel in Jimmy's hand and his foot in the other hand.

"What happened to you, Jimmy?" he asked as he sat down. "Did you get your foot frostbitten?"

"Yes, Grandpa. I sure did. Just a little bit."

Tom looked at Alice, then, back at his foot. The foot looked good. He sat down at the table.

"I borrowed those muskrat traps you wanted," he said, and looked at Jimmy for a reaction.

"Are you sure you still want to go out there where you can freeze your feet off just to get an old muskrat?"

Jimmy put the towel around his foot and rubbed it, then looked at it. "I don't know, Grandpa," he said finally. "I'll have to think about that a while. Grandma said I couldn't trap during the weekdays, only on Friday nights. So I'll wait and see how I feel Friday."

Tom and Alice looked at each other. That grandson of theirs was becoming wise. The cold scared him, that was for sure, but not enough for him to be afraid to go out again if the time was right. They knew he would do the right thing whether he trapped or not.

"I put Mr. Miller's muskrat traps out in the garage. He wishes you the best of luck. He said he tried it one year and did pretty good, but his farm work and other things got in his way, and he quit."

Tom smiled. "Chuck said his wife hid them. That was the 'other things'." They all laughed.

Jimmy started to put his sock back on, but it was wet. He looked up at his grandpa. "I walked up the creek bank behind our house earlier and found over a dozen holes in the banks," he said.

"I'll start there first. That way I won't have to walk a long way to set the traps. I would need a car to trap like Don does."

Soft Feather

"His dad lets him have his car, and Don traps all of the creeks and ditches around here. He makes pretty good money doing it, too."

Tom looked at him and didn't say anything for some time. Jimmy started feeling uneasy, and sat looking at the floor.

Tom cleared his throat. "Jimmy, you know you are not old enough to drive a car. Sure, he's just a year older than you, but he still isn't old enough to drive. Just because his father lets him drive his car doesn't make it right."

"I will let you drive my truck when you are old enough and get your driver's license. I know you drove it the day the spider bit me, but that was an emergency, Jimmy."

He stopped and looked at Alice, and then, back at Jimmy. "If another emergency like that one came up, I'd expect you to drive the truck again. But only in the case of an emergency."

He sat and looked at him. "Do you understand what I'm saying, Jimmy?"

Jimmy didn't answer at first, then slowly said, "Yes, sir."

"I see that you don't, and I'm sorry," Tom answered. "The day will come, though, when you'll understand exactly what I mean. We'll just have to wait for that day to come, and it will be here before you know it."

"But until then, I can't, and I won't, let you drive the truck."

"I do understand that I have to be older before I can do anything. It's always been that way. Why should it change now?"

Tom and Alice didn't say a word. He picked up his shoe and sock and excused himself. He went to his room, and closed the door. Taking off his other shoe and sock, he looked out the window.

Soft Feather

Slowly, he took off his clothes, turned the light off and got into bed. He pulled up the covers, and looked at the ceiling. When was he ever going to be old enough to do the things older people did? Don was his age, and his dad let him use the car. Why wouldn't his grandparents do the same? The things he really wanted to do, they wouldn't let him.

He was just as good a driver, or maybe even a little better, than Don.

There was a tap on his door, and it opened. His grandma turned on the light and came in smiling at him. She carried a piece of cherry pie and a glass of milk.

"You forgot to eat something when you came in, Jimmy," she said. "Would you like to have something to eat before you go to sleep?"

Jimmy sat up with a grin on his face and a twinkle in his eye. "Yes, Grandma, I sure would," he replied.

She put the milk and pie on his desk, went over to the closet and got his bathrobe out and gave it to him. He got up and sat down at his desk. The pie was soon gone, along with the milk.

"You make the best cherry pie in the world, Grandma."

"Thank you, Jimmy." She saw her son sitting at the same desk. Tommy hadn't understood, either, why his father wouldn't let him drive the truck when he was fourteen.

Now Jimmy is fourteen, and he is having the same thoughts his father did.

"Jimmy," she said, softly. "Your father felt the same way you do right now when he was your age. Your grandpa wouldn't let him drive until he had a driver's license. It all goes back to what's right and what's wrong according to the law.

Soft Feather

"You gave up your hawk, Strong Feather Lady Samson, because the law said it was unlawful to hunt with a hawk in Colorado. It's the same thing as driving without a license."

She stopped and watched him for any reaction. Seeing none, she continued. "Don't judge us too harshly, Jimmy. We're doing what we think is right for you. We know you don't feel the same as we do, but the responsibility is ours, not yours.

"If anything were to happen to you, your grandpa could never forgive himself. Not only that, he would be put in jail. So we have to think of that, too. Do you see?"

Jimmy frowned.

"You know your grandpa follows the law. The laws we live by are there for the best of everyone. I believe it all comes down to just one thing. Your friend gets his father's car, and you don't. That's what it's about, isn't it?"

Jimmy thought about it for a while, not saying anything. "I guess you're right, Grandma," he said. "I just want to drive a car now and then.

"When I drove the truck back home that day, I was frightened. But when I drove it after I unloaded the railroad ties, it was easy. I sure did like that."

"Well, Jimmy," she answered, as she picked up the glass and plate and looked at him. "You're going to have to be man enough to wait for about a year. I promise that the minute you turn fifteen years old, we will go with you to the driver's license office in Longmont and sign for you so you can get your license."

She walked over, opened the door and stopped. "What do you say? Is that a deal?"

"Yes, Grandma," he said, taking off his bathrobe and jumping back in bed. "It's a deal! And Grandma, I wouldn't ever want to get Grandpa in trouble."

Soft Feather

"I know you wouldn't," she said. She closed the door and went down the hall.

He looked at the ceiling again. The clouds moved in from the west and covered the moon; so, there wasn't much moonlight coming through his window.

"It might even snow again tonight," he thought pleasantly.

If it did, then the Lone Warrior wouldn't melt. Looking across the room, he saw the soap spool tank and elephant sitting on top of his dresser. "What's wrong with me?"

He looked back at the ceiling. "One moment he disliked his grandparents, the next, he loved them. "What is happening to me?" he wondered. He was fourteen, and he should be acting like a man. He'd have to stop acting like a kid.

People would think there was something wrong with him. Turning over, he went to sleep.

Soft Feather

CHAPTER 6

Don Nix waited for Jimmy when he got to school Thursday morning. He was smiling when he walked up to him. "Got fourteen dollars for those six muskrats after school yesterday, Jimmy," he said.

"I had to fill up the car with gas for my dad so I only had ten dollars left. But I sure had a lot of fun with that ten dollars." Jimmy hoped Don might give him a dollar or two for helping him, but he just kept talking. Anyway, it was already spent.

Jimmy listened. Don was so excited. "Sure wish you'd been up the other day when I came by, Jimmy. You could have gone with me to Longmont, and we'd have had a ball."

"I wanted you to see where I sell all the things I trap." He stopped and slapped him on the back.

Jimmy held back as long as he could, then asked, "What did you do, Don?"

"The fellow who buys my muskrats asked if I was going over to the Boulder carnival. I thought about it, then realized I had money in my pocket. So I told him 'sure'."

"I drove over there to check it out. Man it was nice. There were all kinds of rides and all kinds of girls - - brunettes, blonds, red heads, tall, skinny, short, fat - - I liked them all. You should have been with me. I had two or three gals hanging on me most of the time.

Later there was a street dance all around the courthouse. There were all kinds of food and soft drinks. The biggest thing was after we ate they formed a long Congo dance line. It wrapped all around the courthouse. It was something else, Jimmy. You should have been there," he said again.

Soft Feather

"Of course when it was over and I got home, I was broke. The only problem with having fun, you have to have money and a car. I had both and I had fun."

"How come you get to drive your dad's car when you're not old enough to have a license?" Jimmy asked, frowning at Don.

"My dad doesn't care about that, Jimmy. As long as I put gas in the car and give him part of what I make he's happy."

The school bell rang, and Jimmy made his way to his locker then to his classroom. He waved at Mary as he walked down the hall with Don. She gave him an odd smile, then went into her classroom.

"What's eating her now?" he wondered to himself. "She's off on another one of her things. I'm sure she'll let me know what it is later."

He didn't talk to Don the rest of the morning. At lunchtime he went home, ate, then quickly back to school. He wanted to hear more about Don's good time in Boulder. He looked all around the school but didn't see him.

The school bell rang. Jimmy walked slowly into the school building and up to his locker. "He should have come back from lunch quicker," he thought.

When the dismissal bell rang, Jimmy put everything in his locker and headed for the door. It was a long afternoon. He daydreamed almost every minute of it.

Mrs. Davis got onto him more than once, but he thought more and more about what Don told him and all the things that Don does, that he can't. He wanted to know, and he didn't want to know. He never felt this way before.

Monday after school he walked home, thinking about all kinds of things. Mary walked up beside him. She didn't say a word as they walked. Jimmy felt that she wanted to say something, but held it in.

Soft Feather

He decided to wait and see how long it would take for her to tell him whatever she had on her mind.

When they turned the corner and headed down Main Street toward her father's garage, she frowned each time she looked at him. "It won't be long now," he thought, and sure enough, Mary couldn't wait any longer.

"Jimmy!" she said, almost shouting.

He knew it was coming, but she was so loud it caught him by surprise. He grabbed his ears. "What?!" he shouted back.

"Don't you plug your ears when I talk to you, Jimmy Warrior!" she yelled at him. "I want to talk to you about your friend, Don Nix."

Jimmy looked around at all the other students who walked nearby. "Quit your shouting, Mary. Everyone is looking at us," he said, softly.

Mary didn't say a word; she just left Jimmy. He let her cover a good distance before he started to follow slowly. He didn't especially want to catch up with her.

Then he thought about what she said. "I wonder why she wants to talk to me about Don."

Jimmy wasn't watching Mary now and didn't see her stop and wait for him. He almost stumbled into her.

"Your friend, Don, got my friend, Rose's parents all worried about her this weekend," Mary said, calmly."

"What?" Jimmy asked.

"Well, Rose had a date with Don to go over to Longmont and go to a show, then the dance at Roosevelt Park and this is the story she told me:

"They went to the show but some of their friends at the show told them about a new dance hall over in Loveland. So the whole group went over there. They all had a great time. When it got late they all headed home except Don and Rose. They stayed until it closed.

Soft Feather

"Everything was going great, but they got a couple miles from Longmont and ran out of gas. The problem was he had enough gas to go to Longmont but not Loveland and back. It was after midnight and everything was closed.

"The moon shone and they talked as they walked toward Mercer. It was a good eight miles to Mercer. She twisted her ankle about halfway home. Don persuaded her they needed to go on. She put her arm around his shoulder and they slowly made their way along the road.

"When they reached the bridge across Boulder Creek she told him to go on without her. Well, he didn't want to leave her and she got mad. Then he got mad and walked away.

"He hadn't gone very far when she started yelling. He turned around and ran back to see what was wrong.

"She pointed and said, 'there's something under the bridge splashing around and making a lot of noise. It might be a bear!'

"Don listened and heard some loud grunting and splashing coming from under the bridge. He didn't think it was anything dangerous, so, decided to play the hero. He took off his shoes and socks and put them on the bridge railing. Rolling up his pants, he picked up some rocks and made his way around the bridge and down to the water. The water level was low and he found a small sandy island to stand on. He started kicking the water and throwing rocks and yelling.

"There was a loud squeal when he hit whatever was making the noise. Out from under the bridge came two scared skunks. "Some bear," he thought. He laughed and yelled at them. Then it happened. One of them stopped and sprayed him. He didn't realize they could spray from that far away.

Soft Feather

"He wasn't laughing now. Gagging from the skunk perfume all over him, he turned and jumped into the water and tried to wash it off.

"Rose said she screamed, as the two skunks ran up the bank and across the road in front of her.

"She gagged, and holding her nose, jumped down off of the bridge railing and somehow ran back up the road a ways without limping. Realizing what she was doing she stopped, sat down, and rubbed her ankle.

"Looking up, she saw the headlights of a car come around a bend in the road. She tried to get up but couldn't. Turning over, she got up on her hands and knees and finally stood up."

"Rose told me that while all of this happened, other things happened at her parent's house. They were up and pacing the floor. She said her mom, Lilly, said that her dad, Mike, kept saying he was going to wring both of their necks when he got his hands on them.

"Lilly told her she wasn't paying any attention to him but just kept telling him, 'something has happened. I don't know what, Mike, but something has happened to them'."

"He told her, 'I sure hope you're wrong.' "

"She said, 'we have to go look for them. Hurry! Go get the car out and get that gallon gas can.'

"It wasn't long until they headed for Longmont. When they got near Boulder Creek she shouted, 'There's someone getting down off of the bridge railing. Pull over.'

"Mike pulled up next to Don and stopped. Water was dripping off of Don. Then Mike saw Rose come hobbling toward the car. He opened the door, then, closed it quickly, yelling, 'There's a skunk out there, Lilly! I'm not getting out.'

Soft Feather

"Lilly laughed, and said, 'How come you're not brave now, Mike? Letting a little skunk scare you?'

"Rose came limping up and opened the back door and jumped in the best she could and slammed the door. She rolled the window down and told Don, 'you will have to ride out there on the front fender,' and rolled up the window.

"He yelled through the closed window, 'my car is just outside of Longmont, Do you have any gas?'

"Lillie yelled 'Yes!'

"He picked up his shoes and socks and jumped off the bridge railing. He walked over and jumped onto the fender and off they went. It wasn't long until they spotted his car.

"Mike pulled up next to his car and stopped. Her mother handed Rose the gas can. She rolled the window down and handed it to Don, then quickly rolled it up.

"Her parents looked at her and she shrugged her shoulders, and said, 'I thought there was a wild animal under the bridge. Don picked up some rocks and threw them at whatever was under the bridge. It was two skunks!'

"Her parents looked at each other and shook their heads. No more was said as they watched Don pour the gas into the car. He hopped into his car and cranked it a couple of times, and it started. Don drove away, headed toward home, and they followed.

"It was a beautiful night and they would have enjoyed the ride back home under different circumstances but, being 2 o'clock in the morning put kind of a damper on their moonlight ride.

"Mike told Lilly that he would like to say something to Don, but he thought he'd wait a week or two before he did.

"Rose told me she was surprised to see Don the next day, after it happened. He told her his mother made

Soft Feather

him take a bath in tomato juice with a few other things added. It took all the smell away. 'My mother is an Indian and she knows how to mix up all kinds of things. Of course, she burned my clothes except for my shoes'.

"And that's the end of the story that Rose told to me. She told me that she doesn't think her parents will let her go anywhere with Don for a long time."

Jimmy and Mary laughed as they thought about what happened, especially Don's getting sprayed with the skunk's perfume.

The days went by slowly. School kept Jimmy busy during the days, but the nights were a different story. There wasn't a thing to do. It got dark soon after he got home from school, and outside activities were short.

His room started to feel like a prison cell. It seemed to get smaller and smaller each night.

One evening after finishing his homework, he leaned back in his chair. He looked at his desk. There were some books there. His grandma must have put them there. There were six books, all held up by bookends.

He reached over and picked up one of them up. It was one of his dad's pigeon books. He looked at the front cover. His grandmother told him that he raised homing pigeons. She even made him a quilt with pigeons on it, the one Jimmy used on his bed on the really cold winter nights.

He slowly opened the book, and a feather floated to the floor. He reached down and picked it up and held it up to the light. It was beautiful; half of it was blue and the other half, white.

"It must have come from one of Dad's pigeons." He thought about his dad. He put the feather back in the book, closed it, and placed it back on his desk.

The walls of his room closed in on him again. He undressed, and climbed into bed. Sleep didn't come easily

Soft Feather

that night, but when it did, he slept soundly. He even snored. It was loud enough for his grandma to open his door and look in on him before she went to bed.

Jimmy soon forgot all about trapping. One Friday when he came home from school, his grandpa asked him if he was going to do any trapping.

"Sure I am," he said, as if he already planned it. "Where are those traps, Grandpa?"

"Out in the garage. I hung them on a nail on the left side of the garage as you go in the door."

Jimmy went to his room and laid his books on the desk. He changed clothes and went out the back door and to the garage. He spotted the traps on the nail just where grandpa said they would be. They looked like they were new traps, not like Don's.

He pushed the door open wide and went inside. Taking the chains off the nail, he laid them on the floor and counted them. There were a dozen.

Picking them up, he swung them over his shoulder. He closed the door and walked over to the front porch. He laid the traps down and went inside.

"Those traps you borrowed are almost new. They look like they've never been used, Grandpa," he said.

"They are," Tom answered. "Take good care of them. We don't want to have to buy traps for Mr. Miller."

"No, sir," Jimmy said, nodding his head. "I'll take good care of them."

He walked back to his room and sat down at his desk. He would like to lie down on the bed and wait for his grandma to call him for supper. But he had some homework to get done first. It would be a long night, and he wanted to get some rest, but first things first.

He finished his homework and picked up one of his dad's pigeon books. He lay down on the bed and started

Soft Feather

reading. Before he knew it, his grandma called him for supper.

With supper over, Jimmy retreated once more to his room. The book about pigeons interested him, and he wanted to read more.

There was a knock on his door, and his grandma came in.

"You said you were going to go set the traps before midnight, Jimmy," she said. "It's ten o'clock."

He put the book down and jumped up. He put on a lot of clothes and went over to the closet. He brought the rubber boots out of the back of the closet.

He pulled them on and put on his heavy coat. He took the gloves out of the coat pockets and put them on.

Lastly, he put on his stocking cap and took a deep breath. He felt nice and warm inside all those clothes, boots, cap and gloves.

His grandma led the way back to the kitchen where his grandpa sat at the table.

"Good luck, Jimmy," he said. "Here's a flashlight. It's a dark night. No moon. You'll surely need it."

"Thanks, Grandpa," he said. He went out the front door, closing it behind him, and turned on the flashlight. He picked up the traps, and headed towards the creek.

He hoped he would get a bunch of muskrats. It would feel so good to have money in his pocket again.

The crunching of the cold snow and the clanging of the traps made a funny tune as he walked across the field towards the creek. When he reached the creek, he remembered that he needed some sticks to hold the traps to the bank of the creek. He surely didn't want those muskrats dragging his traps off.

He would have to find some sticks as he walked towards the creek. He needed to get the sticks before he set

Soft Feather

the traps. He didn't want to make a lot of noise. Don said it would disturb them, and they would try harder to get away.

It took some time to find a dozen sticks, but he finally located them. Holding all of the sticks, the traps, plus the flashlight soon became a problem. He started to laugh as he wobbled up the creek, then, stopped. He was making too much noise.

Slowly, he set them one by one just like Don set his. It took longer than he thought it would. He was tired when he reached the bridge. He climbed up the bank and stepped up onto the highway.

As he walked towards home, every part of his body ached from the night's work. It was bitter cold up on the highway. A slight breeze blew as he neared the town.

He looked at the streetlights stretching off down the main street. The night was clear, which made the lights shine like glittering jewels. It gave him a good feeling inside.

When he came to the street leading to his house, he stopped. He took one last look at the glistening streetlights. It was hard not to like this little town when it looked like this.

Too bad it didn't look this good in the daytime.

The breeze picked up, and he moved quickly down the street towards home. His ears were cold; so, he covered them as best he could with his gloves.

As he entered the front door, the warmth of the house embraced him like his grandma's hug. Taking off his coat, cap and gloves, he sat down at the table. His grandma came out of her bedroom and into the kitchen. She stopped and looked at the clock. It was twelve o'clock.

"It took you longer than I thought it would, Jimmy," she said. "Is everything all right? You didn't have any trouble, did you?"

Soft Feather

"No, Grandma," he replied. "I forgot to cut some sticks to hold the traps down. I had to do that before I could put the traps out. It took me some time to find a dozen sticks the right size."

"Oh," she said. "I'm glad that's all it was." She gave him a hug, turned and went back toward her bedroom. As she got to the door, she asked, "When are you going to make your first run?"

Jimmy looked at the clock. "I'll make my first run at two o'clock, my second run at four o'clock and my last run at six. That's only three checks on the traps, but it should be enough."

His grandma nodded and went back to her bedroom. Jimmy took off his boots in front of the wood-burning stove. He got up and checked the wood box to see if it had enough wood in it to last a couple of hours. It did.

"Grandpa must have filled it before he went to bed," he thought.

Jimmy was soon asleep. He woke up when someone shook his shoulder. It was his grandma. "It's one-thirty Jimmy," she said. "Time for you to get ready for your first run on your traps."

Jimmy got up and put on all his gear. He grabbed his flashlight and headed out the back door. The cold breeze he'd left outside earlier met him. His head quickly cleared as he walked towards the creek.

Climbing down the bank and into the water, he searched the banks for his traps with his flashlight. He spotted one after another, but each trap lay in the water just as he placed them.

"No muskrats tonight," he thought. He walked until he checked them all.

"Nothing," he said out loud, standing in the middle of the highway bridge. He turned his light on and shone it

Soft Feather

down at the creek. Maybe on the next run. He turned and walked towards town.

There was a slight mist in the air now, and the streetlights no longer sparkled like jewels. Instead, they all seemed to have a halo around them. As he neared his turnoff, he stopped and looked at them. He smiled, tilting his head a little as he looked.

"Each one is beautiful in a different way," he thought. He continued walking towards home.

Jimmy's steps were slower now, as he made his way up the steps and inside. He put his extra clothes on the back of a chair, sat down and took off his boots. He didn't expect anything like this.

He pulled down the oven door and put his feet on it, then took them off. It was too hot. He waited a few minutes before he touched it. It was just right so he put his feet back up and leaned back in his chair. He closed his eyes and was soon asleep.

Again, Jimmy awoke with someone shaking his shoulder. "It's six o'clock, Jimmy," his grandma said. "Time for your last run on the traps."

"Huh?" Jimmy said, slowly coming out of his sleep. "My last run," he kind of mumbled. "When did I make the second one?"

"You better hurry up and get out there and check those traps, Jimmy," she replied.

"If you did have anything, they may be gone by now. Come on. Get up."

Jimmy sat up, wide-awake now. He'd missed his second run. What a trapper he was. He put on his clothes and boots as fast as he could. Then his coat, scarf, cap and gloves.

Out the door he ran and down the steps with his flashlight beam moving back and forth ahead of him.

Soft Feather

At the creek, he slowed down and made his way down the bank until he stood next to the water. He stood trying to catch his breath.

"Nothing to get excited about," he said to himself, as he leaned up against a tree. "If they got away, they got away."

His breathing slowed. Then he thought he heard something up ahead of him. He stood still and listened. Sure enough, he heard someone a little ways up the creek from where he was.

Kneeling down beside the tree, he turned off his light. He saw the beams of two flashlights up ahead, moving away from him. He stopped breathing but couldn't make out what they were saying. Someone was raiding his trap line.

He stood up, not knowing what to do. He had trouble finding his way back up the creek bank, as he couldn't turn on his flashlight. He stopped and thought again about what those two were doing. Raiding his traps.

No, Mr. Miller's traps. That made a big difference, and he got mad.

From the sound of the splashing water, he realized that they moved down the creek away from him. He barely heard their voices now as he turned and watched the two light beams disappear around a bend in the creek.

"You two are not going to get away with stealing my muskrats," he thought to himself.

Jimmy checked to make sure he couldn't see any lights, then turned his flashlight on and looked around to see where he was. He saw what he wanted and went over and picked up a good-sized stick.

He would use it for a club if he had to. He smiled as he swung the club back and forth. It felt good in his hand.

He turned his light off and slowly moved as quietly as he could. In his mind he followed the bending of the

Soft Feather

creek and planned where he would go to wait for them. He quickly made his way across the creek and up the other bank.

There were mostly tall trees along that side of the creek, and he would be able to move from tree to tree without being seen. He had a plan, and he felt sure it would work. All he had to do was get ahead of them.

He heard the voices up ahead as he hurried along. They sure were making a lot of noise, which covered any he made. Then, without warning, he stepped on a dead tree limb, and there was a loud snap. He froze where he stood and listened, then sighed with relief.

They were still talking.

He quickly moved away from the creek bank, making sure he didn't make any more noise. It wasn't long until he came out on the highway near the bridge. He ran across the bridge and slowly made his way down the creek bank. He found a place not too far from the bridge. He knelt down behind a large tree and waited.

As he did, he became quite cold, so he stood up and moved around to get warm. He saw the light beams coming his way before he heard voices. He knelt down again and waited.

The voices got louder and louder until the boys were right below him.

"It makes me feel good. Taking that Indian's traps is the best thing I've done to him yet."

It was Joe Crow's voice. Jimmy's face got hot as he watched his light move back and forth. The other guy reached down and pulled a trap out of the water. There was nothing in it.

He hit the ground with the trap and it snapped shut. He pulled the stake out of the bank and threw it away, slinging the trap over his shoulder with all the others he pulled. He walked down the creek.

Soft Feather

"As long as I get these traps, I could care less about him," Joe's accomplice said. "He sure isn't a trapper, Joe. We only got that one muskrat earlier, and none this time. I thought that an Indian would at least know how to trap."

Joe turned his flashlight on him and laughed. "He's not any good at anything he does."

It was Raymond Long, one of the kids Jimmy knew from school. "I'll keep an eye on him from now on." he thought.

"This dumb Indian don't know nothing, Raymond," Joe said, laughing. "He can't even fight. I beat him up a month ago downtown. It was great. Everyone in town was there watching me take care of him."

"You should have been there and seen it, Raymond. It was great. I taught him a lesson he'll never forget."

Raymond didn't say anything. He looked for the next trap with his flashlight. Anyway, he heard what really happened and knew that the Indian beat Joe up, not the way he told it. He knew Joe was one who stretched the truth when it was to his advantage.

"There's the last one, Joe," he said. "That one makes an even dozen traps. I'll be able to do a lot of trapping with a dozen traps."

"You'll only have six, Raymond," Joe said.

"But you said I could have all the traps, Joe," Raymond replied. He reached into the water and pulled up the last one.

"All you wanted was the muskrats, remember? You get the muskrats, and I get the traps. That was the deal."

"If there had been some muskrats, I would have let you have all the traps," he snapped back. "But one crummy muskrat is not worth messing with.

"I tell you what, Raymond. You take the muskrat, and I'll take the traps. How do you like that idea?"

Soft Feather

"A deal's a deal," Raymond said, starting to get mad. Then he remembered he was talking to a person who beat someone up just for fun. Even though he knew he didn't win the fight with the Indian boy, he wasn't sure he wouldn't win one with him, so he backed down. "Come on, Joe. A deal's a deal," he whined. He knew Joe was treating him like his friend, Brad Bradley, treated him.

"You make me sick, Raymond," Joe replied. "I'm the one who heard at the service station about him going trapping. Seems like Mr. Miller loaned his grandpa some traps. Well, I kept my eye on his place, checking it out half a dozen times each evening. I saw him leave tonight and got hold of you. I should have it all. You mess with me, and you'll not get anything."

Joe's flashlight searched under the bridge and he thought about what he was going to do to Raymond.

He let his light wander on up the creek on the other side of the bridge. It moved back and forth along the side of each bank, then, stopped.

"I saw something move up there, Raymond," he said. He pointed the beam of light at a certain place on the bank. "It looks like a muskrat. Put those traps down, and we'll go see what it is."

He ran under the bridge, leaving Raymond with the traps over his shoulder. He hurried over to the side of the bank and laid the traps down, then ran after Joe.

Jimmy heard them talking but couldn't see them. He turned on his flashlight and moved out from behind the tree and down the side of the bank to where his traps lay. He reached down and quietly started picking them up.

He put all the rings on the first two fingers of his right hand. "Thanks, Raymond, for laying them down nice and neat," he thought. He picked them up carefully, with only one of them making a slight clang. He turned off his light and waited.

Soft Feather

All he heard was Joe and Raymond laughing and splashing around in the creek on the other side of the bridge.

They didn't hear him, so he quickly climbed back up the bank. He felt his way, trying to find the edge of the bridge. He found it and went up onto the highway.

"Everything worked out just right," he thought.

He made his way out onto the bridge. Without a light, he felt his way along the railing. In the middle he stopped, walked over to the other side of the bridge, and knelt down.

He saw the two lights on the other side of the bridge. One of them held up a large muskrat in the beam of the other's flashlight. They laughed as they danced around, celebrating their find.

Jimmy was glad they were distracted long enough for him to get his traps. "I have to get out before they find out I'm here," he thought.

As he turned to leave, there was a loud bang. Jimmy fell onto his knees on the bridge. "Someone shot at me," he thought. "It must be Joe's friend, Brad." He probably waited for Joe and Raymond to come back and saw me get the traps."

"Somebody in the ditch yelled. "I'm shot in the leg! I've been shot," came a cry from one of the two in the creek. "Joe, wait for me. It hurts, Joe! Help me!"

"Help yourself," he replied, and ran back under the bridge and up the creek. "It's that crazy Indian. I'm not staying around here and let him shoot me. No sir, not me," he shouted, as he ran.

Raymond cried loudly, as he limped along the best he could. Jimmy stood up and peeked over the side of the bridge. He watched the lights of Joe's and Raymond's flashlights disappear under the bridge. Raymond kept begging Joe to wait and help him. Joe stopped and waited

Soft Feather

until Raymond got to him. "Shut up! Quit your bawling! You're going to get me caught," Joe said, as he reached out and grabbed his hand and dragged him along.

"Ouch! You're hurting me!" Raymond said. "You'd be crying, too, if you got shot."

Their flashlight beams appeared on the other side and bounced back and forth on the creek bed.

They made their way up the creek bank and disappeared behind a couple of trees, trying to hide. "I've got to catch my breath," Joe said. "Helping you tired me out."

Jimmy quietly made his way over to the other side of the bridge and knelt down. He wanted to know who took the shot at them.

He heard water splash on the other side of the bridge. Someone entered the creek and ran under the bridge. Whoever was there stopped right below where Jimmy stood.

The light beam searched both sides of the creek bank. Each tree got a good going over before it moved on.

"Ouch," came a voice from behind one of the larger trees on the left side of the creek. It was Raymond.

"What's the matter, low life?" asked a voice below Jimmy. It was Don Nix. "Does a little rock salt in your thieving skin hurt?"

Joe peeked around the tree and saw Don's flashlight beam. He searched the ground and found a big rock. He whizzed it at Don and hit him in the side. "Ouch!" he yelled.

Joe Crow was deadly with a rock. Jimmy found that out the first day he got to Mercer. Joe hit him in the back right after he got off the bus.

Jimmy peeked over the side of the bridge and looked down. Don still had his flashlight on, but he was all doubled over with pain. One of Jimmy's traps rattled as he

Soft Feather

leaned over. Don jerked around and looked up at the top of the bridge.

Jimmy ducked down. He didn't know if Don saw him or not. He sure didn't want any rock salt shot at him.

"That'll teach you to shoot at me," Joe yelled.

Don's attention returned to where the rock came from. He moved his light from tree to tree as he looked for him. Then it found Joe as he peeked out from behind a tree next to where Raymond hid.

"I'll blow you in two!" Don yelled.

Joe realized it wasn't Jimmy's voice. He knew he was in big trouble. He jumped out from behind the tree and headed for the top of the creek bank. Don kept him in his flashlight beam as he raised his shotgun and fired. Bang!

It looked like Joe jumped clear over the top of the creek bank when the load of rock salt hit him in the seat of the pants.

"Ye-o-w!" he yelled. "I'm on fire! I've been shot! I'll find out who you are. I'll never give up. You'll see. I'll get Brad Bradley after you," he cried. He ran a short distance and stopped to rub where he'd been shot.

He took off again, holding the seat of his pants. His flashlight beam zigzagged through the trees as he ran.

Don ran up the side of the bank. He wanted to get another shot at him.

When Raymond got to the top, his fear outweighed the pain, and he found new energy. His light bobbed along as he ran down the bank and across the creek, then up the other bank.

Don didn't know if it was Joe or Raymond, but he took off after the one whose light beams he saw on the other side of the creek.

Jimmy stood up and smiled as he watched the three light beams disappear between the trees. "Go get them, Don," he said aloud.

Soft Feather

He breathed a sigh of relief and turned his flashlight on. Swinging the muskrat traps over his right shoulder, he walked across the bridge and down the highway towards town. He felt good about getting Mr. Miller's traps back. Very good.

Then he remembered that Raymond talked to Joe about how they got a muskrat from his traps earlier that night. "If I made my second run like I was supposed to, I would have that muskrat now instead of them," he thought.

He thought about it for a minute. It was worth a muskrat to see Joe jump when Don hit him in the seat of the pants with the rock salt.

Jimmy stopped and laughed out loud. He continued thinking, "Raymond was right about one thing. I'm not a trapper. Sure, I'm Indian, but being Indian doesn't assure me or anyone else that we're good at all things."

Don was the hunter, trapper and anything else he seemed to want to be, and he was only half-Indian. Jimmy felt good when he thought about Don. He liked him. Especially after what he did this early Saturday morning. He would never tell him, but he was grateful. Sure, Don might do some things he didn't like, but who didn't?

"A friend is a friend, and that's what counts," he thought.

Jimmy walked down the highway towards Mercer. It started to get light in the east. Once again he stopped and looked at the lights on Main Street. He was amazed at what he saw. A fine mist hung in the air, and around each of the streetlights was a multicolored halo. He saw each color of the rainbow shine clear and bright.

"Sure, it's a small town and there's not much to do, but it surely does look nice on a cold misty morning," he thought.

He headed towards his grandparents' house. He smiled at the sight that lay before him. It wasn't just

Soft Feather

knowing it was nice and warm in their house that attracted him, it was knowing that there was, also, love there---a deep love that was real.

The cold breeze that blew earlier stopped. An orange glow filled the eastern horizon. It would be a nice day.

"I'll probably sleep and miss most of it," he thought.

"What am I going to tell Grandpa and Grandma?" he wondered. If he told them what happened, his grandpa would get mad. He didn't want that. It didn't matter, anyway. He surely didn't plan to do any more trapping.

He realized that he didn't care too much about being out in the cold like this. He'd rather be in his warm bed. If people wanted muskrats to make coats, they could get Don to catch them.

He walked to the garage and opened the door. After he put the traps back where he got them, he went into the house. His grandma was in the kitchen, cooking breakfast.

"How did it go, Jimmy?" she asked. She looked at his face and knew without his saying a word.

"I didn't get anything, Grandma," he answered. "All that work for nothing. I could have stayed in bed last night for all the good I did."

"I don't think I'll do any more trapping."

Alice didn't say anything for a while. Jimmy took off his outer clothes and boots. He set them near the hall entrance. He wanted to go to bed, but he didn't want to miss breakfast.

Alice hummed as she set the table. She cooked pancakes and put them on separate plates. When she thought there were enough, she set them on the table and sat down next to Jimmy. She watched him pick up the syrup bottle.

"Let's say grace for the food, Jimmy," she said.

"Yes, ma'am."

Soft Feather

"Thank you, Lord, for this food," she started, "and I thank you for letting Jimmy find out that trapping is hard work. We usually don't get something for nothing here on this earth. But Lord, you gave us the most important thing there could ever be--your love forever. All we have to do is accept your gift. We're grateful. Amen."

"Amen," Jimmy said. Then he realized what she said. "I guess you're right, Grandma. I wanted to get a dozen muskrats tonight so I could have some money. I did want to get some money. Christmas is less than two weeks away, and it sure would come in handy."

"I know, Jimmy," she said. "We all would like to have a lot of money come our way. It would be nice if someone would give us a lot of money, or if we could just find it. But usually it doesn't work that way. We have to work hard for it. When we do, we've earned it, and it's a lot different then. We take better care of it and we don't go on a spending spree. People who don't work very hard for their money usually don't take care of it very well."

Jimmy thought about what she said. That was exactly what happened to the money Don made from selling the muskrats they caught earlier. He took the money and spent it as if there would be more where that came from. There might be, and, then again, there might not be.

He ate his breakfast without saying another word. Alice knew he thought deeply about what happened to him that night.

After breakfast, Jimmy went to his room. His clothes were soon off, and he curled up under the blankets trying to get his feet warm as fast as he could.

He fell asleep before they were warm.

Soft Feather

CHAPTER 7

Tom was in the kitchen looking out the window. It snowed, and there was a good foot of it on the ground.

In each corner of the window there was some frost on the windowpane. He scratched T O M in it. "How many times have I done that?" he thought. Even as a child, he scratched his name, not someone else's. He nodded his head. "Yep, I sure do like my name."

Tom sat down at the kitchen table as Jimmy came in looking at the floor.

"Good morning, Jimmy," he said.

"Huh?" he said. "Oh. Good morning, Grandpa."

"You sure are in a good mood this morning. I hope you don't go through the rest of the day like that."

Jimmy didn't answer. He was somewhere else.

"What could be wrong now?" Tom wondered. He frowned and tried to figure it out. Then he nodded his head. It was his hawk. He had not gotten over the loss of his hawk.

He remembered that he had a part in Jimmy having to give it up, and because he agreed that he had to give it away, Jimmy blamed him for his loss.

If it hadn't been that Mary talked him out of leaving, they would have lost their grandson. Tom sat and shook his head as he looked at Jimmy. That was close. He sure didn't want that to happen again. "Something needs to be done, but what?" Tom wondered.

Jimmy was depressed before, and Mr. Miller brought him out of it. He took him deer hunting. That trip ended up with Jimmy being lost for three days in the mountains. There had to be something else.

Alice came out of her bedroom and stopped as she entered the kitchen. She looked at the two sitting at the table and put her hands on her hips. One of her "men"

Soft Feather

frowned, and the other stared at the tablecloth. This was serious.

She walked over to the stove and picked up a skillet and dropped it. "Bang!"

Tom and Jimmy jumped and looked up at her. "Now that I have your attention, I want you two to get together and do something today. I'll not have a couple of sad faces around here."

"Yes, dear," Tom said.

Jimmy looked at his grandpa, then back at the tablecloth.

"It snowed last night, and I know that the two of you can find something to do out there in that beautiful snow. Remember how much fun we used to have when we had an overnight snow, Tom?"

"I sure do, Alice. We use to go sledding on Judge Brown's hill. We used to slide all the way down to the bottom, then pull the sled back up to the top."

"Now and then, we caught hold of the bumper of a car going up the hill," Alice added.

"We sure did," Tom said. "I remember the times we tied our sled to the back bumper of one of our friend's car, and he pulled us all over town. That surely was a lot of fun."

That was what he needed to do to get Jimmy out of his depression. "How would you like to help me build a sled today, Jimmy?"

Jimmy didn't know what to say. "Build a sled, Grandpa?"

"Sure. We'll build us a good-sized wooden sled. Then, we'll tie it onto the back bumper of the truck, and I'll pull you all over town."

Jimmy's eyes lit up. "You'd let me do that?! That sounds like a lot of fun, Grandpa. Let's go build it."

Soft Feather

"Not that fast, you two," Alice said. "First things first--- food before play. Have you two cleaned up?"

Without a word, they headed for the bathroom. Running water was soon heard, along with eggs and bacon frying.

After breakfast Tom got some notebook paper and sketched out the form of a sled. Jimmy watched him work on the drawing until it was a fine-looking sled.

"We will make it all out of wood. 2X4's for the runners, 1-inch boards nailed on top of the 2X4's to sit on, and another 2X4 across the front to put our feet on."

"That looks good, Tom," Alice said. "But you forgot one thing."

"Oh, yes. I'll also have to round off the front of each runner so they won't dig into the ground whenever we hit a bump."

"That's right, Tom. But you also need a hole in the footrest to put the rope through."

Tom nodded his head in agreement as he finished the drawing.

"I have some old boards in the garage. They're underneath my workbench. They've been there for a long time. I didn't know why I was keeping them, but now I do."

Jimmy's long face turned into a happy face.

"Let's get on some heavy clothes, Jimmy."

"Yes, sir," he said, and they got up and headed for their bedrooms. "This is going to be a grand day," Jimmy thought.

Tom backed the pickup out of the garage and turned off the motor. He hopped out and went into the garage, and Jimmy followed. He pointed at the boards under his workbench.

Soft Feather

They soon had them in a pile on the garage floor. Tom handed Jimmy a hand saw and picked up a 4-foot folding ruler. "I'll mark the boards, and you cut them."

The 2X4's were first. 4 feet long with an angle cut on one end.

Then the 1- inch thick by 6- inch wide boards were cut into 2- foot lengths.

A rasp and a scraper came from one of the drawers in the workbench.

With everything cut, they looked at the pile of wood in front of them. Tom shook his head. "Looks like we still have a lot of wood left over. Let's put it back under the workbench."

They used a little over half of the wood, and they soon had the leftover wood under the workbench again.

Tom laid the 2X4 runners on the floor. "Get me a hammer and that red coffee can of nails over there, Jimmy."

He placed one of the boards on top of the runners. Jimmy handed him the hammer and placed the can of nails near him. "Here we go, Jimmy," and he drove a nail halfway into the board.

Making sure the other side of the board was lined up with the other 2X4, he drove another nail halfway into the board.

Everything lined up, so he drove another nail into each side of the board. That made sure it wouldn't move, and he drove the other two nails all the way in.

The rest of the boards were quickly nailed, and it was finished. There before them was a great-looking sled. "Let's put up the tools and bring your grandma out here to see her new sled."

"OK," Jimmy said, and grabbed the saw and put it up.

Soft Feather

Tom put away the hammer, nails and ruler. He saw his drawing lying on the workbench, and he picked it up. His smile disappeared. "Get the saw, Jimmy," he said. "We forgot something."

Jimmy took the saw down and handed it to him. "What did we forget?"

"The footrest across the front of the sled. We have to have a good sturdy footrest to keep you from falling off."

"With a hole in it," Jimmy said.

They laughed as they dug out a 2X4 from under the workbench. It was soon marked and sawed and the hole drilled. Instead of nails, Tom put long screws into the footrest to make sure it wouldn't come off.

The tools again found their home, and two proud carpenters stood beside their masterpiece.

Tom put his arm around his grandson, and they headed for the front door. They stepped inside and asked Alice to come out and look at their sled. She put down the paper she was reading and followed them out to the garage.

"That looks just like the one we used to have, Tom," she said.

"It is just like it. Why change when you have a winner?"

"Who's going to be first?" she asked.

Tom looked at Jimmy and winked. "I think your grandma wants to be first. What do you say? Should we let her be first?"

"Yes, sir," Jimmy said.

Alice went in to put on warm clothes, and Tom went over and started the truck. He came back and looked at the sled. "Let's pick it up and put it on the snow."

Jimmy grabbed hold of one side and tried to lift it, but couldn't. "It's heavier than I thought it would be, Grandpa," he said.

Soft Feather

"Squat down and pick it up, Jimmy. Just take it easy. We sure don't want to get hurt before we have our first ride."

They both squatted down, and slowly picking the sled up, carried it over to the snow and put it down. "All it took was some muscle, Grandpa," he said.

"That's right," Tom said. He got in the truck and started it, as Jimmy got in on the other side.

He backed up and drove around the circle in the front yard. He drove out onto the road and up and down it a few times. "I'm packing the snow down a little, Jimmy. It's probably packed down all over town, but not here. It's a lot better riding on packed snow than on loose snow."

He drove back to the house and pulled up in front of the sled. Alice came out and ran over to the truck. Tom grabbed the rope and started pulling the sled towards the truck.

Jimmy ran over and helped him as Alice watched. They soon had it behind the truck. Alice sat down on the sled and grabbed the rope. Tom pulled the rope over to the back bumper and tied it.

"You're an old hand at this, Alice, I'll let the tailgate down. Remember to turn loose when it gets too rough. We don't want you to get hurt."

"I will, Tom," she said. "Let's go. I can hardly wait."

Tom grinned, shaking his head, and got in the truck. Jimmy jumped in the bed of the truck. He wanted to see his grandma zipping along on the sled he helped build. He wouldn't have dreamed she would do anything like this. She was acting like a teenager.

Alice looked up at him and winked, "I'm a teenager at heart, Jimmy," she said, as if she read his mind. She did it before, and here she was doing it again.

"Let's go, Tom!" she shouted.

Soft Feather

Tom put the truck in gear and drove slowly. When they got out on the road, Alice shouted, "Faster, faster!"

Tom sped up a little, and the snow from the tires flew up, hitting the tailgate. Now and then a patch of soft snow sprayed her face. She laughed and tried to brush it off but stopped. She didn't want to fall off.

Tom slowed down at the main street, then, turned and sped up. As they approached Mr. Wilson's filling station, Alice started yelling. Bill stepped outside and laughed when he saw who it was. He was like Jimmy; he could hardly believe his eyes.

"I'm going to arrest you, Alice," he yelled. "No one as old as you should be having that much fun. You get right back here and let me have a turn!" he shouted, as they drove by.

"Do you hear me?"

Alice just waved as she slid on past. He shook his fist at her. Jimmy stood up behind the cab of the truck and waved.

Bill went back inside and got on the phone and called his wife. "I want you and Mary to get down here right now. Put on your warmest clothes."

Helen asked why, but he just hung up. He sat down in his chair in front of his stove and recalled being pulled behind a car when he was a child. What a special time that was in his life.

Tom stopped at the edge of town, and Jimmy got on the sled. Grandma got in the truck. She was cold, and she wasn't going to ride in the back of the truck.

When Helen and Mary arrived, Bill didn't tell them what was happening. He just told them to stand there and wait. They stood outside with Bill, and when Jimmy went sliding by the garage, Mary shouted and waved.

Jimmy gave a short wave at all of them as he passed. He was kind of afraid to let go of the rope.

Soft Feather

Helen realized there was a lump in her throat. She remembered the days when she and Bill went sledding like that. She grabbed his hand and squeezed it. He knew why.

Tom turned around and came back, pulling up to the garage and stopping.

"Bill, I want you to go find us the best place in town to pull this sled. It could get dangerous pulling it up and down on this highway," Helen said.

"O.K.," he said. He got in his truck and drove away.

He would find the best place in town for them. No one wanted anything bad to happen to any of them.

"It's your turn, Helen," Tom said.

She hurried over to their car and got her coat. She put it on and came running back.

Mary went over and helped Jimmy get up. He handed the ropes to Helen and stepped back. "That sure is a lot of fun. Wait until you get your turn. You'll see. The only problem is it was too short. I wanted to ride a long way."

"I'm sure we will get to," Mary said. "My daddy went to look for a good place in town to pull the sled."

Bill came back, and Tom soon drove up with Helen on the sled. "I'm next," he said, and walked over to her.

"Did you find a place, Bill?" Tom asked.

"Sure did---the block around the high school. Pull me up there, and we'll check it out."

Alice got out of the truck, and Jimmy and Mary got in the back. They wanted to see how her dad rode the sled.

"Helen," Bill said, "follow us in the car."

Tom drove away before she answered. They were both cold from their ride so they went into the station and sat by the stove.

When Tom got near the school, he turned the steering wheel to the right, then to the left a couple of

Soft Feather

times. Bill slid one-way, and then another. He started yelling, but he didn't yell to stop.

"Do it again, do it again!"

Helen and Alice finally warmed up and went outside. Helen locked the door to the station, and they drove up to the school. There they saw Bill's great ride, back and forth across the road.

Tom pulled up beside them, and Bill got off and staggered up to his car. "Man, oh, man, was that a lot of fun, Helen," he said.

"I'm next," Mary said.

"O.K.," Tom said. "Get on the sled."

"I've got to go back to the filling station," Bill said. "Thanks a lot, Tom. You've made my day."

Helen and Alice got out and into the front of the truck. Bill honked his horn as he drove off.

After an hour passed, everyone had a turn riding on the sled. In fact, a few of their friends came by and got a ride.

By noon it was time to stop and eat. They went by the station and told Bill that they were headed to the Warrior's house. They would have sandwiches, with potato chips and a cold drink.

He closed his filling station for lunch. He made sure that the cold drinks were Nesbitt Orange, Jimmy's favorite.

It would be a long lunch break as tale after tale was told, of not only the good old days, but the great time they had today.

Soft Feather

CHAPTER 8

Jimmy's grandma came up to him and was very excited. "Look what I have here," she said, as she handed him an envelope. "It's a letter from your father. He plans to come see us during the Christmas holidays.

"Your Christmas vacation at school starts this Friday. Tommy said he plans to be here Friday or Saturday. That's going to work out real well for all of us, Jimmy."

Alice went back to the sink, where she peeled some potatoes. "It's an answer to my prayers, Jimmy," she said softly.

"It's an answer to mine, too, Grandma."

Jimmy opened the letter and read it. It was just a few lines saying that he would be coming to see them. It, also, said he could hardly wait to see all of them again. Jimmy put the letter back in the envelope and placed it on the table.

"It's going to be a great Christmas, Grandma," he said, his voice showing his excitement.

They looked at each other and giggled a little. It was going to be a long week for all of them. He decided he would keep busy, and the days would pass a lot faster. He went over and checked the wood box. It needed filling, so he went out back and brought in a couple of loads of wood.

When Jimmy finished, Alice had a big hamburger and French fries fixed for him. He ate and returned to his room and picked up the pigeon book he read a couple of days earlier. Time passed fast for him when he read, so he intended to read a lot the next week.

Sunday came and went, and Jimmy went back to school Monday. He didn't know what he was going to tell Don about his bad trapping experience. By the time he got to school, he decided he wouldn't even mention it. To his surprise, Don was not in school.

Soft Feather

Tuesday, Don came to school with a bandage on his left hand's ring finger. It looked like part of his finger was missing.

When Jimmy asked him how it happened, he said he was setting a large trap for a wolf, and the trap shut on his finger, cutting the end off. He had to go to the doctor and have it sewed up.

He wiggled his bandaged finger at everybody that day. He laughed a lot, but Jimmy could tell it really bothered him. He now knew for sure that he was through with trapping. He liked his fingers too much to lose one of them in a trap.

As the school days passed that week, Don changed. Each time Jimmy talked to him, he wasn't the way he was before he lost part of his finger.

He frowned when he told Jimmy that he tried to scratch the part of his finger that was missing. He said it was an odd feeling, not being able to scratch it.

Don didn't come to school Thursday. Jimmy was surprised to see him hanging around after school Friday. Don told him that he quit school. He said he decided to go to work with his dad in the coal mine.

"I don't need any education to do that. And I can trap whenever I want, not just on weekends."

Their friendship didn't end with his quitting school. Their goals in life were just different now. But that didn't matter. The only difference was that one stayed in school, and the other went to work in the mines.

Friday arrived, and Jimmy suffered through the school day, counting almost every minute. Even his lunchtime seemed to bother him. He wanted to get back to school so it would be over that much sooner.

Finally, the last bell of the day rang, and Mrs. Davis wished them all a very merry Christmas and happy New Year. She gave each one of them a small stocking full of

Soft Feather

candy as they left the room. That made the students even more excited as they ran out the school door.

There was no other time of the year like Christmas holidays. Two weeks out of school was the best part of all, and this year Jimmy would have his dad with him.

Jimmy saw Mary walking ahead of him as he came out of the school building. He ran up to her and offered her some of his candy. She had two large suckers that her teacher gave her for Christmas.

"Which one do you want?" she asked, as she held them out to him.

"The orange one," he said.

They exchanged candy and walked together eating candy and having a happy time. As they neared Mary's father's garage, they laughed with joy, talking and thinking about all they were going to do during the holidays. Jimmy told Mary he could hardly wait to see his dad.

"I wonder if he is in yet," Mary said.

"I don't know. Let's go in and ask your father. He will know."

They ran into the office and looked around. To their surprise, Mr. Wilson was nowhere to be seen. So they hurried out into the garage. No one was there, either.

"This sure is strange. I wonder where he could be," Jimmy said.

Just then a car pulled up outside and stopped. Mr. Wilson got out and came into the garage.

"Hello, kids," he said. "What are you two up to now?"

"Where have you been, Daddy?" Mary asked.

"Oh, I had to check out Mr. Miller's car," he said. "It needed a tune up, and I just drove it around the block to see how it runs. I also checked the brakes, and everything else works O.K."

"Did Jimmy's father come in yet?" she asked.

Soft Feather

"Not yet, Mary," he answered. "The last bus through here will be in about an hour. If he's not on that bus, then he won't be here until tomorrow morning about eight o'clock. We'll just have to wait and see, won't we?"

Mary looked at Jimmy. "Yes, sir," he said.

They walked back outside as Mr. Wilson went over to his desk and started working on some of the paperwork on Mr. Miller's car. "I'll go home, Mary, and come back later," Jimmy said.

"OK," she answered. "If I don't see your father when he gets in, tell him hello for me. I'll see him tomorrow, for sure."

"I'll do that. See you later." He walked towards home. When he turned the corner, he took off running as fast as he could. He wanted to tell his grandparents his dad hadn't arrived.

When he got home, he found his grandma starting supper. "Well, Jimmy, no school for two weeks," she said.

"Some people have it good around here. I wish I had two weeks off. Maybe I'll take off the next two weeks, Jimmy."

Jimmy started to say, "sure," then, caught himself. If she took off the next two weeks, who would cook all that good food and bake all those good things they expected at Christmas time?

He wanted to say something, but didn't know what to say. He was at a loss for words, and his grandma saw it.

"Don't worry, Jimmy," she said, laughing. "I'll wait until after New Year's Day, and then I'll take some time off. Would that be better?"

"Yes, ma'am," he answered. "That's a lot better idea than the first one."

Tom listened to them and came out of the bedroom. "Surely am glad you talked her into waiting until after New

Soft Feather

Year's, Jimmy," he said, sitting down at the table. "I'd hate to eat my cooking over the holidays." They all laughed.

"I checked with Mr. Wilson on the way home, and he said that Dad hasn't come in yet, but the next bus will be in about an hour, less than an hour now. Are we all going to go down and see if he's on that bus?"

"I'm getting the food fixed so if he is, all I have to do is put it on top of the oven, Jimmy," Alice said. "I'd like for all of us to go down and meet the bus."

Tom nodded his approval. He headed back to the bedroom when he heard a car pull up. He turned and headed for the front door. Before he reached it, the door flew open, and there stood Tommy.

"Hello, Dad," he said, grabbing him and hugging him tight.

"Hi, son," Tom said, hugging him back.

It was a great surprise.

Tommy looked into the kitchen and saw Jimmy get up from the table.

Alice and Jimmy ran into the front room as Mr. Wilson stuck his head through the door and said, "The bus came by a little early, so I picked him up and brought him right over."

"Hope you don't mind. I can take him back if you want."

Tom let go of his son so Alice and Jimmy could hug him. He stuck his hand out and shook Bill's hand. "Thanks a lot, Bill. You saved us a trip. Now anyone that would do that for someone else can't be all bad," he joked.

Bill and Tom laughed as they stood and watched the sight in front of them. Alice had tears in her eyes, and Jimmy had a good grip on his dad.

Alice wiped her eyes with her apron as she stepped back. "Thank you, Bill," she said. "Come in and have

Soft Feather

something hot to drink. I have a pot of hot coffee and some hot apple cider."

"No, thanks, Alice," Bill replied, as he set Tommy's bag down. "Helen is waiting for me in the car. We're heading to Longmont to see a movie. It's Friday night, and we're going to howl. That is, if our daughter will let us."

They all laughed. Bill said good-bye and shut the door.

"Jimmy, you've grown since I last saw you," Tommy said, messing his hair up with both hands. He stepped back and stood there and studied his son's face, then, looked him up and down.

"Mom, what are you feeding my boy?" he asked. "He's just about as tall as I am. I don't know what I'll do if he gets to be taller than I am."

"Oh, you'll learn to live with it, son," Tom said, laughing. "I did. You were taller than I was, you know, and I thought the same thing when you were a teenager. "It may hurt your ego a little, but you'll get over it."

It was a happy Warrior family that night as they sat down at the table.

"It sure is good to be home," Tommy said. He looked around at each one. "I have waited for this day. I planned earlier to come Thanksgiving but couldn't work it out. I was glad I didn't when Mom wrote me about Jimmy getting lost in the mountains."

He looked at Jimmy and smiled. "I would have worried myself sick if I'd been here. It's better that I came now. Now we can do some things together that we wouldn't have been able to do Thanksgiving."

He paused, then, said, "It doesn't seem that it bothered you too much---you look good, Jimmy."

"He had a little setback," Alice said, as she got up from the table, "but he has recovered." To answer the question you asked a while ago, I'm feeding him pretty

Soft Feather

much the same thing I fed you when you were a teenager. You know. Everything I can find to cook, and then some more. He'll probably be quite a bit taller than you are, Tommy."

They smiled at Jimmy. Alice got up and went about her business of getting supper ready. "Anyway," she continued," we need a tall Indian around here."

Jimmy was pleased with the praise. Not many people praised him that he could remember. He agreed with her, thinking that it surely would be nice to be tall.

Supper was soon on the table. Tom asked the blessing, and they talked and ate and enjoyed this time of being together. Soon, Alice cleared the table and put things away.

Tom and Tommie got up and washed and dried the dishes, and Jimmy helped put them up. Alice sat down and enjoyed it until Jimmy started putting things in places where they weren't supposed to go.

"No, Jimmy," she said. "That goes up on the second shelf. Here, let me put them up for you." He then handed them to her. When she finished, she closed the cupboard doors, and looked at Tom and Tommy sitting at the table. "Men!" she exclaimed, and laughed.

Each took their turn telling Tommy what happened since the last time he was home. Then, he told them about his part-time job as a plumber's helper in Big Spring, Texas. During the summer months, he helped the plumber work on air conditioners. Then in the winter, he helped work on heating systems. He also helped install hot water heaters and did small plumbing jobs. Though part-time, it was a year-round job.

When he finished, Tom looked around the table. "Time for me to be in bed. I've got some cleaning to do tomorrow. The rest of you can stay up if you want, but I'm going to bed. See you in the morning."

Soft Feather

They all got up. "Where do I sleep, Mom?" Tommy asked.

She looked at Jimmy.

"With me, like you did last time, Dad," Jimmy said. "You know that. It was your room before it was mine."

"So it was, Jimmy," he said, and picked up his bag.

Tom and Alice gave him a hug, and Jimmy and his dad walked to their room. Jimmy opened the door, and his dad stepped in and looked around. "It's still the same, Jimmy," he said. "Thanks for not changing it. I have a lot of good memories of this room."

"I need as many good memories as I can get, and as often as I can get them. Yep. This is home."

Jimmy closed the door, got undressed and put on his pajamas. Tommy put his bag on the desk and opened it. He took out his clothes and laid them on the desk.

"Do you have some extra room in the chest of drawers for my stuff, Jimmy?" he asked.

"Sure, Dad. The bottom drawer is almost empty."

He put some things in the bottom drawer and hung some clothes in the closet. Jimmy went and brushed his teeth. When he got back, his dad did the same. Upon his return, he had on his pajamas, too.

"I see you're reading one of my books about pigeons," he said.

"Yes, sir," Jimmy answered. "I think I may be interested in having my own pigeons someday if we can ever afford to buy some."

"Before we get into bed, Jimmy," his dad said, "do you know about this quilt on the bed?"

"I know Grandma made it for you," he answered, sitting back in his chair.

"Yes, your grandma made it for me when I was about your age." He sat down on the bed and ran his fingers

Soft Feather

over the quilted bird in the middle. "I raised homing pigeons, you know."

"Grandma told me you raced them."

"I worked really hard with my pigeons trying to win some races, but something always seemed to happen. I was always second. I was second so many times I began to think I could never win first place with any of my birds. But the day came when Lilly won first place."

Tommy stood up and looked at the quilt. "That's her there on the quilt, Jimmy. Lilly was my first winner," Tommy continued. "She not only won a lot of races for me, but hatched some of the best homers ever born around these parts. She was my darling Lilly."

Jimmy put the book down and stood beside his dad. For the first time, he took a close look at the bird on the quilt. He looked at it before but paid no attention to the details. This time he looked at the bird differently. It now had a story behind it, and knowing the story made it look altogether different.

"Maybe your grandma will make a quilt for you with your hawk on it, Jimmy," his dad said, smiling at him.

Jimmy was surprised his dad didn't know what had happened to Lady Samson. "I don't have my hawk any more, Dad," he said. "In fact, I don't have anything at all."

"The game warden found out that Mary and I hunted with them, and we had to give them away." We gave them to the Air Force Academy down at Colorado Springs right before school started."

"I'm sorry to hear that, Jimmy," his dad said. "That's too bad. I don't care that much for hawks, you know, but that was the most beautiful hawk I ever saw. I wondered why you're reading about racing pigeons, because hawks eat pigeons."

They sat down on the bed and looked at the quilt for some time. Tommy ran his fingers along the sewn edges of

Soft Feather

the bird. He stopped and looked over at the book Jimmy read. Jimmy turned and looked at the book then he looked at his dad. "I am reading your books. Grandma put them on my desk last week. I guess because you were coming. I finished reading a couple of them. Reading makes the time pass faster. Time has a way of dragging by here in Mercer. Anything that can hurry it along, I like."

Tommy looked at his son with love in his eyes. "Don't make the time go by too fast, son," he said. "One day, when you're older, you'll wish you could find something that will make it slow down."

"You've had a lot happen to you since I was here last summer. Your grandma wrote me that you won a lot of contests with your hawk. Now you tell me that you had to give it away.

"I got a letter from your Mom a couple weeks ago, before Thanksgiving, saying that you'd gone on a hunting trip with Mr. Miller and got lost. She said it was three days and two nights before they found you. That must have been quite an experience for you, Jimmy."

"Yes, sir," he said. He then told his dad all about the time he spent in the woods at Mr. Miller's cabin in the mountains. He, also, told him about Mr. Wilson's dog, Goldie.

He got up and showed his dad the plaque Mr. Miller made for him. It was a dog with the words 'Lost Feather' on it.

Jimmy put the plaque back on the wall, and his father got up and came over to his son's side. He pointed to another plaque. On it were the words 'Strong Feather Jimmy Warrior'.

"Where did you get this one?" he asked.

"Mr. Miller made that for me, too, Dad," he replied. "That was the first plaque he gave me. You can see that it looks like Lady Samson."

Soft Feather

His dad looked at it for some time before he said, "The name fits."

"Thanks, Dad," Jimmy said.

"I see that you have two feathers on your desk." He walked over and picked up their wooden holder."

"Grandpa gave them to me."

"If he gave them to you, son, you earned them," Tommy said, smiling.

Jimmy hugged him and didn't say a word. He didn't have to. The hug said everything.

"Come over here and sit down in the chair again, Jimmy," he said, putting the feathers back on the desk.

Jimmy sat down as Tommy sat on the bed. "You know what I think you need?" he asked.

He shook his head. "No, sir."

"I think you need another hobby. You've had a good time working with hawks. Now let's see how you are at working with another type of bird. How would you like that?"

"Pigeons?" Jimmy asked.

"Yes, pigeons," he said. "I'm only going to be here a few days, but during that time I can teach you all you need to know about pigeons. Would you like to do that? It will give us something to do while I'm here. Something to pass the time faster, like you talked about."

Jimmy thought about it for a moment. "That sounds good, Dad. Grandma said that you were the best trainer around these parts. Were you, Dad?"

"That's what they say," he answered. "And who am I to say that I wasn't? They wouldn't lie, would they?"

They both laughed. It felt good to have something to do together. Jimmy yearned for something to do with his dad for a long time. He didn't know what it would be, because his dad was always off somewhere else. But now

Soft Feather

he was here with him, and they talked about doing something together.

"Seriously, Jimmy. I worked hard to learn what I know about pigeons. I've forgotten a lot since then, I'm sure, but I'll read some of those books again, and get myself thinking like a pigeon trainer."

"I feel like I can really help you become a good trainer. There's a lot of work to it, Jimmy. Are you sure you want to do it?"

"Yes, sir. I want to be like you, Dad. You teach me all you know about homing pigeons, and I'll work hard at being a good trainer. Maybe I'll be the best one around here. What do you want me to do?"

"Well, first," he said, putting his arm around him, "let's get some sleep. It is way past midnight, and here we are talking about homing pigeons. There must be something wrong with people who sit up past midnight talking about pigeons. They probably have featherbrains."

They looked at each other and laughed again. Jimmy was so excited that he didn't want to go to bed now. It was just getting interesting. But he didn't want to stay up all night like he did last Friday when he went trapping. He pulled back the quilt and slid in between the sheets, and his dad followed.

He and his dad had a good time today, and tomorrow would be even better.

Tommy reached over and turned off the light. They lay there thinking their thoughts about what they'd be doing the next few days. Tommy found himself caught up in the time problem they had. He, too, could hardly wait for tomorrow to come.

As they lay there, Tommy said, "You know what, Jimmy?"

"No, sir, what?"

Soft Feather

"I once knew some good pigeon trainers around here. A couple of the best trainers lived over in Boulder. We could go over and see if they still live there. They could tell us what's going on in this area in homing pigeon training and competition. I think that's what we should do, Jimmy. What do you say?"

"That sounds great, Dad," he said, sitting up.

Tommy reached over and turned the light back on. "Yes," he said. "We'll go over to Boulder and see if some of my old friends are still around. Let's see-- tomorrow is Saturday. I'd say that some of them would be home for sure."

"How are we going to get there?" Jimmy asked.

"Well, let's see. We need to borrow a car or truck. How's your grandpa's truck running?"

"He hasn't driven it for some time. I don't know if it's because he can walk to work or if it's because there's something wrong with it. It should be OK, but I don't know for sure."

"Well, son, first thing tomorrow morning, we'll find out how it's running. If it's running all right, we'll ask him if we can use it to go to Boulder. He will be working tomorrow so we will be going by ourselves."

"That's great," Jimmy said, lying back down. He now wanted the night to pass even faster than his dad did.

Tommy leaned on one elbow, thinking. He reached over and turned the light off again. As he lay back down, he thought about people he used to know in Boulder who owned pigeons.

Both of their minds were filled with what the next day would bring. To Jimmy, it meant getting out of Mercer and going to a city. He hadn't been anywhere in such a long time, and this time he would be with his dad.

For Tommy, it meant renewing old acquaintances, seeing people he had not seen in twenty years.

Soft Feather

That was a long time ago, but most people around these parts didn't move around like he did. Many who were born in this area lived here all of their lives. They might travel away from Colorado for a short period of time, but they always came back to what they considered the best place in the world.

He thought about that for a few minutes and came to the conclusion they were right. He was back.

They fell asleep thinking of all kinds of things that might happen the next day.

Soft Feather

CHAPTER 9

Alice didn't bother knocking on their door when breakfast was ready. She heard them talking way into the night so she waited until ten o'clock, and couldn't wait any longer.

When she knocked, she heard a faint sound, then, nothing more. She opened the door and found both of her boys still in bed.

Pulling the curtains back, she asked, "Are you going to sleep through this beautiful day? The sun has been up for hours. Come on, you two. Get up before you miss it," she said, as she went back to the kitchen.

Tommy realized they slept a good portion of the morning away. "Come on, Jimmy," he said. "Get up. We've got to go to Boulder today. Come on, get up."

They jumped out of bed and rushed in and out of the bathroom in record time. Down the hall they went, and entered the kitchen to find Alice cooking biscuits and eggs.

She made some cream gravy and put it on the table as they sat down. Tommy looked at the food before him and shook his head.

"Mom, you remembered my favorite breakfast."

She went around the table and gave him a hug. "When my prayers are answered, I'm overjoyed. Cooking what you like for breakfast is just a way of showing my thanks for having you with me for a while, son.

"Where's Grandpa?" Jimmy asked.

"Oh, he got up early," Alice said, and walked over and gave Jimmy a hug. She didn't want to leave him out. "He went down and did his work early. Then he went with Mr. Miller up to his cabin in the mountains."

"He said they would be back later this afternoon. He just went along for the ride, as far as I know."

Soft Feather

"Did he take his...?" Tommy said, then stopped. "You said he went along for the ride. That means he didn't take his truck. That's great. Jimmy and I want to borrow it today and go over to Boulder for a while."

"Oh," she said, looking at Tommy "What do you want to do in Boulder?"

"Jimmy and I would like to try to locate one of my old friends who used to fly homing pigeons. I used to have some good friends in Boulder, and if anyone is still around, we'd like to talk with him. Jimmy thinks he might be interested in learning about racing pigeons."

"Oh," she said again, thinking about what he said. "Well, the truck hasn't been out of the garage for some time, Tommy. I don't know if it will start, since it's been parked for so long."

Tommy jumped up and motioned for Jimmy to follow him. "We'll go push it out into the sun so it can warm up while we eat," he said, and went out the door with Jimmy right behind him.

Alice went over to the kitchen window and watched as they ran around the house to the garage. She was glad she placed those homing pigeon books on Jimmy's desk. She could see that she did the right thing.

They opened the door and disappeared inside the garage. Tommy opened the driver's door and put the truck in neutral. He closed the door, and they went around to the front of the truck and pushed.

With a lot of grunting and puffing and pushing, the two managed to slowly roll the truck out of the garage and into the sunshine. Tommy opened the hood and checked out everything. When he finished, he looked over at Jimmy and smiled.

"Everything looks OK. Let's go get something to eat." They were breathing hard as they went back to the kitchen and sat down.

Soft Feather

"I want to thank you again, Mom, for cooking my favorite breakfast," he said, taking her hand and kissing it.

"You're welcome, son," she said. "You know I love to spoil you a little. You two enjoy your breakfast, and I'll go get the key to the truck." She hurried to the bedroom.

Jimmy bowed his head and waited for his dad to say the blessing. Tommy started to eat, then saw his son. He bowed his head and talked to the Lord. When he finished, they both enjoyed the good meal.

Alice stopped outside the bedroom door and waited until her son finished the prayer. Then she walked over and laid the keys on the table. "Even though he got off on the wrong track for a long time, he didn't forget how to pray," she thought. She felt proud of him.

The two of them ate everything she cooked. She cleared the table and sat down. "There's a small can of gas out on the work bench in the garage, Tommy," she said. "You can use some of the gas to prime the carburetor. Tom always does that when the truck hasn't been used for some time."

"Thanks, Mom. That way we won't run the battery down trying to start it." He got up and hugged her again. "We'll be back later this afternoon. I don't know when, but we won't miss supper."

"That's for sure," Jimmy said, grinning.

"Well, I'll see if I can find something to cook for supper," Alice said, enjoying the hug.

They knew she would have a good meal waiting for them. They went out the door and over to the truck.

Again, she stood at the window and watched. Tommy tinkered around with the truck a while, then got inside and tried to start it. The truck growled a couple of times, then started. "That didn't take long," she thought.

Tommy got out and checked everything under the hood again, then put the hood down. They climbed in and

Soft Feather

sat there letting it idle for a while. When it warmed up, he backed up, shifted gears, and drove around the big tree in the front yard.

As they drove past the window where Alice stood, they waved at her. She waved back and smiled.

The truck slowly moved down the lane and into the street to the highway and stopped. They turned right, and the truck picked up speed and was soon out of sight. She went back to her work humming a little tune. She was a happy woman.

The truck moved along really well after it warmed up. The snow disappeared except for some fairly large patches out in the fields. The last snow melted fast, which made the farmers happy. It was like the Lord sent snow to irrigate every inch of ground around Mercer.

Jimmy sat beside his dad and shook his head.

"What's the matter, Jimmy?"

Jimmy looked over at his dad. "It's nothing, Dad."

"Oh," he said frowning at him. "Tell me, anyway."

"Well," he said, then stopped. He looked at his dad to see if he really wanted to hear what he had to say. His dad looked back and nodded his head.

"I made a large snowman two weeks ago. It's across the creek up on the hill behind the house. When I went up to check on it last weekend, I found it melted a little. I named the snowman 'Lone Warrior' because I left him alone so much of the time. He was to guard the hills and creek for me while I wasn't there."

Jimmy looked out the window of the truck. "I don't think he's guarding anything now. He's probably a puddle of water."

Tommy didn't answer for some time. "When I was a boy, I made snowmen up on one of those hills, Jimmy," he said. "You're probably right. He may be melted by now.

Soft Feather

But the great thing about your Lone Warrior, son, is that you can build another one just like him the next time it snows. And you know, when he melts, he runs down into the valley streams, which water the crops, and the farmers gather those crops. Your grandma goes to the farmers' market and buys peas, corn, tomatoes, peaches, pears, and all that good food. So, really, all the snowmen just keep doing all of us a favor every year. He may be gone to the valley today, but someday he'll be back on the hill."

He hadn't thought of it that way, but he knew his dad was right. His Lone Warrior would not be gone for good. When it snowed again, he'd make sure he returned.

"My dad sure is a great person," he thought, looking at him. "It sure feels good sitting next to him."

When they came to a road that went off to the right, he said, "That's the road that goes up to Mr. Miller's cabin in the mountains."

"I'm glad to know that," Tommy answered. "It must be up by Ward. I've gone different ways to get to Ward, but that's the best way. It's the shortest."

They soon passed the place where a black widow spider bit his grandpa. His grandpa drove the truck out here to get a load of railroad ties. When the ties got old, they were pulled out from under the tracks and laid alongside the fences.

He told his dad all about how he learned quickly how to drive that day. They laughed when Jimmy told how he almost knocked the right rear fender off when he hit the railroad crossing sign. It was the fender that his grandpa and Mr. Wilson just welded back together after another accident.

They talked and laughed as they drove, having a good time. It wasn't long until they came to a large road that crossed the highway. Tommy slowed down and turned right. The truck picked up speed, and now they passed

Soft Feather

large farms. The fields were bare, but all of them were plowed. They were ready for planting when spring arrived.

There were large haystacks in many of the fields. They had no fences around them, so the cows could feed anytime they got hungry. He saw a couple of haystacks where the cows ate their way up under the hay.

Jimmy wondered as he rode along if any of those haystacks ever fell on the cows and covered them up.

When they topped a hill and started down the other side, he saw a large lake off to the right. On the west side of the lake was a building with the largest smokestack he had ever seen. Smoke came out of the top and drifted off towards the north. "What's that, Dad?"

"That's the Valmont power plant, Jimmy," he answered. "It's where the electricity for this area is generated."

Jimmy looked at the magnificent sight as they drove towards it. High above the smokestack was a flock of birds. They turned and headed toward the lake on the far side. It was a beautiful sight.

"Look at that flock of geese, Jimmy," Tommy said.

"I saw them when they were high above the smokestack," he answered.

The truck picked up speed going down the long hill. When they reached the bottom, houses and large trees blocked the view of the lake. Now and then there was a break between the trees and houses and Jimmy tried his best to see the geese again, but being at the same level as the geese, he couldn't see them.

The Valmont plant disappeared behind them, and the truck soon passed the Boulder City Limits sign. Tommy slowed down and tried to get his bearings. He turned right for a couple of blocks, then left. They soon drove down one of the main streets of downtown Boulder.

Soft Feather

There were people everywhere. It was Christmas shopping time. The sound of holiday songs came from some of the stores.

Tommy drove slowly around the courthouse square. He took a close look at everyone on the street. "I don't recognize anyone, Jimmy."

He drove around the square until he spotted someone backing out. He stopped, then pulled into the parking space.

"Here's a quarter, Jimmy. I want you to go across the street to that popcorn wagon and get us some popcorn."

"Yes, sir," Jimmy said, with a big smile on his face. He hadn't had any popcorn for a long time. He jumped out and quickly made his way across the street, dodging cars as he went. Soon he was on his way back with both hands full.

Tommy opened the door for him and he got in. He handed his dad a box of popcorn. "Here's your change, Dad," he said.

"You keep it, son," his dad said. "You'll need the change for later. We'll probably need another box of popcorn before we leave Boulder, won't we?"

"Yes, sir," he replied, putting the money in his pocket and grinning his best grin.

Tommy smiled back as he started the truck and backed up, then drove down the street. "I know where I am now, Jimmy," he said. "We'll go over one street and turn right. That's Canyon Street. One of my best friends that I told you about used to live on that street. He had a house high up off the road."

"There are a lot of steps we'll have to climb to get up to his place, but it's a good place to raise and fly pigeons."

Before long he stopped the truck, and they got out. Jimmy looked up at the house. It was on the side of a

Soft Feather

mountain. His dad was right, there were a lot of steps that led up to it.

They climbed the steps fairly fast at first, then slower and slower until Tommy stopped to catch his breath. They looked down at the truck. "It's a good place to live if you don't want people to bother you," he said.

"No one in their right mind would climb all of these steps just to ask for a cup of sugar."

Jimmy pondered what his dad said. It didn't make sense, but it did. Up they went again, only a lot slower this time. Finally, the door to the cabin was in front of them.

"We should have begun slower," Tommy thought, leaning up against the railing. "I should have quit that nasty habit, smoking cigarettes, years before, and maybe I wouldn't be so short of breath."

Tommy looked around and shrugged his shoulders. He knocked on the door. They listened but heard nothing. He knocked harder the second time. Then they heard someone moving around inside the cabin.

Slowly, the door opened and an unkempt man stood there looking at them. "What do you want?" he asked.

"I'm looking for Jack Starr," Tommy replied, smiling at him.

"I'm Jack Starr," the man said. "What can I do - - don't I know you?"

"Well, the Jack Starr I'm looking for is not as ugly as you are. He sure is a lot better-looking than you are."

Jack looked at Tommy, then Jimmy, and back at Tommy. "It seems like I should remember a punk like you," he said.

"Who's a punk?" Tommy said, narrowing his eyes.

"Who's ugly looking?" Jack said, looking real mean.

"I guess we both are," Tommy answered. "I'm Tommy Warrior. I used to raise and train homing pigeons.

Soft Feather

You bought some of my best homers from me more than once."

"I know," Jack said, and stuck his hand out and shook his hand. "Nobody could forget an ugly face like yours, either."

"How are you doing, Jack?" Tommy asked, and they both laughed.

"I'm doing fine. Come on in. It's good to see you again. Where have you been and what have you been doing? Are you still in the pigeon business? Where are you living now?" Questions just overflowed from him.

"I'm living in Texas right now. I'm not in the pigeon business anymore, but my boy is interested in learning as much as he can about homers. Are you still in the business?"

"Sure am, Tommy," he replied. "I don't have any of the pigeons you sold me, but I have their offspring. They do real well in the races around here. I don't win them all, but I win a lot of them."

"That's great," Jimmy spoke up.

Jack opened the door, and they followed him into the living room, where they sat down. He looked at Jimmy and smiled. "Another competitor, huh?" he said, looking at him real mean. "Well, if you're anything like your dad, I'd better watch out. Your dad was one of the best."

Pride showed in Jimmy's face as he looked at his dad. Tommy gave him a wink. "Could we see what you have, Jack?" Tommy asked, looking around the room.

"Sure can, Tommy. It's about time for their daily exercise flight. I'm sure they'll enjoy going out a few minutes early, it's such a beautiful day. Follow me, and I'll show you some great homers."

They got up and followed him through his cabin to the back door. They went outside and around the side of the

Soft Feather

cabin and down a narrow walkway. Attached to the back of his cabin was a nice pigeon pen.

Having the roosts at the top, it was a nice size and tall enough to stand up in. The pigeons started cooing as soon as they saw him.

He opened the door to the pen and held it open until Jimmy and his dad were inside. He closed it behind them and started talking to his pigeons as he walked around the pen. He reached into his coat pocket and pulled out some feed. Some of the pigeons flew down and landed on his hand and began to eat.

As he stroked them, he talked to each one like it was his favorite pigeon. He placed the remaining feed back in his coat pocket and looked at Tommy.

"What do you think?" he asked.

You have some outstanding birds, Jack," he said, as he looked at each bird separately. "I can see you put a lot of work into getting where you are today. Your hard work paid off."

"Thanks, Tommy," Jack said. "It means a lot to hear you say that. Yes, I have worked hard, and I'm proud of my birds."

He walked over and opened a part of the cage near the top. The pigeons, one by one, flew out the opening, and in a flock, flew around above them. They flew off a short distance and came back and circled above the pen again.

The three of them watched them fly gracefully back and forth and then around and around.

Then, as though someone gave them a signal, they flew over a nearby hill and were gone. Jack and Tommy headed for the door.

Jimmy stood there not moving, waiting for the pigeons to return.

Tommy reached over and grabbed his arm. "Come on, son. They'll be gone a while. It's a nice day for flying."

Soft Feather

He slowly followed them out of the pen. They walked over and sat on some chairs that were around a large stone-top table near the cabin but not next to the pigeon pen.

Jack looked at Tommy and asked, "What are you looking for, Tommy?"

Just then they heard a flapping noise inside the pigeon pen. Then a pigeon flew out of the opening at the top of the pen.

"Look at that beautiful pigeon, Dad," Jimmy said, pointing at it.

They watched it fly away, with Jack shaking his head.

"That is the most beautiful blue color I've ever seen."

Tommy looked at the pigeon as she flew off. "Yes, son," he said, "but color doesn't mean it's a good homer."

"Your father is right, Jimmy," he agreed. "She is the worst I have. She's the last to leave the pen for her exercise flight, and the last to return. She is pretty, though. That I have to admit."

Jack looked back at Tommy "Well," he said, "I'm waiting for an answer."

Tommy looked at him as if to say what do you mean, then he remembered his question. "I just want my boy to see some good homing pigeons, Jack," he said. "He has read most of my books, but they are old.

"He needs to know what's happening in the pigeon world now. Maybe later on he'll get his own pigeons, but we're just looking this time."

There was a noise above them, and they looked up. The pigeons were returning. One after another they flew down and entered their pen. They strutted around inside the coop on the ledges, cooing and pecking at each other.

Soft Feather

Some of them paired off and didn't have much to do with the others. Jimmy turned and looked at his dad.

"How come those over there don't have anything to do with the others?" Jimmy asked. "Is there something wrong with them?"

"No, son," Tommy replied. "Pigeons are different from almost all other birds. They choose a mate, and when they do, it's for life."

That impressed Jimmy, as he watched them.

Jack and Tommy went over to the pen and looked at all of the pigeons. They discussed how some of the birds were so different from the others.

But Jimmy looked up into the sky. He wondered where that lovely blue pigeon was.

He wondered why she was so different from the rest. "Maybe she's a loner," he thought, "and doesn't want anything to do with the others."

Jimmy thought all kinds of things about her as he watched for her return. Then he realized what her problem probably was---she didn't have a mate. She was lonely, just like a person who doesn't have someone to care for him. Maybe she was like he used to be and just wanted someone to care for her.

Tommy and Jack talked for a while before they realized what was happening. They watched Jimmy. He just searched the skies for the lone pigeon that flew off alone. They both knew exactly what happened. Jimmy was hooked.

He sat waiting for a specific little bird to fly into his sight. They knew the feeling, oh, so well. In fact, it still happened to them.

They, too, sat many times and waited and watched the sky for the return of that one bird that they loved so much. Neither said a word for a while. They cherished that

Soft Feather

moment with him. They sat and looked into the sky with Jimmy, searching for that beautiful blue pigeon.

Jack and Tommy just looked at each other and remembered. They talked about some of the good times in their early days of training pigeons. Tommy told Jack that Jimmy had a hawk and some of the things he did with it. Jack looked at him, raised his hand and thought a minute.

"You know, Tommy," he said, "I remember seeing his picture and reading about him in the local newspaper. I wondered if he was related to you. But you know us pigeon people. Anyone who has anything to do with hawks is not much interest to us pigeon lovers."

"The game-warden made Jimmy get rid of his two hawks, and the hawk his girlfriend had. They took them down to Colorado Springs and gave them to the Air Force Academy right before school started."

He stopped and looked at Jimmy, then, continued, "I didn't know about this until I got here yesterday. The way I look at it, my boy needs something else to occupy his time. I can think of nothing better than having a few homers around to do that. He's real good with birds, and I'm hoping this will be something he will enjoy."

They looked over at Jimmy and grinned.

His face had a big smile on it. Slowly, he stood up and watched a distant speck get closer and closer. The beautiful blue pigeon returned from her own exercise flight. She flapped her wings as she landed on the special landing ledge just outside the pen opening, and hopped inside.

She then headed for her corner in the back of the pen. She almost disappeared from view when she settled down in the corner.

Jimmy walked up to the pen as she settled down. Tommy looked at Jack and he nodded. He would sell the blue pigeon to Tommy. How could he refuse, when Jimmy stood and looked so wistfully at her? He remembered that

Soft Feather

wonderful day the first time he'd looked at a pigeon like that.

It is a special time pigeon owners cherish all of their lives because it's an ongoing love. Each new pigeon they get brings back some of that old feeling, but it's never the same as with their first pigeon.

They walked to one side and talked for a while. Jimmy just remained outside the pen and stared at the dark figure in the corner. Now and then he saw her look at him. He began talking softly to her to let her know he liked her. Suddenly, she got up and came to the edge of the walk board by the coops.

She stood motionless and looked at him. She seemed to know he was talking to only her.

She cooed a couple of times, then went back to her corner. He kept on trying, but nothing Jimmy could say or do brought her out of the corner again.

"That's more than she ever did for me," Jack said. "I talked to her over and over, but she just ignored me. "Maybe she doesn't like my voice," he laughed.

"I told you he was good with birds," Tommy replied, grinning.

Jimmy finally told her goodbye and walked over to his dad and Jack.

"Thanks a lot, Jack," Tommy said. "We appreciate your showing us your pigeons. I know Jimmy learned a lot just by watching them today." He headed back toward the cabin.

Jack and Jimmy followed after him. Jack opened the door and they went in the back door of his house. "I promised my mother we'd be back before supper. If we hurry, we'll make it," Tommy said.

"Jack, I don't know when we will be back. Christmas is only a couple days away, and you know what happens at Christmas time. I'm looking forward to it."

Soft Feather

Tommy did all of the talking, and Jack did all the listening as they headed for the front door. Finally, he said, "Tommy, it's been good seeing you again. You and Jimmy come back any time. He's going to be just like us if he doesn't watch out."

Jimmy didn't want to go, but his dad opened the door and walked out onto the porch. "Let's go, Jimmy," he said. "We've got some popcorn to buy before we head back to Mercer, or maybe you don't want any?"

That was the magic word. His eyes showed it as he walked out the door after his dad. He walked past him down the steps. Tommy watched him disappear below.

"I'll see you in a couple of days, Jack," Tommy said. "I'd like to have a couple more to go with the blue pigeon. She'll need some company. Pick out a male and female. She seems kind of lonely, so you might pick the male for her."

"I'll leave it up to you. My boy deserves the best, Jack, but I can't afford that right now."

Jack looked at him and nodded. "Her blood lines are the best, Tommy," he said. "She just doesn't have the drive she needs to be the best. Maybe you're right; a mate might help pull her out of her troubles. I'll see what I can do, and don't worry, your boy will get the best."

Tommy nodded his head and smiled. "Thanks." He turned and headed down the steps after Jimmy.

"You're welcome, Tommy," Jack shouted after him. "I'll see you later."

He watched Tommy's back as he disappeared down the steps. Soon he heard the truck start and saw them drive off. He thought about the popcorn they would be eating. "A good idea," he thought. Back inside he went and got out his popcorn popper.

Soft Feather

The sun was going down as Jimmy and his dad turned off the highway in Mercer and headed down the street toward their house. Tommy slowed the truck when they entered the lane that led up to the front porch.

They saw something shining through one of the windows in the front room as they got close to the house.

"What is that?" Jimmy asked, pointing at the house.

Tommy looked and smiled. "That looks like Christmas tree lights on a Christmas tree," he answered. Then he laughed out loud. "Sure. That's what your grandpa and Mr. Miller went up in the mountains for."

"I should have guessed what he was up to when we got up this morning, but I was too interested in going to Boulder."

Jimmy looked closer as the truck passed the house and parked in front of the garage. He got out and opened the door. His dad drove the truck inside and came back outside while Jimmy closed the door.

They headed for the front door, excited. When they walked into the front room, the sweet smell of spruce reached their nose. A large spruce tree stood in front of the window.

Tom and Alice put all kinds of decorations and tinsel all over it. The lights were all different colors, and Christmas scenes turned around on the top of each light. Jimmy had never seen anything that pretty before.

Tom and Alice went into the front room to see the expression on their faces. "Thank you, Mom and Dad," Tommy said. "So many times I lay awake at night, and remembered this scene."

"Not only when I was overseas during the war, but also those lonely Christmas nights when I was in the states far away from home. Thank you. Thank you," he said slowly, as tears filled his eyes.

"You're welcome, son," Tom said, softly.

Soft Feather

Alice walked over to Jimmy and put her hand on his shoulder. "Well, Jimmy, what do you think about all of this?" she asked.

"Mom and I used to have a Christmas tree, too, Grandma," he said, looking at the tree. "But nothing like this. It was a small one with just a few decorations. Mom didn't have money for more. But I was always proud of the one we had."

The mention of his mother brought a silence to the room. They each wondered where she was and what she was doing. "I pray your mother has as nice a Christmas as we're having, Jimmy," Alice said. "I love her very much."

Nothing was said for a couple of minutes. Then they heard Jimmy say very softly, "So do I, Grandma."

Soft Feather

CHAPTER 10

Monday morning found everyone busy around the Warrior household.

"Jimmy," Alice said, "Helen and I are going to Longmont to do some Christmas shopping. You may go along and buy some presents if you would like. I saved some of the money the Air Force Academy gave you as a gift for giving them your hawks."

Jimmy thought she spent all of that money long ago. He surely was glad she hadn't.

His heart filled with joy as he realized he would now be able to buy some gifts for everyone.

When Alice told him Mary would be going along with them, he was even happier. He remembered the last shopping trip they took just before school started. He hoped that today would be even more fun than that one was.

He quickly finished his breakfast, put the dishes in the sink and washed them. Alice dried them and put them up.

He looked at the wood box behind the stove and saw it needed some wood. He brought a big armload from outside and put it in the wood box. His dad came into the kitchen.

"Fill it up to the top, Jimmy," he said. "We surely don't want it to run low. Your grandma might not be able to cook us those good meals."

Jimmy went over and hugged his dad. "Grandma sure can cook, can't she?" he said.

His dad hugged him back and said, "Yes, Jimmy." He looked at his mother and then back at Jimmy. "What's happening around here today?"

"We're going to Longmont to buy some Christmas presents, Dad," Jimmy answered. "Are you and Grandpa coming along?"

Soft Feather

"No, Jimmy," he said. "Not this time. Your grandpa and I planned to do a few things around here. It seems like every time I come home, there's always something that needs to be fixed. I'm glad that I can help out a little."

A car pulled up in the driveway, and the horn blew. It was Helen Wilson and her daughter, Mary. "What are you going to fix, Dad?" Jimmy asked.

"Don't worry about it now," Alice said. "Go get your coat. They're waiting for us." She hurried Jimmy away toward his room. She winked at Tommy and went to her bedroom to get her coat.

When Jimmy returned, he met his grandma coming out of her bedroom. "Let's go," she said. Jimmy went out to the car, but Alice stopped to talk to Tommy.

"We'll be back home kind of late, Tommy. Be careful. Will you have everything done by the time we get back?"

"We plan to, Mom," Tommy said. "Don't worry."

"OK," she said, and went out to the car and got in. She waved at him as they drove off. "It's so exciting," she thought. "I love all of the secrets and surprises that come at Christmas time."

The four of them talked all the way to Longmont. Alice and Helen sat in the front seat. They talked about all the things that happened, or were about to happen, in Mercer.

Jimmy and Mary sat in the back. Jimmy told Mary all about the beautiful, blue pigeon he saw when his dad took him to Boulder.

Mary didn't say much. She just listened to Jimmy. She knew he didn't care much about girl stuff.

When they almost reached Longmont, Mary asked, "Jimmy, do you have your Christmas list made out?" Jimmy shook his head "no." "Don't worry, I'll help you

Soft Feather

make your list." She got some paper and a pencil out of her purse and gave it to him.

"Write down the name of each person you want to buy a gift for. Put a price by the name so you'll know about how much you can spend." He made the list the way she told him to do it.

When they arrived in Longmont, they all got out of the car. Jimmy looked at his grandma. Before he asked, she said, "Here's twenty dollars, Jimmy. That should be plenty. It's not how much or how little you spend for a present, it's remembering the person that counts. Just buy a little something for everyone. Don't worry about not being able to pay much."

He took the money, and they walked a short distance. They stopped and looked back to see if Alice and Helen followed. "I know you two want to go off by yourselves," Helen said. "That's OK. But be back here at the car in an hour. We'll go get something to eat then. If we have more shopping to do, we can do it after we eat."

They all agreed, and Jimmy and Mary disappeared into the crowd. Alice and Helen stood and watched until they disappeared. They looked at each other and walked into the nearest store. They, too, liked to shop, and planned on doing a lot of it.

An hour later, they all met back at the car with their arms full of packages. Helen opened the trunk of the car, put her packages in first, then, she helped the others. Each one put theirs in a separate place so they wouldn't get mixed up. "We need to get a few boxes," Helen said.

They each had a hamburger and an ice cream sundae. They soon were back at the car with some boxes. Another short shopping trip was all they needed to complete this buying spree. So off they went, and returned shortly with a few more packages.

Soft Feather

Into the boxes they went. Helen closed the trunk lid. "Let's go home. I like to shop, but I also want to go home."

Again the car was filled with conversation as they drove along towards Mercer. Alice and Helen talked about the things they bought, and Jimmy again talked about the blue pigeon he saw when his dad took him to Boulder. Mary sat and listened politely.

Helen pulled up next to the front porch of the Warrior home. Tom and Tommy came out and helped take the boxes into the house. The Wilsons drove off as Alice and Jimmy went into the house with an arm around each other. It was a fun shopping trip.

The boxes were put on the couch in the front room. Jimmy looked to see which box was his. He picked it up, excused himself, and headed for his room. He didn't want anyone to see what he bought. He placed the box on his bed and went back to the kitchen.

"Grandma," he said, "do you have any wrapping paper?"

"Sure do," she said. She got her stool, and, reaching up to the top of the kitchen cupboard, took down two pretty rolls of paper. It had all kinds of pretty winter scenes on it. "Will this do, Jimmy?" she asked, and handed one to him.

"Yes, ma'am. It sure is pretty." He turned and ran back to his room and started wrapping his presents. Soon he was back, asking for string to tie them. His grandma gave him some, and back he went to his room. It wasn't long until he had them all tied, with names on them.

His grandparents watched him run in and out of the front room as they sat at the table wrapping presents. Each one of them was having a grand time. What really touched their hearts was watching their grandson. It was some time since they saw Jimmy so happy.

Jimmy stayed in his room for some time. When he came out he had the box filled with wrapped presents. He

Soft Feather

walked over to the Christmas tree, and with care, took them out of the box. He put each one under the tree.

When he finished, he stood up and looked at all of the presents. "It looks even prettier with presents under it, doesn't it?" he said.

The three who watched him said in unison, "It surely does."

After supper, each one told something funny that they remembered from the past. Laughter rang throughout the house. It was the season to be merry, and the Warrior clan was merry.

It then grew quiet as they watched the fire dance in the fireplace. It wasn't long until Jimmy headed for bed. It was a long day, and he was tired. He didn't know when his dad came to bed.

It seemed like before he turned over in bed, it was time to get up. It was the day before Christmas, and Alice was already in the kitchen making cookies and candies in and on the kitchen stove.

The smell just made the three men do nothing but lie around and wish Christmas day was today. They could have gone outside since it was a nice day, but they just stayed around the house.

Later that afternoon, clouds moved in and hid the sun. Just before the sun disappeared, it started to snow -- softly, at first, then harder. As the last rays of light faded away, Jimmy looked out the front window and saw that the ground was covered with snow.

"Now I can rebuild Lone Warrior," he thought. He looked forward to seeing his snowman again.

Alice finished her last cooking chore and came into the front room where all the men were taking it easy. They sat around the Christmas tree just looking at it for a long time.

Soft Feather

Softly, she started singing 'Silent Night', and they all joined in. Other Christmas carols followed, and soon it was time for bed.

Jimmy jumped up and headed for bed. "I'm going to get in bed and go to sleep as fast as I can," he said. "If tonight is like last night, tomorrow morning will be here before I know it. See you all in the morning. Goodnight."

They wished him "goodnight" as he headed for his room. He got in bed and turned off the light, but sleep didn't come as easily as it had the night before. He tossed and turned for a long time and finally went to sleep.

Tommy came to bed later and marveled at his son's ability to go to sleep so fast. He didn't know that he tossed and turned for quite some time.

The next thing Tommy knew, Jimmy was climbing over him to get up. "It's Christmas morning, Dad! Let's go see what we got for Christmas!"

Tommy got up slowly and headed for the door. Then his son's excitement began to rub off on him. His steps became quicker as he headed down the hall towards the front room. When he got there, he found that Jimmy already turned on the lights. "What time is it, Jimmy?" he asked.

"Five o'clock," Alice said, coming out of her bedroom. Tom followed, rubbing his eyes. They came into the front room and sat down with their eyes half-open. Tommy sat down beside them and watched, as Jimmy pulled a present out from under the tree and looked for a name.

Alice and Tom's eyes were now open wide, and they got just as excited as their grandson. They sat on the edge of the couch and watched Jimmy.

"You go ahead and call the name that's on the present, Jimmy," Alice said.

Soft Feather

He found it and did as she asked. It wasn't long until everyone had his or her presents. As each one carefully opened theirs, trying to not tear the paper, they exclaimed joyfully over each gift they received. Jimmy got more clothes than anything else.

After they opened all of the presents, the excitement died down a little. Alice stood up and started picking up the paper. Everyone helped and gave her theirs. She took it all into the kitchen and folded it up nice and neat.

With an armload of wrapping paper, she went over and opened the hall closet door. She placed the pretty paper up on the top shelf. She would use it again next year.

Tom got up and walked into the kitchen. He lifted a lid on the wood-burning stove and checked the fire. It was low so he put a couple sticks of wood in and put the lid back on the stove.

Alice returned to the kitchen and started breakfast. "Since you got me up this early, Jimmy," she said, "we might as well eat and get it over with. That will give me plenty of time to fix the turkey your grandpa got yesterday for today's dinner."

He picked up his presents and took them to his room. He placed all of them on top of his desk and separated his clothes from the other presents. He placed them in his chest of drawers.

He had plenty of clothes that should last him until next Christmas. He went over to the desk and looked out the window. It stopped snowing during the night, and the sun now shone brightly. Water dripped off the roof as the snow melted. It wouldn't be long until the beautiful snow would be gone.

Leaving his room, he opened the back door and went out onto the porch. The majestic Colorado Rocky Mountain range rose high into the sky. The green of the pine trees reached up almost to the top of many of the

Soft Feather

mountain peaks, and snow covered the rest. He admired that which lay before him.

He took a deep breath and smiled. "God sure painted a beautiful Christmas picture this morning for all to see," he thought.

His grandma called, letting him know that breakfast was ready. He sat down at the table and sat quietly as he ate. He didn't want to disturb anything by talking.

After breakfast he listened to his dad and grandparents tell stories. Most of them he heard many times before, but now and then, there was a new one. He really enjoyed them.

Alice got up and started getting dinner ready. Soon the kitchen got too hot for the men, and not just from the heat, so they got up and went into the living room. It was what Alice wanted. "The kitchen is where I cook good things for my men, and I love to do that," she let them know. "I don't need a lot of talking going on when I'm working. If I need help, I will ask for it."

It was about ten o'clock when Jimmy heard a car pull up in front of the house. He paid little attention to it, thinking it was the Wilsons or the Millers. He sat in the sofa chair in the front room and read a book on pigeons his grandpa gave him for Christmas.

Someone knocked at the door, but he kept reading, hoping someone else would answer it. But no one did. Again, someone knocked, only harder.

Tommy sat on the couch. "Answer the door, son," he said.

Jimmy looked up at him and said, "Yes, sir."

He slowly got up and went over to the door. He wondered why his dad didn't answer the door. He was closer, and he knew that Jimmy was interested in the book he read.

Soft Feather

Jimmy opened the door and there stood Jack Starr with his hands behind his back. "Hello, Mr. Starr," he said. "Dad, it's Mr. Starr."

"Tell him to come in, Jimmy," Tommy said, not getting up from the couch.

"Come in, Mr. Starr," he said, and opened the screen door. "Please come...oh, look, Dad, he brought Lady Blue with him!" he exclaimed, as Jack slowly brought the pigeon cage around so Jimmy could see it.

Tommy got up and went over to the door where Jimmy stood. "Merry Christmas, son," he said. "I hope you like the present I got you."

Jimmy turned and hugged his dad. "Oh, Dad!" he said. "It's the best Christmas present I've ever received! Thank you, Dad! Thank you."

He turned around and opened the screen door and let Jack in. Then he saw the other pigeon. "There's another pigeon with her, Dad!" he exclaimed. "Are they both for me?"

"Yes, Jimmy," he answered. "Jack and I talked about it and agreed that your blue pigeon needs some company. He picked out another pigeon for her. She seems to be a lonely loner."

"I felt like she needs a pigeon she is used to. One that can help her get used to her new home."

Tommy looked at the other pigeon and then at Jack. "You sure meant what you said, didn't you?" he said. "It looks like they are the best you have."

"No, Tommy," he answered, smiling. "They're only two of my best. I have plenty left."

Tommy nodded, knowing what he meant. "Thanks," he said.

"You are welcome," Jack said.

Alice and Tom came into the front room and looked at the pigeons. "Good morning," Alice said. "I believe we

146

Soft Feather

know you. You came to see Tommy some time ago when he raised pigeons. It's good to see you again, Jack. You know my husband, Tom, don't you?"

"Yes, of course, Alice," he said. "I remember Tom, and I remember you. I remember the great meals you fed me every time I came over here. I couldn't forget such a good cook."

"You sure know the right words to say," she replied. "You men go out and put those pigeons in their new home and come back in here. I'll have a little something for you to eat. Can you stay for dinner?"

"No, Alice. My housekeeper fixed me a big Christmas dinner. Thank you, anyway."

Alice nodded, got up and went back into the kitchen. She motioned for Tom to follow her.

Tommy, Jimmy and Jack went outside and around the garage. There were patches of ground here and there where the snow melted. They walked up to the old pigeon pen Tommy built, only it wasn't old and run-down like it was earlier. It was all fixed up and painted. It looked like new.

"Your grandpa and I worked on that pen while you were in Longmont yesterday, son. I would say there is probably not a better pen around here. It will keep them out of the cold on this side of the house."

"I made sure that each pigeon box is draft-free and has plenty of nesting material, Jimmy. You have to have a place where they can stay warm during the cold months.

"We got some feed for them; so, all that pen needs now is a couple of pigeons. Do you know where we can find some?"

Jimmy ran over to the pigeon pen and opened the door. "Let's see how they like their new home, Mr. Starr," he said.

Soft Feather

They went into the pen, and he shut the door behind them. Tommy watched from outside the pen. Jack opened the cage, reached in and took out the blue pigeon. He handed her to Jimmy.

Jimmy noticed how soft she was. He talked to her like he talked to his hawk, Strong Feather Lady Samson. She looked at him as if to tell him she remembered he talked to her before. Slowly, Jimmy opened his hand as he talked to her. She cooed and walked back and forth on his palm.

She enjoyed the attention he gave her. Then she flew up onto his shoulder and turned around. Jimmy turned his head toward her, continuing to talk, and she watched his mouth."

"Lady Blue," he said softly, "you have the softest feathers I have ever felt. They are nothing like the hawks'. They have rough feathers. I think that's what I'll call you. Yes, I'm sure that's what I'll call you. "Soft Feather Lady Blue. Now that's a name to be proud of," he said.

Tommy and Jack stood and watched. This pigeon, a loner, sat on Jimmy's shoulder acting like a well-trained pigeon. It was nothing but amazing the way Jimmy handled her.

Slowly, he reached up and held out his hand. Lady Blue walked off his shoulder onto the palm of his hand. Lifting her up to the walk board next to the nesting boxes, she stepped off onto the board and turned around and looked at him. She cooed as she walked back and forth, watching everything he did.

She was a different pigeon than she'd been over at Jack Starr's pigeon coop in Boulder.

Jack took out the other pigeon and placed it on the boardwalk near Lady Blue. She walked away a short distance, then, turned and watched Jimmy again.

Soft Feather

They stepped outside the pen and closed the door. "You have a great talent for working with birds, Jimmy," Tommy said. "Cultivate that talent, son."

Jimmy looked at his dad. "I'll do my best, Dad," he said, as he looked at Lady Blue.

He put his hand on Jimmy's shoulder. "I don't believe you will have much more to do, Jimmy," he said. "You've done more with that pigeon in a few minutes than I've been able to do with her since I've owned her. It was a pleasure to watch what just happened."

Jack looked at Tommy, and he nodded agreement. "Thanks for coming over today, Jack. I really appreciate it."

"As I said before, it's been my pleasure, Tommy. I wouldn't have missed seeing Jimmy and Lady Blue. He's a natural trainer. They are hard to find. Over the years I've only met two. I think I've just met number three."

Jimmy started to say something but stopped when Jack shook his dad's hand. Turning he patted Jimmy on the back and winked at him.

"I'll be going now," Jack said. He turned and looked at Tommy. "Don't know when I'll see you again, but I'll be seeing your son now and then. I promise."

"Thanks," Tommy said.

"Jimmy, if you need any help, drop me a line or call me. I'll be glad to do what I can to help you get started."

They thanked him again, and he left. They stood there outside of the pigeon pen and looked at the two new arrivals of the Warrior household. It made both Tommy and Jimmy feel good to have birds around the house again.

"There's something you need to realize, Jimmy," Tommy said. "Those two pigeons don't know this pen as their home. If you released them right now, they would fly back to Jack Starr's coop. That was their home, and as far as they know, it still is."

Soft Feather

"You'll have to keep them penned up for some time before they'll forget Jack's pigeon coop. It will be better and faster if you work with their offspring. Those born here will know it as home from the beginning."

"They will return to this pen no matter where you take them. Do you understand that?"

Jimmy nodded his head. "I understand, Dad," he answered as he thought about it. He began to realize that Lady Blue might not be the great racer that he fleetingly thought she could be. But, he also knew that one day she would consider this her home, and that made him feel good inside.

Tommy knew that his son accepted the reality of the problem and probably was working out a solution in his own mind. That was the way it should be.

"Now, Jimmy, let me go over a few things for you so you'll understand pigeons better. If you're a careful observer, you'll find pigeons are a lot like people. There are all kinds, including greedy, generous, meek, loving, warlike, good, and bad."

"But the ones you'll be looking for are the fast ones. They are like people. There are some people who run faster than others. But if the fast ones were put to the test in a long- distance race, they would probably quit before the end. So you must train your faster pigeons just like a racer must train for a race."

"A good homer can fly over sixty miles an hour. That's right, son. They can fly a mile a minute."

Jimmy began to daydream while he listened to his dad. He saw his pigeons fly like the wind, winning race after race. He smiled at the thought of winning.

Tommy brought him back to reality when he said, "You're going to have to put up a screen between the pigeons in one of the nesting boxes, Jimmy."

Soft Feather

He picked up a piece of chicken wire he didn't use the day before and opened the door to the cage. Jimmy followed him inside the pen. He picked up the male pigeon and placed him in one of the three nesting boxes he built.

He folded the screen so it fit into the box, and placed it so the male pigeon couldn't get out.

"Get Lady Blue," he said.

Jimmy reached up, and Lady Blue came to him. He picked her up and placed her into the nesting box. Tommy handed him a nesting bowl, and Jimmy placed it inside with her. He stood and watched to see what she would do.

Lady Blue stuck her head out of the box and looked at Jimmy. In a low voice, he assured her that everything was all right. She looked over at the other pigeon and saw that he strutted back and forth, showing off for her.

She seemed to like it as she pulled her head back inside the nesting box, and became very interested in the other pigeon.

"They probably would find each other if we leave them outside, but it would take longer," Tommy said, looking at them.

"But now, just being separated caused them to notice each other. If it works, you'll see the male pigeon try to feed her through the openings in the screen.

"Even though she has plenty to eat, she will coyly allow him to insert his bill into hers like it was the best food in the world.

"When that happens, remove the partition you've put in her nesting box, and they will rush together as if they had been separated for a long time."

Jimmy enjoyed listening to his dad tell him about pigeons. He read some about it. But this was what he always wanted--- his dad to tell him things he didn't know.

"They mate for life, Jimmy," he continued. "When a pigeon leaves its mate, it's because of a long period of time

Soft Feather

apart. Short periods, like races, seem to make them fonder of each other.

"After they are put together, there will be a lot of activity for the next week. They will be making their nest in that nesting bowl. At the end of the week the male will begin to drive the female to the nest. Then in about ten days, she will lay her first egg, always white, and, within forty-eight hours, the second. There are always two, no more, no less.

"The hatching takes about eighteen days. The youngsters are fed what is called pigeon's milk.

"It's a yellow substance that looks something like pale cheese. Even though it is not milk, it has all the nutrients of milk. It's made only when they have youngsters to feed.

"They grow rapidly, Jimmy. They increase in size and weight one hundred percent in the first two days. From less than an ounce at birth, they'll easily weigh more than a pound within thirty days. "You'll need to band them when they're a little over a week old. I have some bands I'll give you.

"Each band must have a number and the date of birth. You must enter the number and date in a pedigree book. Do you understand everything I've told you so far, Jimmy?"

"Yes, Dad," he said, smiling. "I've read your books. But it makes more sense when you tell me."

Tommy shook his head. "Here, I've been trying to tell you all about raising pigeons, and you already know. You amazed me with the hawk you raised, and now you're doing the same thing with pigeons."

"I must be like my father," Jimmy said, smiling.

"Let's go see what your grandma has for two hungry pigeon trainers to eat," Tommy said, giving Jimmy a quick hug.

Soft Feather

They ran around the garage toward the house as fast as they could. Jimmy won, and they laughed. Tommy wasn't as fast as he used to be, but that was all right, that's the way it should be.

Soft Feather

CHAPTER 11

The day after Christmas, Tommy got his suitcase out of the closet. Jimmy sat at the desk and watched his father pack his bag. It seemed like only yesterday when he sat and watched him unpack. Time for Jimmy usually went by slowly, but never at Christmas time, and it went unusually fast because his dad visited him. He didn't want their time together to end.

Tommy looked around the room to make sure he had everything. Then, he closed his bag and set it by the door. "It has been good to be here with you, son," he said.

"Maybe we can do it again real soon. I've thought about coming up to the veteran's hospital in Denver, but with the job I have in Texas, I can't do it right now."

"It would be great if you could come up to Denver, Dad," Jimmy said. "We could see each other a lot then."

"It's something to think about, son," Tommy replied. "We'll see."

Jimmy walked over to his dad. He put his arm around him and gave him a big hug.

"I need to say good-bye to your grandma and grandpa," Tommy said, as he returned the hug. With his bag in hand, he opened the door.

As they walked toward the kitchen, Tommy gave Jimmy some last-minute instructions. "Don't forget, Jimmy, you have to keep your pigeons well-fed when it is cold like it is now; especially, keep their water unfrozen so they can get a drink when they need it. It will freeze over quickly, so check the water before you go to school each morning.

"Some nice warm water will really help them after a cold night. Then check it again at noon when you come home for lunch, and then feed and water them when you come in from school."

Soft Feather

"I'll do it, Dad," he said, as they walked into the kitchen where Tom and Alice were. "I'll take good care of them."

"They're hardy birds," Tommy continued, too interested in what he talked about to notice that his parents were at the table. "But that doesn't mean they can't get hurt. They depend on you for their care.

"If you are not going to properly care for your pigeons, you should set them free. Then they can take care of themselves. But as long as they're caged, they're your responsibility."

"That was good advice your dad gave you, Jimmy," Alice said.

Tommy realized where he was when he heard his mother's voice. "Sorry, Mom," he said. "I forget where I am when I talk about pigeons. Remember how I used to carry on about my pigeons and what great and wonderful plans I had for each one of them. Well, it was a lot of fun, and a lot of my plans came true. It worked out good for the pigeons and me."

"That it did, son," she said. "Tom and I sat here this morning and talked about the times when you went to contests and came back with all those ribbons. What ever happened to them?"

"Oh, they got lost," he sadly answered. He looked at his dad. "Those were good times, weren't they, Dad?"

"Yes, son," Tom said. "They surely were. I'm glad Jimmy can carry on where you left off. It makes your mother and me proud of both of you."

Tommy looked affectionately at Jimmy. Nothing was said for some time. They enjoyed just being together. Then Tommy looked at the clock over the sink. "It's time for me to go down to the highway and flag down the bus. Anyone going with me?" he asked, looking around the table.

Soft Feather

They all got up and put on their coats. They weren't going to let him go by himself.

They strolled down the lane to the street and then up the street to the highway. They looked down Main Street to see if the bus was coming.

It was nowhere in sight. It wasn't long until they talked about things that happened during the time Tommy was home this time. A lot happened in the short time they were together.

Snow on Christmas Eve was a special treat. It was a time they would remember for a long time. There was still some snow alongside the road.

Now and then Tommy looked down the road. Then, he saw the bus come slowly through town.

He waved, and the bus driver slowed even more and stopped right beside them.

Tommy said goodbye and hugged everyone. He went up the steps on the bus, turned to Jimmy and said, "Remember what I told you about taking care of your pigeons, son," he said, looking him in the eye.

"I will, Dad," he said. "I promise I will remember."

Tommy climbed up the rest of the steps, and the bus driver closed the door. Slowly, the bus moved off. He sat down and looked out the window and waved.

They waved back until the bus was out of sight. It surely was nice to have him home, even though it was a short time.

They didn't say much as they walked back to the house, each one deep in thought.

"I sure am grateful. Thank you, Lord," Alice said. Tom and Jimmy knew what she meant. They felt the same.

As they reached the house, a car pulled up behind them. Mr. Miller got out of his car. "It looks like I missed him," he said.

"Yes, the bus just left," Tom replied.

Soft Feather

"I'm sorry I didn't get to see him again," Mr. Miller said, "but my truck wouldn't start. Had to drain the glass bowl under the carburetor. I guess some water got into it from the cheap gas I bought the other day. It never fails, when I try to save a penny, it costs me one way or another."

They all agreed with him.

"Anyway," he continued, "I'll see him next time." He looked at each of them and smiled. "Tommy asked me to help Jimmy with his pigeons. I told him I would help as much as I can. I sure would like to see those two pigeons Jack brought."

"If I remember correctly," Alice said, "you had some of the best homing pigeons around when Tommy trained and raced his. In fact, you worked together on a couple of your pigeons' breeding, which paid off later on."

"You have a good memory, Alice," he said. "But your boy was the trainer. I just followed along, learning as much as I could at that time." He paused, but continued. "Maybe I can repay him by helping Jimmy now."

Tom looked at Mr. Miller and said, "Chuck, you two pigeon nuts go on around the side of the garage and look at those pigeons. Get it over with. I know for sure we won't hear anything from either of you from now on but pigeon talk. So go on."

They laughed as Tom and Alice went into the house. Jimmy and Mr. Miller walked around the garage to the pigeon pen. Mr. Miller looked inside. He watched the two pigeons for some time.

Jimmy opened the cage door and went inside. Mr. Miller closed the door and stayed outside. He looked closely at them. "What are their names?"

"Lady Blue, and Big Boy," Jimmy answered.

"Hmmm," Mr. Miller said. "It looks like you have two of the best homing pigeons I've seen in some time, Jimmy. I see you've separated them with a small piece of

Soft Feather

chicken wire. I used that kind of screening technique with some of my birds, and it works. I read about it in one of your dad's books he lent me. I see he started you off right. If everything works out, you'll have some little ones running around the coop in a month.

"Then in another month or two, they'll be ready to race. You may want to see if they will return to their coop by then. Turning them loose for the first time is a hard thing to do, but you have to do it."

Jimmy took the covering off the hole on the nesting box. He talked to the blue pigeon as he came closer to her. She came out of her nest and flew onto his shoulder and looked at his mouth. She seemed to know what he said. Whether she did or not didn't matter; she got the attention she needed.

"Come on in, Mr. Miller," Jimmy said.

He came in and shut the door. He walked up to Jimmy and put his hand out to the blue pigeon. She wouldn't have anything to do with him. She even backed up a little, lowered her head and looked at him.

Jimmy talked to her. "Don't be afraid of Mr. Miller, Lady Blue. He's one of my best friends, and he'll be yours, too, one of these days."

She seemed to perk up as she heard his voice. She didn't go to Mr. Miller, but she raised her head and looked at him. That was a big step. Jimmy knew he had more work to do with her, but it would work out.

Mr. Miller saw that Lady Blue wasn't going to come to him, so he went over and talked to the male pigeon in the next nesting box. The bird came to the opening and looked at him.

Jimmy walked over to the corner and got a handful of feed. He gave some to Mr. Miller, then held some of it in his hand for Lady Blue. She flew down and ate from his hand.

Soft Feather

When she finished, she strutted back and forth on his hand, cooing as she went. She listened when he talked, and now, she talked and Mr. Miller listened.

She stopped and looked up at him. He reached over and stroked her head gently. She ducked his hand the first two times, but realized he meant her no harm, and raised her head higher each time he stroked it.

He opened his hand, and she stepped up onto it. He lifted her gently, placed her back in her nesting box, and replaced the screen over the hole so she couldn't get out. He would keep it covered a few more days. She had to learn that this was her home now.

The two pigeons got along nicely, and he didn't want to disturb them any more than he had to. It would be hard to have to leave her alone until her babies arrived. He could hardly wait for that day to come. Jimmy took a couple steps back and waited for Mr. Miller.

Mr. Miller finished feeding the other pigeon and followed Jimmy out of the pen, who closed the door and told Lady Blue he would see her later.

They watched as she went back to her corner and sat down. Only now, her head didn't droop like it did at Mr. Starr's. She held it up and looked around at her new home. She settled down and seemed to be content. "Maybe she likes not having other pigeons all over the place," Jimmy thought.

Jimmy and Mr. Miller walked around the house to his car. Jimmy wondered what Mr. Miller really thought about the pigeons.

Mr. Miller said, "You know your dad got me interested in pigeons again the other day when he told me he was going to get you a couple of homers. I've always had pigeons around my place. It hasn't been long since you and Mary came over a couple of times and caught some of them for your hawk.

Soft Feather

"I still have a few pigeons flying around in my barn that are homing pigeons. The rest of them are just regular pigeons.

"I believe you could tell by my having them around my place, that I kind of like pigeons. I told your dad I'd help you get started training and racing; so, I built a small pen by the side of my house.

"I used to have one in that same place, but I tore it down when I stopped working with homers. I'd like for you to come over and see it sometime, Jimmy."

"I'd like that," he replied, getting excited.

"Jump in, and I'll take you over and show it to you right now," he said. "I'll bring you right back so your grandma won't miss you."

"OK." Jimmy said, and ran around the car and got in. He looked at the kitchen window and saw his grandma looking out at them. He waved at her, and she waved back. "Grandma doesn't miss too many things that go on around here," he thought.

It didn't take long to drive over to Mr. Miller's farm. He drove up next to his house and stopped. They got out, and he led Jimmy across the yard and around to the south side of his house and showed him his pen.

It was a small pen, hardly big enough for one person to walk around in.

"It's not large, Jimmy," he said, seeing his frown. "But it doesn't need to be large. It's big enough for a few pigeons. I do have something though, that you don't have."

He reached over and pulled a string. A buzzer sounded inside the house. Jimmy wondered what it was for.

"When a pigeon lands on the board into my pen, it won't ring the buzzer," he said. "But when it enters the pen and steps on this board here, it trips the lever that rings the buzzer over there. That way I know when a pigeon has come into the pen. I don't have to stand around in here

Soft Feather

waiting for them to come in. If I have five birds out on an exercise flight, all I have to do is count the rings, and I'll know when all five of my pigeons return."

"It surely helps. Of course, you have to put up with the noise. You might want to make one for your pen."

"That's a neat idea, Mr. Miller," Jimmy said. He thought about it. "I think I'd like to make one of them. I can see where it would help later on."

"I'll help you put one together, Jimmy," Mr. Miller said. "Let's go out to the barn, and we'll make one right now. Then we'll take it back to your pen and put it on the entrance."

They headed for the barn and excited to be doing something together again. Before long they returned with a bunch of wires, boards and a buzzer. They quickly loaded all of it into the back seat of the car.

Then they drove back to the Warriors' house. They unloaded the things and carried them around to the pigeon pen.

They hammered, and sawed and rang the bell a lot to see if it worked. Finally, they finished. They stepped back and looked at their handiwork. Mr. Miller smiled, and Jimmy frowned. He wondered if it would work. Mr. Miller knew it would.

He stepped outside the pen, and Jimmy followed. He reached up and touched the lever, and the buzzer buzzed. He looked at Jimmy. "Only one pigeon can come in at a time. As they walk over to the end of this board, it trips this lever that is attached to that switch. Their weight will cause the switch lever to close the contacts and cause the buzzer to buzz. It won't buzz until the pigeon is inside."

"It will continue to buzz until the pigeon jumps off the entrance board. So, each time it buzzes a pigeon has entered your pen. Most pigeons don't stay on the board very long, as they want to get over to their roost and their

Soft Feather

mate. The other buzzer goes inside the house, so let's go hook it up.

"I have a switch inside our house so we can turn it off. We'll put a switch inside your house so you can turn yours off, too."

When they finished in the house, they went back outside. Jimmy reached up through the entrance hole in the pen and put his hand on the board attached to the lever. The buzzers rang each time he touched the board.

Mr. Miller smiled. "I think yours works better than mine," he said. "I'll really get to be a whiz if I build many more of these things."

They started to walk around the house when Jimmy stopped and went back to the pen. "I'll see you later, Lady Blue," he said. He then hurried back and followed Mr. Miller to his car.

He started his car. "I'll see you tomorrow, Jimmy," he said. "I'll need your help in catching a couple of homing pigeons that are in the top of my barn. Bring Mary with you if she will come. You two can catch them for me. I'll show you which ones."

"I have to go to Longmont tomorrow morning, so come by early. If you can do that for me, we'll have more time when I get back to talk about how to train your homers."

"OK," he said. "I'll go over this afternoon and let her know what we plan to do. I know she'll want to help. I told her all about my pigeons, and she was really interested."

"That's fine, Jimmy," he said. "I'll see you two in the morning. Don't forget now."

"No, sir," Jimmy said, laughing. "I won't forget."

Mr. Miller smiled at him. "I didn't think you would," he said, as he put the car in gear. Slowly, it moved

Soft Feather

down the lane and out onto the street. Jimmy waved, then ran into the house.

As he entered the kitchen, his grandma came out of her bedroom. "What's all that buzzing for? I thought you two would never stop buzzing that thing. It probably has something to do with the pigeons, doesn't it?"

"Yes, Grandma," Jimmy said, and looked at her to see if she was really mad. He saw a slight twinkle in her eye, and he knew she kidded him. "It's to let me know when a pigeon lands on the entrance passage and goes into the pen."

"That way I'll know when all of the pigeons return without having to go outside. Mr. Miller has one on the pen he built when he had homers, and it works. I told him I'd like to have one on my pen, and he helped me build it."

"It works real well, Grandma."

"It sure buzzes. I know that for a fact. I had to go into the bedroom to get away from it," she said.

"Mr. Miller has a switch inside his house so they can turn it off. We put a switch on mine over there by the window. That way we can turn the buzzer off when we want."

Alice walked over to the window and looked at the switch. She nodded and looked at Jimmy. "I like that idea. Of course, it has to be painted white so no one can see it."

"Yes, ma'am. I'll paint it right now."

"Not right now, Jimmy. You go wash up."

He hurried to the bathroom as she took some dishes off the back of the stove. She was keeping something warm for him.

When he returned, she said, "I kept your lunch warm for you while you and Chuck buzzed that buzzer. Sit down and eat. If that thing works, it will be worth the noise. I can see where it would be a great help on a cold day. Did you try it with the pigeons to see if it works?"

Soft Feather

"No, Grandma," he answered. "Dad said to not fly the pigeons for a couple months, and then only fly one at a time. After they get used to their new home, I can fly one at a time for a week or two. When they accept this pen as their home, I can then fly them together on daily exercise flights."

"Oh," she said, nodding her head. "That makes sense. I kind of remember Tommy doing the same thing when he first got his pigeons. Yes, I remember. That's the way to do it."

"I surely hope it is, Grandma," he said. "I don't want to lose either of them, especially Lady Blue. Her feathers are the softest I've ever touched."

"Lady Blue?" Alice said. "So you named her already." She thought a while and then continued. "Another "Lady" around here. I like it, Jimmy. It fits her. She sure is a beautiful blue color. In fact, I've never seen a pigeon that color. She's one of a kind, Jimmy, and I can see you're proud of her already."

"I sure am, Grandma," he said. "She was sad when I first saw her over at Mr. Starr's in Boulder, but now she holds her head high when I talk to her. She likes me a lot, and I like her, too."

Alice watched Jimmy say the blessing and start to eat. She knew he felt better than he had in a long time. Nothing else they tried worked.

She was happy to see that gleam in his eye again, the one that was there last summer when he trained and worked with his hawks. "Working with birds seems to bring out the best in my grandson," she thought.

When Jimmy finished eating, he picked up the plates and put them in the sink. Alice told him she'd wash them for him. He started to leave, then stopped. "Grandma," he said.

She stopped and looked at him. "Yes, Jimmy."

Soft Feather

"I want to thank you for all you do for me."

She gave him a big hug. "You are welcome, Jimmy. I love to do things for you, just like you love to do things for me."

He hugged her back. "There's nothing like having a grandma that loves you," he thought. "Nothing."

After breakfast the next morning, he said to his grandma, "Mr. Miller asked me to come over to his place this morning. He wants me to help catch a couple of the homing pigeons that live in the top of his barn.

"He asked me to see if Mary can come over and help. He has to go to Longmont. Is it all right if I go over and ask?"

"That sounds like a good idea, Jimmy," Alice replied. "Mr. Miller helped you build that buzzer, so you need to help him catch some pigeons so his buzzer will be buzzing, too."

Jimmy laughed at her little joke, and she got tickled at him.

"Mary would probably be disappointed if you didn't let her help, so you run along and find her. Don't be late for dinner, though."

"I won't." Jimmy walked out of the house, laughing at his grandma. She was a nice person, and he enjoyed talking to her. He wondered why he and his mother didn't have good times together like he and his grandma.

As he thought about his mother, he walked slower, then stopped.

He remembered some of the good times with his mother. When he was younger, they played games and laughed all the time. But as he grew older, everything gradually changed. She soon found she had problems with his getting older.

Soft Feather

"Maybe it was because she didn't want me to grow up. Just wanted me to stay her little boy," he thought. "But I wanted to be grown-up."

When he turned eleven, things changed. She started working all night and sleeping most of the day. It wasn't long before he wandered the streets on the weekends. During the summers, he spent more time on the streets.

In a nearby park, he started begging for quarters. He got so good at it that he had money in his pockets all the time. But it all changed when he turned twelve. He got taller, and no one would give him quarters.

He had no money, and one day he got caught stealing two apples.

The vendor called the police, and they took him to the police station and put him in jail to scare him. A policeman called his mother, but she didn't come until the next day. Spending the night in jail really scared him.

She had a big problem with his stealing. It was the last straw. She was getting a drinking problem, and she said she didn't want him around any more. She told the policeman that she just couldn't handle Jimmy since he was older and for him to send him to a reform school. She told Jimmy she didn't ever want to see him again.

Instead of sending him to a reform school, the policeman made arrangements for him to be sent to live with his grandparents. He didn't want to live with them at first, but soon realized that it was the best thing that ever happened to him.

He looked back at his grandparents' house. The house was so pretty all covered with snow. Behind the house, rolling hills stretched off toward the mountains.

The beautiful mountains rose into the sky like giants looking down on him. The snow-covered peaks looked as if they had their nightcaps on for a long winter's

Soft Feather

nap. It was beautiful compared to living in Newark, New Jersey. He was so glad to be here.

But deep down inside, he missed his mother, especially at this time of the year. Sure, he loved his dad, how could he not love him? But he loved his mother, also, and missed her very much.

He walked down the main street of Mercer and up to Mr. Wilson's garage. He saw Mary inside the office looking out the window at him. He went in, smiling at Mary. "Hello, Mary. How are you?" he asked.

"Fine, Jimmy," she said.

"Mr. Miller would like for you and me to go over to his place and catch a few pigeons. Would you like to go?"

Mary remembered when she went up in top of his barn and shooed pigeons out so they could catch them. "Sure," she said. "Only you have to go up there this time. Not me."

"It's a deal," he said, laughing.

Mr. Wilson sat in his chair and laughed, too. He remembered her talk about how scared she was. "Now, she's getting even," he thought, "but maybe not. He just might like being up there with all those pigeons. If Jimmy is anything like his father, he will love it."

Soft Feather

CHAPTER 12

Mr. Miller pointed out four homers that he would like them to catch. Wishing them luck, he drove off, on his way to Longmont. They waved as he drove down the lane and stopped at the highway. He turned right and headed north.

They ran into the barn, and Mary picked up the pigeon cage that was on a bench. Jimmy climbed up the ladder, but Mary just held the cage. Halfway up, he stopped and looked down and frowned at her and started back down.

"Go on up," she said, walking over to the ladder. She handed him the cage, and both of them laughed. "Glad you woke up," he joked. As they entered the barn loft, some of the pigeons flew around them and out the opening at one end of the barn.

Jimmy put the cage down and ran over to the opening. He shooed some of them back into the loft. Mary walked over to him, shaking her head.

"It's my turn to stand here and watch you catch them, remember?" she said.

"O.K.," he answered, and looked around. He tried to catch one of the pigeons Mr. Miller pointed out to them. All he caught was air as the pigeon flew up and landed on one of the crossbeams.

"This is not going to work," he thought. He hurried over to the ladder and climbed down.

He remembered that he saw a fishing net hanging on the wall above the bench. He took it off the nail and hurried back up the ladder. "I'll show those pigeons who is the boss around here," he thought.

When Mary saw the net, she clapped her hands. "Why didn't we think about that before?" she said. "I

Soft Feather

remember how hard it was to catch just one pigeon. I sure hope it works."

"I hope it does, too," he said, as he walked over to where the pigeon sat above him. He gathered the net up into his right hand and stretched his arm out. Holding onto one end of the net, he quickly turned around a little and threw the net as hard as he could.

It opened as it flew through the air towards one of the pigeons. It was so quick that the pigeon didn't know which way to fly. The net was all around it before it knew what happened.

The net and pigeon fell onto the loft floor. The bird flopped around on the floor as it tried to fly, but it couldn't.

He picked up the cage and opened the door. Then, oh so slowly, he picked up the net and untangled the pigeon. Gently, he grabbed it and put it into the cage and closed the door. "That's number one!"

"That sure was easy," Mary said. "I should have used the net. It sure would have saved me a lot of work."

He remembered her running all over the loft chasing pigeons. He picked up the cage, and they looked at the pigeon. "It wasn't hard at all," he said.

He spoke too soon. Of course, there's a difference between homing pigeons and regular pigeons. It seemed that all of the homers flew out of the barn. They had to catch ten more before they had another keeper.

With the two pigeons in the cage, they climbed down from the loft. They hurried over to the house and put them in Mr. Miller's pen. They looked at them with pride.

Now Mr. Miller and Jimmy each had two great-looking homers.

Mary went over and checked to make sure the gate was closed. They walked around the house, and Jimmy went up onto the porch. He knocked on the door and stepped back.

Soft Feather

Jackie opened the door. "We caught two homers for Mr. Miller," he said. "They're in the cage and seem to be enjoying their new home."

"Thank you, Jimmy." She opened the screen door and looked at Mary. "You, too, Mary."

"You're welcome," she said. "Jimmy did all the work. He cheated, though. He used a fishing net to catch them."

"That's a great idea, Jimmy!" Jackie said. "I'll have to remember that. I've had a time catching them myself."

"I just thought of it when we were up in the loft, and it works real well. Of course, you need to know which pigeons are homers. We had to catch a bunch of them before we got two."

"That's another good thing to know," Jackie said. "I'll tell Chuck what you two did. He'll be glad to know what to use to catch them. Thanks."

"You're welcome," Jimmy said. "Bye."

"OK," she said. She watched as he made his way down the steps.

Jimmy heard the screen door close, then the door. He smiled, knowing they did something nice for the Millers.

Jimmy didn't say anything as they thought about what they did. He thought about his homers, and a frown appeared on his forehead.

He had a problem that Mr. Miller didn't have. He would have to wait until he hatched out some pigeons. Then he would have to wait until they were old enough to fly. Then he would have to train them to race. His grandpa said that patience was something everyone needed to learn.

"That's true," he thought. "I am certainly going to have my patience tried."

Soft Feather

His excitement about raising pigeons continued, and Jimmy stayed busy. He tried to find out as much about pigeons as he could. He read all of his dad's books and worked hard at trying to put what he read into practice.

His grandma told him at breakfast one morning that their friends were coming over that evening. It would be a New Year's Eve get-together. He could hardly believe that the Christmas holidays were almost over.

Jimmy felt a little sad, but it soon passed, and he was his old self again.

"The Millers and the Wilsons will be coming over to help us welcome in the New Year, Jimmy," she said. "They will be over here about ten o'clock tonight. I'll fix a few treats for everybody and something special for you and Mary. Would you like that, Jimmy?"

"Yes, ma'am," he said, not knowing what it would be. But if his grandma said it was something special, he knew it would be good. It did have an effect on him as he could hardly wait until they came over so he could see what the surprise would be.

He worked around the pigeon pen most of the day, stopping a few minutes for dinner. Time passed quickly when he stayed busy doing what he liked. It wasn't long until his grandma called him for supper. He went inside and washed up.

As he came to the table, he could hardly resist asking his grandma what kind of surprise she had for him and Mary. But when he looked at her he saw that she was waiting for him to sit down. He swallowed the question and didn't ask. It went down hard.

All through the meal his grandma had a smile on her face. She was enjoying watching Jimmy fight off asking her about the surprise.

Tom sat there and watched both of them, shaking his head now and then. "They have another secret," he said

Soft Feather

to himself, "but if they think I'm going to ask them what it is, they're mistaken."

After supper Tom and Jimmy went into the front room while Alice cleaned up the kitchen. When she finished the dishes she started getting things ready for the company that was coming.

She hummed and sang as she worked. Tom sat in his easy chair with his eyes closed, listening to his wife. She had the sweetest voice he ever heard.

Jimmy wasn't caught up in the sweet melodies she sang, though. His mind raced along, daydreaming about his pigeons.

A knock at the front door brought Tom and Jimmy out of their daydreams. Tom got up and opened the door. It was Chuck and Jackie Miller. They came in, and Jackie went in to help Alice, while Mr. Miller sat down by Jimmy.

That was Jimmy's chance to ask Mr. Miller some more questions. He answered them the best he could. He looked over at Tom now and then.

After a few minutes, Tom said, "Jimmy, let Chuck have a breather. I'd like to talk to him, too."

Jimmy hung his head and said, "I'm sorry, Grandpa."

He sat quietly as Tom and Mr. Miller talked about the weather and how things were going around his farm. He felt that he had more important things to talk to him about, but he bit his tongue and listened.

As he sat there, he heard another car pull into the driveway. He got up and looked out the window. Bill and Helen Wilson came up the steps. He opened the door and was greeted with a happy "hello" from Mary.

He stepped aside and said "hello" to each one as they came in. He closed the door as Alice and Jackie came into the front room. It was a happy time for all.

Bill sat down next to Chuck and started talking.

Soft Feather

Jimmy stood there, shaking his head, and Mary looked at him, wondering what was wrong. "Let's go into the kitchen, Mary," he said. "My grandma said she has a surprise for us tonight. Let's go in and see what it is."

As they walked into the kitchen, Alice knew exactly what Jimmy had on his mind. She walked over to the stove and picked up a potholder. Grabbing the handles of one of the pans on the stove, she carried it over to the sink and set it on a folded towel on the counter.

She opened one of the cabinet doors and took out another pan. She filled it with cold water. Then, she put the hot pan in the cold water, waiting for it to cool a couple minutes.

Jimmy wondered why she did that.

"Get the butter out of the refrigerator, Jackie," Alice said, as she put the pan of cold water on the cabinet.

She looked at her grandson. "This is the surprise I told you about, Jimmy."

Jimmy looked in the hot pan. "What is it?"

"It's taffy," she said, "I'll bet you don't know what taffy is, do you?"

He shook his head. "No, Grandma, what is it? Is it something to eat?"

Helen walked over to the cabinet. "Yes, it is," she said, and picked up the butter dish and put it on the table. "It is some of the best candy there is."

"Oh, boy!" Mary said. "We're going to have a taffy pull, Jimmy! Come on and get some butter on your hands. When your grandma gets the taffy cool enough, we'll get to pull it until it's just right."

They sat down, and she put butter all over her hands. Jimmy just looked at her and shook his head.

She reached over and smeared butter all over his hands. He pulled them back, looking for something to clean them.

Soft Feather

"When the taffy is just right, we can eat it; you'll see how good it is then. Come on. You need to put more butter on your hands."

Alice filled a cup with cold water, then took a spoon and dipped it into the taffy. She let a drop of the taffy fall into the cold water. She took the cooled candy out of the water with her fingers.

She felt it, then put it in her mouth and chewed it.

"It's ready," she said. "All it needs now is to be pulled."

Mary picked up the stick of butter and rubbed it all over Jimmy's hands, making sure he had some extra butter on all of his fingers. She then put more butter on her hands and fingers.

When she finished, the taffy was cool enough to pull. Alice poured it out onto some wax paper on top of a towel. She formed the taffy with a big wooden spoon. When it was the way she wanted it, she put it in front of Jimmy and Mary. Mary picked up one end of the roll of the candy and gave one end to Jimmy.

He got a good hold on it and Mary pulled. It slipped out of his hands and onto the table.

Everyone laughed as they looked at the expression on his face. Jimmy reached for the taffy and grabbed it. This time when he pulled, it stretched into a fine string and broke, leaving half of the taffy in his hand.

"Don't pull so hard, Jimmy," his grandma advised. "Pull it gently until it starts to harden. Then I'll check it and see how much more it will have to be pulled before we can eat it."

Jimmy and Mary started pulling it. It seemed the more they pulled, the funnier it got, until they laughed more than they pulled. Helen came over and looked at them. She didn't say a word, but they knew what her look meant.

Soft Feather

It was time for them to become more serious about pulling the taffy. They still had a good laugh now and then as the slippery, stringy stuff slipped out of their hands.

It wasn't long until the taffy started changing from a stringy mess to a more solid state. Even the color changed from brown to a lighter color. Here and there, it had some light red streaks in it.

As it hardened, they had to work at pulling it.

Alice checked on the taffy now and then in addition to her pies and cakes in the oven. Another inspection, and she told them to stop. The taffy was ready to be cut.

Jimmy and Mary washed the butter off their hands. Alice cut the taffy and placed it on a large dish. She then put the pies and cakes on the table next to the taffy.

She looked at Jackie and Helen. "I think we're ready, girls," she said. "Let's call the men in here and get set for the midnight hour."

Jackie went into the front room and motioned at the men. When they were all in the kitchen, they looked at the food on the table and were quite pleased at what they saw.

"A person can get fat around here this time of the year," Tom said. "It's good fat, though."

They laughed as Alice looked at the clock over the sink. "Two minutes until midnight, Tom," she said, as he walked over and took her hand.

"Let's all join hands," Tom said. When everyone joined hands, Tom said a prayer for everyone there and for many not there.

When he finished, they looked at the clock. It was midnight. They looked at each other and started laughing. The Miller, Wilson and Warrior men kissed their wives. It was great to celebrate the coming of another new year.

Jimmy watched them, and before he knew it, Mary came up to him and kissed him. He turned red and didn't

Soft Feather

know what to say. They all laughed except Mary, she was serious.

Tom let go of Alice's hand and ran into the bedroom. In a minute, he came out with a shotgun. Jimmy eyes got big as he put his hands over his mouth and backed up. His grandpa ran over to the front door, opened it, and stepped out onto the front porch.

Boom! Boom! Boom!

He came running back in and closed the door. "Happy New Year, everybody!" he shouted.

"Happy New Year!" they all shouted.

Jimmy was relieved. This was all new to him, and for a minute he didn't know what was going to happen. It had been a night of surprises, that's for sure.

Tom took the empty shells out of the shotgun and went into the bedroom. He returned and saw everyone smiling at him.

Alice looked at Jimmy. "It wouldn't be New Year's Eve for us if your grandpa didn't go outside and shoot his shotgun. That's how he says 'Happy New Year' to everyone in town. Now they can all sleep well tonight, knowing that Tom Warrior said 'Happy New Year' to them."

They all gathered around the kitchen table and filled their plates. The food quickly disappeared, and soon there was nothing left but empty pie pans, cake dishes and a plate half full of taffy.

They joined hands and sang 'Auld Lang Syne'.

They sat in the front room and talked about all the great things that happened to them during the last year.

The Wilsons and Millers looked at each other. It was time to head for home. They exchanged good-byes, with a promise to do it again the next year.

As the Miller's left, Chuck looked at Jimmy. "I want to thank you for catching those pigeons for me. They were two of my best homers, and maybe they still are."

Soft Feather

"You're welcome," he said, as he remembered how he caught them. "Mary and I had a time trying to catch them at first, but then I got one of your fishing nets, and that really helped."

"I told him how you two caught them so fast," Jackie said. "Looks like he'll be catching a couple more, now that he knows how."

"That's great," Jimmy said, with a big smile.

"Thanks to you and Mary," he said.

They said goodnight and headed for their cars.

It was cold outside, so they watched them leave from the open front door. Tom closed the door. It was a great night.

Jimmy picked up a piece of taffy and excused himself. He walked down the hall to his room, chewing on the taffy. He sat down on his bed, and the taffy sweetness made him feel good.

It tasted a little like the kiss Mary gave him. She tasted like taffy. It was his first kiss, and he would remember how sweet it was.

As he crawled between the sheets, his mind was still on Mary. He wondered why she kissed him. "I'll never understand girls," he thought. "Never."

Lying there, he thought about his mom. It sure would have been great if she could have been there tonight, his dad, too, of course. He sobbed quietly. Maybe someday.

The next morning found Alice up and making plans. While her two men slept, she got her jar from the cupboard that had change she saved. She counted it and there was $9.55. That surely would be enough. It being New Year's Day, she would have to go to the Wilson's house.

Putting the money back in the jar, she placed it back in the cupboard, picked up her purse, left the house and

Soft Feather

went up the street. She knocked on the Wilson's door. When Mary answered the door, she went in and found Bill & Helen at the kitchen table.

`"Sit down and join us, Alice," Helen said.

"Thanks. I've come over to ask a favor."

"It must be a good one," Bill said. "Let's hear it."

"Well, it's New Year's Day, and I know that you're enjoying a day off. But I'd like to make a telephone call to Jimmy's mother today. If you could open your station for a while, I sure would be grateful."

"Now that's a great idea," Bill said. "That boy needs to talk to his mother, and this is the best day of the year to do it."

"I've got her phone number. There's a two-hour difference between here and there. It will involve two calls. One, to set up a time with her, and the other, the call."

"Do you have the number?" Helen asked.

Alice opened her purse and got her address book out. She found the number and handed it to Helen. She went over to the phone, got the town's operator on the line and told her what she wanted to do. "What time do you want to call back, Alice?"

Eleven o'clock here would be one o'clock there. My men should be up by then," she said, and they all laughed.

Helen got it confirmed, and Alice stood up. "Thanks. My grandson needs to talk to his mother. I try hard to take her place, but a boy needs his mother. It's been too long since he talked to her. I've heard him crying at night. I asked him one time why he was crying the night before. He just said that he missed his mother, and he got up and went outside. He didn't want to talk about it.

"Last night after everyone left, I heard him again. I opened his door and stood there looking at him. He was asleep, hugging his pillow. A pillow is a poor substitute for a mother."

Soft Feather

Helen walked her to the door, and Bill and Mary followed. "The station will be open a little before eleven o'clock."

"Thanks," Alice said, and walked back home. She hoped her men didn't arise while she was gone. That would ruin everything.

She sighed as she walked into her kitchen. It was empty. She soon had breakfast cooking. Next came the knocking on the doors and the grumbling from two sleepyheads who did not want to get up.

It took a second call to get them up. Tom grumbled when Jimmy beat him into the bathroom, again. Standing in the hall waiting, he looked at Alice in the kitchen. "One of these days, I'm going to beat him. When I do, I'll just mess around like he does, and he'll have to wait on me. I'll teach him a lesson," he griped.

She shook her head while her husband acted like a little boy, and went about finishing breakfast. It was ten o'clock.

After breakfast she let them know that she had a surprise. Mr. Wilson wanted them to come down to his filling station a little before eleven o'clock.

They both wanted to know what the surprise was and why they needed to be at Mr. Wilson's garage before eleven, but she would not tell them. Tom got upset, but it didn't do him any good.

At 10:45, the three of them sat in the Wilson's filling station, along with the Wilsons. Tom, of course, asked Bill what was going on. He wouldn't tell him.

The phone rang, and Alice got up and answered it. Tom looked at Bill, and he just sat there. "What's going on here?" Tom asked.

"Hello," Alice said. "Yes. Thank you. Is that you? It is so good to hear your voice. Yes, right here with me. Oh,

Soft Feather

I'm so glad to hear that. That is wonderful. Would you like to talk to him?"

She handed the phone to Jimmy and said, "It's your mother, Jimmy."

He reached for the phone then stopped. "My mother, Grandma? She wants to talk to me?"

"Yes, Jimmy. She wants to talk to you."

He took the phone and slowly put it up to his ear. "Hi, Mom."

"Hello, Jimmy. How are you doing?"

"I'm doing fine, Mom. It sure is good to hear your voice. Are you alright?"

"Yes, son. I'm doing fine. I have a new job working at a grocery store. I'm also going to night school to be a secretary."

Jimmy smiled and looked at his grandma. "Mom's got a new job. She's working at a grocery store and going to school at night," he whispered.

"That's great, Mom!"

"I love you, Jimmy, and miss you."

"I miss you, too, Mom. I thought about you last night. I wished you were with us Christmas and New Year's Day."

There was a silence on the phone before she said, "I miss you so much, Jimmy."

"Don't cry, Mom. I'm doing OK. Dad got me a couple of homing pigeons for Christmas, and I'm going to learn how to race them. They are beautiful. One is the prettiest blue I have ever seen. She likes me a lot, and I sure like her."

"Racing pigeons. Just like your dad. That's wonderful, Jimmy. He was one of the best, you know."

"Yes, ma'am. He told me, and everyone else told me. He's doing fine. He's working some now."

"I'm glad to hear that. He needs that."

Soft Feather

There was someone talking in the background. "I've got to go, Jimmy. I'm on my lunch break. Tell your grandma that I'm grateful she called me. I'll try and write you a letter."

"That would be great, Mom."

"I love you. Goodbye."

"I love you, too, Mom. Goodbye," he said, choking up. He hung up and stood there, trying to get composed.

Mary came over and stood next to him. His lips quivered, as he smiled at her. "Mom said she misses me and loves me, Mary."

"Of course she does, Jimmy."

He went over and hugged his grandma. "Thank you Grandma," he said, tears filling his eyes again. She hugged him back. "Everything is going to be all right, Jimmy," she said.

She handed Bill a $5 dollar bill and thanked him for the use of his phone. He took it and didn't say anything. As Tom shook his hand, he put the bill in Tom's hand. Tom knew Bill wanted Alice to have her little savings back, so, he took it. He nodded at Bill, then looked towards Alice, letting him know it would turn into a present for her.

As they walked back home, Jimmy thought about all he and his mother talked about. He knew in his heart that grandma was right. "'Everything is going to be all right.'"

When Jimmy worked with his pigeons, time passed quickly. He was glad that Mary started to like them, too. It made him feel good that they worked together again. Just like it was with their hawks.

One day when he got up, he thought about Lady Blue. He watched her very closely for about a week. He felt that something was wrong with her, but he didn't know

Soft Feather

what it could be. After he ate breakfast, he was about to leave when his grandma stopped him.

"Last night I remembered that there is an old chair out in the garage that your father used to sit in when he watched his pigeons. He spent a lot of time watching them, and I believe that is how he came to know so much about pigeons, Jimmy," she said, looking at him.

"I'm sure that chair is still there, because your grandpa doesn't throw anything away."

"Thanks, Grandma," he said. He was soon in the garage looking for the chair. Then he saw it and was glad his grandpa hadn't thrown it away. It was dusty, but he carried it outside and soon had it clean.

Placing it under the tree next to the pigeon coop, he sat down. He was very pleased; it was just right to sit in and watch his pigeons.

This became his daily ritual, especially, when it was nice outside. He tried to sit out there a couple times when it was cold. That didn't last long, though, and he soon found himself back inside where it was nice and warm.

At times his grandma came to get him when it was time to eat. Time passed so fast he wondered where it went.

One day as he watched them, he realized something changed. Both pigeons started liking each other. At first, the male tried to feed Lady Blue through the screen covering her nesting box.

She refused for some time, but one day she accepted his offering. Everything in their lives changed. She now sat in front of the screen watching the male.

He showed he liked her by strutting back and forth in front of her.

Two days later, when Jimmy returned to his chair, he saw the male feeding Lady Blue regularly. He got up, opened the gate and went inside. Going over to the nesting

Soft Feather

box, he took off the screen his dad placed there to keep his female pigeon inside.

With the screen gone, she stuck her head out of the box and looked around. She looked at Jimmy, then Big Boy.

Jimmy spoke to her, but she didn't seem to pay any attention to him. She walked out of her box and stood there. She was more interested in the male pigeon than him.

He reached up and gently grabbed the male pigeon and placed him next to her nesting box. The two pigeons ran together. They acted like they were so happy to finally be together.

Jimmy reached into her nesting box and took out her nesting bowl. He cleaned out her box and put the bowl back. He went over to a pile of straw he'd put in the pen and grabbed a handful. He placed it in the nesting box for her to make her nest.

Stepping back, he watched to see what they would do. All they did was coo at each other and gently peck each other's beaks. "She will make her nest later," he thought. He walked over and closed the gate and latched it.

He sat down in his dad's chair and watched them for some time. Then, they flew off the boardwalk, landing on different objects in the pen. It was a small area. Not that good for an exercise area, but it was all they had.

They returned to the boardwalk and strutted around, acting happy to be out so they could fly around. Jimmy's grin grew bigger as he watched them enjoying being together.

Day after day, he watched them get acquainted. Lady Blue's attitude changed. She no longer was a shy loner. She had someone that liked her now and someone she liked. It was good to see her prancing around the cage.

It wasn't long until there was a lot of activity in the nesting box. A nest began to appear in her nesting bowl. It

Soft Feather

took about a week for her to get it the way she wanted. Then a funny thing happened. The male started pushing her toward the nesting box every chance he got. She soon couldn't do a thing that she wanted to do.

It was all happening just like his dad told him. The male pigeon wanted her to lay her eggs.

Lady Blue finally gave up and stayed on the nest. Jimmy checked to see how she was doing every day. About ten days later, he noticed a small white egg under her. "It won't be long now until there are baby birds," he thought.

The next day when he got home, he went out and checked on his pigeons. Lady Blue was still on her nest. He reached up into her box and put his hand under her. He smiled when he felt two small eggs.

He was so excited that he left the pen quickly and ran inside the house to his room. He flipped through the pages of his pigeon books until he found the one he wanted. He read several pages and finally found the information he looked for. They would hatch in about eighteen days.

"Another waiting period," he thought. He wondered if he would ever have any pigeons big enough to train for racing.

On the eighteenth day, he ran all the way home from school. He was sure there would be two little pigeons under Lady Blue. He found there were only the two eggs under her. "That's not fair," he thought. "It's just not fair."

The next day was Saturday, and he was up early. Before he ate, he went outside to check on Lady Blue. As he entered the pen, he knew something happened. Lady Blue was different towards him. She pecked his hand when he put it in her box.

Slowly, he lifted her and saw why she pecked him. There, under her, were two little babies with their mouths open. They didn't have any feathers, so there was no way

Soft Feather

he could tell what color they would be. He ran into the house and told his grandma about the two baby pigeons.

Then it was over two weeks before he saw what they might look like. One looked like it was blue and white, and the other might be pure white. He shook his head when he walked out of the pen and shut the gate.

Shrugging his shoulders, he entered the house. He found his grandma in the kitchen.

"One is blue and white like its father, but the other is snow white," Jimmy said. He frowned as he sat down and looked at his grandma. "How come, Grandma?"

"How come 'what'?" Alice asked.

"I don't understand why one is snow-white," he said. "She's all blue. He's blue and white. I was hoping for a beautiful blue-colored pigeon just like her. That would have been nice. Lady Blue is so pretty, Grandma."

"I know she is, Jimmy," she said. "But I'd say that the snow-white pigeon will be just as pretty when she's grown. Just wait and see."

He felt some better after she said that. He hadn't thought about how the snow-white pigeon would look. He got up and went back to his bedroom.

He looked through the books again and found that in about thirty days they would be flying.

"Another long waiting period, but at least the babies are here," he thought. "All they have to do now is grow up."

School was now getting in his way. Mrs. Davis made him stay in after school one day and tell her why he was daydreaming in her class. She shook her head when he told her. She let him know that he must pay more attention in class or he might fail.

He told her he would, and he did study harder at home. He tried to quit daydreaming in class. His grades

Soft Feather

didn't go down, but now and then he had to stay after school.

As the days passed, Jimmy was amazed at how fast the babies grew. It wasn't long until they were cheeping to be fed. They let their parents know they wanted it 'right now'.

Jimmy was having a great time watching them grow.

When the two babies' feathers came in, one was white. Just like his grandma said, she was beautiful. "How could I not have wanted her?"

It wasn't long before they ate by themselves. The blue and white baby looked just like its father, Big Boy.

Jimmy watched the male pigeon. He noticed that he was herding Lady Blue back to the nesting bowl. He looked at the way they acted. Sure enough, he wanted her to lay some eggs. It wasn't going to be long until he would have a large group of pigeons.

It made him feel good to know his wishes were coming true.

Digging into the pigeon books, he studied some more and came to the conclusion that the blue and white baby was a male, and the snow-white baby was a female. He put the book down and took a good look at them again.

They were not little babies, anymore. They started to try their wings. They would soon be flying. He sat there and looked at them for some time.

Then he remembered what his dad told him. He ran around to the back of the house and up the porch steps into the house. In his room he got the bands and pliers his dad gave him. He ran back outside to the pen and went inside.

He caught the white one first and put a band on her left leg. The white and blue one was next. With that done, he looked at them.

Soft Feather

"What shall we call you two?" he wondered out loud. "'Blue Boy' will be the male's name; now what shall I call the little snow-white female?" Then he thought about what he just said. "Of course... 'Lady Snow White'. Sure. That's what I'll call you."

He went back inside and put the bands back in his desk. He got out some paper. It was time for him to write a letter to Jack Starr telling him about his two babies, and that he banded them. He wanted to join a club so he could race them. He got an envelope out of his desk drawer and placed the letter inside. All he had to do now was have his grandma address it. Then, of course, wait for Mr. Starr to answer his letter.

The next day he turned both of his pigeons loose for their first exercise flight. He let Big Boy out first. If he flew off to Mr. Starr's, he would have to go get him. If he didn't, Jimmy would be one happy pigeon owner.

He was eating when the buzzer buzzed, and he knew Big Boy was home. He ran out to the pen and released Lady Blue. He went back in and finished eating his sandwich. He breathed a sigh of relief when the buzzer finally buzzed.

Two days later, he let both of them out. This time he sat in his chair and watched them fly around the house, then, head for the creek. They were gone for about fifteen minutes. Again, he was a happy pigeon owner when he saw them. He watched each one enter the pen, making the buzzer buzz.

They were now his. All his. It was a great feeling.

It wouldn't be long until the two young ones would join their parents. They flew around in their pen like they knew what they were doing.

A week later he let the four of them go on an exercise flight. He might as well find out now if they would all return. It was exciting to see his new pigeons fly off for

Soft Feather

the first time. Jimmy knew he could always get them from Jack Starr, but he felt confident they would return to him.

It was even more exciting when all four of them returned. A big load was lifted off of his shoulders. Jimmy's coop was now Lady Blue's, Big Boy's, and their offspring's home.

Soft Feather

CHAPTER 13

When school let out, Mary came running up beside Jimmy. She walked along with him as they headed for home. "What do you plan to do this weekend?" she asked.

"I don't know," he said. He looked at her and smiled. "All four of my pigeons flew together yesterday and returned fifteen minutes later. Well, all but Lady Blue. She came home five minutes later."

"I like her," Mary said. "She's thinks like a woman; she likes to do things her way."

"That's good for you to say, but not for a racing pigeon. I want her to be the fastest pigeon there ever has been. Sometimes when I talk to her, she comes right back. Other times, she's a half-hour late. I don't know what to do to get her back earlier."

"Just love her, Jimmy. She loves you," Mary said.

"Not like she used to. She loves Big Boy now."

"That's different, and you know it. She watches everything you do. She has since the first day you got her."

"Mary was right," he thought. The first time he saw her over at Mr. Starr's house, he loved her. She was the most beautiful pigeon he ever saw. She let him know she felt the same way about him.

When they were a block from Mary's dad's service station, Mr. Wilson came out of the door and motioned for them to hurry. They took off and ran over to him. "You've got a phone call, Jimmy," he said. "Jack Starr is on the phone. He wanted me to have you call him back, and he gave me his phone number. "We talked, and then I saw you two. I told him that I wouldn't have to have you call him, as you and my daughter were headed down the street towards my station."

Jimmy hurried in and picked up the phone. "Hi, Mr. Starr."

Soft Feather

"I guess I called at the right time, Jimmy," he said. "I sat and wondered if I should call you or not and decided I would."

"I'm glad you did," Jimmy replied. "How are you doing?"

"Fine, Jimmy, just fine. The reason I called was to ask you if you might be interested in going with me to a homing pigeon race over at Loveland tomorrow."

"I'd love to go, Mr. Starr. But I have to ask my grandparents."

"Of course. I would expect you to do that. I gave Mr. Wilson my phone number so you can call me back."

"I'll do that, Mr. Starr."

"How are those two homers doing I gave you, Jimmy?" he asked.

"They are doing fine. In fact, they have two babies. One is a blue and white male, looks like its daddy. The other is a snow-white female. It sure surprised me it was white. I thought it would be blue like its mother."

"Well, what do you know about that," he said.

"I named her Snow White, and him, Blue Boy, because his body and wings are blue, and his breast is white."

"I like that, Jimmy. I really do."

"Mary and I went over to Mr. Miller's barn and caught two pigeons for him. He has a lot of pigeons in his barn loft. We caught two homers. He and my dad raised homers when they were kids."

"I remember Chuck Miller," he said.

"He helped me put a buzzer on my pen. It works just great. He has one on his pen, too."

"You really are getting serious about working with homers, Jimmy," Jack said. "I'm sure glad I called. This is all working out real well. You said something about Mary. Who is she?"

Soft Feather

"Mary is the daughter of our friend, Mr. Wilson. We work together. When I caught my hawk, it had three babies in the top of a dead tree. We captured two and trained them together. We went all over the state showing them."

Jimmy looked over at Mary and smiled. "We're kind of a team. We love working with birds."

There was silence on the phone, then Mr. Starr said, "Ask her if she'd like to go with us to Loveland tomorrow and help me with my pigeons. Have her ask her dad right now, Jimmy."

Jimmy looked at Mary, and she was still smiling from what he said. "Mr. Starr wants me to ask you if you want to go to a homing pigeon race tomorrow at Loveland. If you want to go, he would like for you to ask your dad for permission."

The smile disappeared as she sat there and thought about what Jimmy said. Then the smile returned even bigger. She looked at her daddy and was about to ask him when he nodded his approval.

"Tell Mr. Starr that I would love to go with you and him. In fact, you couldn't keep me away, Jimmy," she said. "You know that."

Mr. Wilson shook his head. "She knows us better than we know ourselves, Jimmy. I believe she's related to her mother."

"Mr. Starr, Mr. Wilson said it is OK for her to go with us. That is, if I get permission from my grandparents," he said.

"I'm sure you will, but I want to make sure. It will take most of the day. It's going to be a great race. We should be back for supper. You call me back as soon as you can."

"Yes, sir," he said.

Soft Feather

"I'll bring a 'Boulder Creek Pigeon Club' form. Call me back. Bye for now."

"I have to go get permission from my grandparents and call him back," he said, hanging up the phone. "Mr. Starr said he will be here early in the morning, and the racing events will take most of the day. It is supposed to be a great race. We should be home for supper."

"That sounds great, Jimmy. I've never been to an event like that," Mary said, looking over at her daddy.

"I sure hope they have a lot of things going on for you two," Bill said. "If they don't, it's going to be a long day."

"I do, too," Jimmy said, smiling. "I'm sure there will be, and we're going to be able to see how they run a pigeon racing event. There should be all kinds of trainers there. I hope we'll be able to talk to them. I think we will learn a lot more from them than we can from the books we read."

"That's true," Bill said.

"I'll run home and be back as soon as I can, Mr. Wilson."

"See you later," he said to Mary. He opened the door and ran down the road towards home. He sure hoped his grandparents would let him go. If they didn't, it would be O.K. He knew Mr. Starr would understand.

He ran up the porch steps and into the house, banging the door. His grandpa was sitting at the kitchen table. He looked up at Jimmy and was about to get onto him when he saw the smile on his face.

Alice just filled a glass with water when the door slammed. Turning quickly, she spilled some on the floor. She was irritated at what she did, and, also, at Jimmy for slamming the door.

"Watch out, Alice," Tom said to his wife. "Here comes our grandson with a big smile on his face. I'd say he wants something. Don't give in right away."

Soft Feather

She looked at him, then Jimmy. "Well, is your grandpa right?"

"Yes, ma'am," he said, out of breath. "Mr. Starr called Mr. Wilson's garage and wanted to talk to me. He asked me if I would like to go with him to a homing pigeon race in Loveland tomorrow. He wants me to ask you for permission to go. Mr. Wilson gave Mary permission.

"Mr. Starr wants me to call him back as soon as possible and let him know what your answer is."

Tom looked at Alice and smiled. "Looks like we better not say 'no', Mother. Even though I'm a little disappointed that I wasn't asked to go. Especially with all the knowledge I have of homing pigeons. I know you know more than I do, Mother, but I'm the one Mr. Starr should have asked first."

Alice shook her head at him and took one step towards the table. Her foot stepped in the spilled water and slid a little, then, stopped where the floor was dry. She lost her balance and put her hands out in front of her.

When she stopped, the water in the glass continued on, and Tom was right in its path.

The water drenched Tom from the top of his head, down the front of his shirt. It was cold, and he gasped and just sat there.

Alice was in disbelief, as she watched the water drip off his hair, nose and chin, onto his wet shirt. Tom stared down at himself with a strange look on his face.

"I'm sorry, Alice. I think Mr. Starr should have asked you first. Of course, you know more about water birds, like the duck. Me, I never did know much about ducks. You can tell, because I didn't duck."

Jimmy never heard his grandpa joke much, and he couldn't help laughing. Alice put her hands up to her mouth and just looked at what she did. She started to say something, then stopped. She grinned at Tom, and slowly it

Soft Feather

became a little laugh, which was catching. They all laughed so hard that tears welled up in their eyes. Alice and Jimmy sat down at the table with Tom.

Tom pulled his wet shirt up to wipe his face.

"You have my permission, Jimmy," Tom said, and sat up straight in his chair.

"Mine, too," Alice said. "How can we refuse a nice boy like you who bangs the door and causes laughter like this?"

She got a towel and wiped up the water she spilled on the floor. She then went over and got some change out of a glass on top of the stove. She handed it to Jimmy. "This is for the telephone call."

"Thanks, Grandma," he said, reaching up. He sat back and looked around the room. "Now I have to run back and tell them I got permission to go, but I'm kind of weak. I think I'll rest a little."

They laughed again.

Tom and Alice got up and led Jimmy over to the door, and he opened it. No one said anything as he walked out onto the porch and down the steps. They watched him run a short ways, then stop and start walking.

When he reached the highway, he stopped and waved at his grandparents, who came out onto the porch. They waved back, then went inside.

He hurried on, thinking about what just happened. It was great to have grandparents like his. He walked toward Mr. Wilson's garage, not noticing where he was.

"You must have gotten permission," Mary said.

Jimmy looked up and saw Mary standing in front of him.

He stopped. "I didn't see you," he said.

"Can you go?" she asked.

"Yes," he said. "Let's go call Mr. Starr."

Soft Feather

They hurried into the office, and Mr. Wilson dialed the number Jack gave him.

"Grandma gave me some money to pay for the call," Jimmy said, and put the change on the table next to the phone. Mr. Wilson handed him the phone, picked up the change and went behind the counter.

"Hello," Jack said.

"It's me, Mr. Starr," Jimmy said. "I have permission to go with you."

"Fine," he said. "I'll see you two around 7:00 o'clock in the morning."

"Okay. We will be here at Mr. Wilson's garage on the highway."

"I'll see you then, Jimmy." He hung up.

"7:00 o'clock in the morning," he said to Mary. "I hoped I wouldn't have to get up that early on Easter vacation. Oh, well, one day won't matter that much."

"Do we need to take food?" Mary asked.

"Yes, I'm sure my grandma will make me a lunch. If we're going to be there all day, we might need more than one sandwich."

"I'm sure your grandma will fix enough for you, Jimmy," Mr. Wilson said. "I know Mary's mother will fix enough for her."

They both smiled at him, knowing he was right. They were going to have a great time.

Jimmy and Mary sat inside the service station and waited for Mr. Starr. They were early, but they wanted to be there just in case he was early.

Mr. Wilson banked the fire in the heating stove the night before. The room was a little cool, but a good stirring of the embers, along with a couple pieces of wood, made it nice and warm.

Soft Feather

Mary looked at Jimmy and said, "My daddy told me something last night that I think you need to know."

"What's that?" he asked.

"You probably know that Brad Bradley and Joe Crow quit school. Joe only being fifteen and Brad sixteen, they couldn't get a job around here. Brad's dad got them a job up in Wyoming working on a ranch. They got fired a couple of days ago. They were way back in the hills so they took a couple of the horses from the ranch. They got caught last week and were sent to a reform school up in Casper, Wyoming."

"Wow," Jimmy said. "Do you know if they're still there?"

"No, I don't, Jimmy. I'll ask him if you want me to."

"No, Mary. I'm sorry to hear about their being in a reform school. I sure hope it helps them change for the better."

"I do, too," Mary said.

Just then Mr. Starr pulled up in front of the service station. Jimmy hurried out the door, and Mary locked it. They got in the front seat of his station wagon.

"I see you brought lunches," Mr. Starr said. "Put them on the back seat."

They put them on the seat, then looked at the three pigeon cages in the back of the station wagon. The pigeons cooed at them. "Why do you have three pigeons?" Jimmy asked.

"Well, I wanted to surprise you. I didn't tell you everything yesterday because I like surprises. I sure hope you two do, too."

"I do," Jimmy said, looking at Mary.

"Oh, yes," she said. "I love them. I always get something nice when I'm surprised. Are we going to get something nice, Mr. Starr?"

Soft Feather

"Well... I don't really know. Maybe..." and he looked at them seriously.

Mary and Jimmy giggled with excitement. They knew he was having fun with them.

"Well, you see we're not going to have a homing pigeon race today," he said. "I'm sorry to tell you that."

They looked at each other, then back at him. "If you're not going to have a homing pigeon race today, why are you here with three pigeons, Mr. Starr?" Jimmy frowned.

"Well, you see, that's the reason." We're not going to have a homing pigeon race, we're going to have three of them."

It took a moment for what he said to sink in. "Three races!" Jimmy said. "I knew this was going to be a great day. How about that, Mary?"

"Boy, oh, boy," she said. "Tell us all about it, Mr. Starr. We sure didn't expect this, did we, Jimmy?"

He was about to answer when Mr. Starr put the car in gear. "Let's talk as we ride along," he said. "We've got to be there on time if we want to qualify for the first race. If we make the first, then, we'll have to be at the second to qualify for the third."

Mr. Starr let out the clutch, and the car moved out onto the highway and headed towards Longmont with three happy homing pigeon trainers.

"Well, Mary, it's like this," he said. "We have to sign in at 8:30 AM to qualify for the Loveland race. Then we have to drive up to Estes Park and be there by 11:30 AM to qualify for the third race. Next, it's over the Continental Divide to Granby by 2:30 PM.

"The way I figure it, we should be back here between four and five o'clock in the afternoon."

Soft Feather

She looked at Mr. Starr, then Jimmy. "Wow," she said. "I believe this is one of the best surprises I've ever had."

Jimmy nodded his head. "Three separate races," he said, looking at her. "We are going to see three races at three different places."

Mary looked at Mr. Starr and asked. "How do they know how far the pigeons fly, and how do they determine who won? How do they know it's the same pigeon, and how…?"

"That is too many 'how's', Mary," he said. "I'll answer all your questions, but you know what is the best teacher? Seeing and doing.

"The answer to your first question of how far they fly is figured with a map. All maps have a scale they are drawn to. If you look closely at a map, you'll see there is a scale that tells you how far an inch is. Like, 10 miles per inch. But we need a more exact map than that."

"Now, to figure out the speed, every competitor will have the exact location of his loft marked on the most up-to-date Ordinance Survey map of the area."

"Then, to find out how long it takes the pigeon to get to the loft, a tag is placed on the pigeon's leg before it is released. The time is logged in a book when the pigeon is released.

"The trainer has a special clock at his house. The pigeon flies into its loft, and the tag is removed from the pigeon and placed in the clock which records the exact time it arrived. That way only that bird's number and time is recorded."

"Knowing when it left and how far it flew, and when it arrived, we come up with the speed of the bird. The pigeon with the fastest speed is the winner."

She thought about what Mr. Starr said, and tried to figure it out. "How come it's not the shortest amount of

Soft Feather

time for the pigeon that gets to his loft first that makes a winner?" she said.

"Mary, not all the pigeons will have the same distance to travel," he said. "As I said, you figure the time released, the distance and the time of arrival. The one with the lowest amount of time taken to arrive at the furthest distance is the winner. "

"Now I think I understand," she said. "I wasn't considering the distance each traveled."

"You also asked some other questions, and we don't have time to go over them right now," he said. "We'll do it later."

"Okay." she said.

Jimmy nodded his head. He was glad Mr. Starr went over it with Mary. Maybe now he could do it himself.

"I sure hope your pigeons win today," Mary said.

"I have a good chance, Mary. All three of mine have been in the top three many times. Only one of them has won first place. That's the one in the green cage. His name is Handsome. He struts around like he is the best pigeon around. Sometimes, he is."

Mary looked at the green cage. Handsome just sat and looked back at her.

"What's the name of the other two pigeons?" Jimmy asked.

"The one in the yellow cage is Celia, and in the white cage is my love, Annie."

They looked at her. "Annie was very tiny when she hatched," he said. "I had to baby her and make sure her mother, Sally, fed her a lot more than usual. Having to take care of her like that, I grew very fond of her."

"Then when she took her first exercise flight and returned, I was so proud of her."

Soft Feather

"I worked with her more than any other pigeon I had. It paid off. Now she is one of my top three pigeons." He looked over at them, and then at the road. "I think she kind of likes me, too."

Jimmy and Mary nodded their heads. They were beginning to know exactly how he felt. Jimmy caught a wounded hawk and took care of it until it healed. Then, he and Mary caught two of her babies and raised them. It took lots of time and work, but during that time, a bond grew between them that only a bird trainer understands.

They did above and beyond what was expected of them. Many times, they won the first three places where they showed their hawks.

"Mary and I know how you feel, Mr. Starr." Jimmy said. "We raised two baby hawks and taught them to hunt."

"That's right, Jimmy," he said. "I remember your dad told me about them. The only thing different---you trained hawks, and I trained pigeons."

"But we have pigeons now," Mary said.

"That's right Mary. One of these days we'll be racing against each other. That will be a great day. That's the reason I asked you two to come with me today. Trainers like to see the pigeons they raise leave and become someone else's winning homers.

"It's like seeing your children grow up and move off and start their own family. It can be a lot of fun."

The sun peeked over the horizon and soon burst into a big orange ball. It would be a beautiful day.

They saw a sign up ahead. As they passed it, they were happy to read the words, 'Loveland City Limits'.

Jack slowed down as they entered Loveland. "We have to drive through town until we come to the red light. Then, we'll turn left and drive until we come to City Lake." He looked at his watch. It was 8:05 AM. "We're a little

Soft Feather

early, but I would rather be early than get here a couple minutes before takeoff time.

"All of the officials will be here. I'll have to sign in and fill out some forms before we get the tags for each pigeon."

They came to the traffic light and turned left and drove on until they saw a large lake on the right side of the road. It was a beautiful lake surrounded by trees.

There was ice in a few places around the edge of the lake. A gentle breeze blew out of the west, causing small waves on the lake's surface. The waves slowly ate the ice away. It would soon be gone when the sun got higher.

"There they are," Jack said. "I sure am glad they're on this side of the lake. "That makes it a lot easier to head on up to Estes Park from here."

"All we have to do is keep on this road into the mountains. This is turning out real nice."

Jack pulled into a large parking lot. A few people walked by carrying cages towards a large tent. He found a place to park and pulled in. They got out and went around to the back of the station wagon. He opened the back door and locked it in place. Picking up the white cage, he stepped back. Mary got the yellow one, leaving the green one for Jimmy.

He closed the door and locked it. They went in the direction everyone else headed.

There were four tables with people standing in line registering their pigeons. Jack walked over to the first line and set his cage down.

He reached into his shirt pocket and brought out some papers. He unfolded them as they moved along.

"These are the forms they sent me to fill out. It helps get all of the trainers registered fast."

Soft Feather

"The line is short right now, but it will get longer very soon." The person in front of them moved up. He picked up his cage and followed.

Before long, they were next. Jack stepped up and said, "Hello, Mac. They must have needed help real bad."

"That's right, Jack. I'm just being a nice guy. I volunteered until you got here."

"Now, Mac, I'm glad to hear that. But you ought to know you should never volunteer."

They both laughed. "Who do you have with you, Jack?"

"I have a surprise for you, Mac. You remember Tommy Warrior."

"I sure do, Jack. He was one of the best homer trainers around these parts."

"Well, this is his boy, Jimmy. Tommy came by my place right before Christmas and talked me into giving his boy a couple homers. He hatched out two nice homers and is starting to train them."

Mac stood up and stuck out his hand towards Jimmy. "I'm Mac Reedy, and I'm proud to know you, Jimmy. Your dad was a close friend of mine and Jack's."

"It's a real pleasure to meet one of my dad's friends," Jimmy said, shaking his hand.

"This is his friend, Mary Wilson," Jack said, and stepped aside.

Mac tipped his hat to her. "Glad to know you, Mary."

"Thank you, sir," she said and shook his hand.

He looked at Jack. "So, Tommy came by to see you. How is he doing?"

"He's in a veterans hospital in Texas, Mac," he answered.

Mac looked him in the eye and slowly said. "What for?"

Soft Feather

"Shell shock. He got it bad in Iwo Jima."

"I had it, too. You remember. But I got over it. My pigeons helped me."

"He's doing fine. He's in rehab and has a good part-time job as a plumber. If everything works out, he'll be released so he can work full time. It just takes time."

"I'm glad to hear that, Jack. Speaking of time, will you quit taking up so much of mine? Those guys behind you are getting tired of hearing you go on and on," he said, grinning.

One of the guys with a cage shook his head. "You two have made my day. Nothing like a GI hearing that another GI is getting better. Especially knowing he will soon be back in society where he belongs."

"Thanks," Mac said. "It made me feel better, too."

He sat back down and looked up at him, then handed him his papers, and he checked them. Nodding, he picked up three tags and wrote Jack's name down with the numbers. He handed them to him. "They will release the homers from here at 9 A.M. Good luck," and shook his hand.

"Thanks, Mac. I sure hope you don't have any homers in these races. I don't want to beat my best friend."

"All I can say to you is just watch the dust my pigeons are going to leave yours in."

Jack turned and looked at the guys behind him. "I think I wouldn't want to make him mad," he said, and walked away, laughing. Mary and Jimmy followed.

He smiled when he heard them laughing behind them. There was nothing like having fun with friends and little birds.

Especially, a friend that fell in love with pigeons like Mac did. A little bird helped him pull him out of the darkness he lived in for years. Out into the light of day.

Soft Feather

Just a little bird that didn't do anything but coo, helped him come out on top again. "Nope, there's nothing like it," he told himself.

Maybe Tommy's son having pigeons will help him remember the good times he had with his. He sure hoped it would.

They walked over and stood in line at another table where a worker placed a tag on each of his pigeon's legs. When they finished, he handed them another paper. They read it and handed it to him. He signed it and gave it back.

"That's it," he said. "Let's go look at some of the things that are on display. A lot of these guys have nothing else to do than make things for pigeons. Do either of you have any money?"

They both said, "No."

"Good. I'm sure you're going to see something you'll think you just have to have for your pigeons, but I can tell you right now, you don't. What you do is look at it real close and see how it's made.

"If it is something you have to have, go home and make one. I've bought all kinds of things, and when I got home and looked at them, I saw how they were made, and then made a few extra for myself.

"Oh, yes, if you see me start to buy something, be sure and tell me to think twice about it. If you don't, we could be going home with a car full of stuff.

"Remember, we have two more places like this that we will be visiting today. Okay?"

They all smiled. Mary looked at Jimmy and said, "We sure don't want to have to walk home, so we better see that he doesn't fill his station wagon full of stuff."

"I agree. Maybe if we hold his money, that would help."

Soft Feather

Jack frowned. "Now wait a minute. If I'm going to spend my money, I want to spend it on things I want. Not on things you two want."

He looked at them seriously, then, laughed. They walked away laughing, headed for the station wagon. They placed the homers in the station wagon and walked towards the area where vendors' goods were on display.

They had a big half-hour to see everything others took all day to see.

Soft Feather

CHAPTER 14

The three of them returned ten minutes before nine o'clock. Jack chose to release Handsome. He told them he was sure that he would fly right home and not stray off the course.

He was different than most pigeons his age. He hadn't found a mate yet.

There was one problem. Handsome had two girl pigeons that kind of liked him, but they started to look at a couple other male pigeons. If he didn't watch out, they would both get tired waiting for him and strut off with another pigeon.

He wrote the time down on his note pad when they opened all of the cages at the same time. Then, he checked the time with the lady recorder and wrote it down.

He closed his pad and motioned for Mary and Jimmy to follow him.

They went to his station wagon and got in. Mary sat next to the window this time. If they were going to go up the mountains, she wanted to see everything.

Jack left the parking lot and turned right, headed towards the mountains. A fairly large creek ran along on the left side of the road. It wasn't long until they passed the 'Loveland City Limit' sign. The houses soon thinned out, and then there were none.

The road twisted and turned, and it wasn't long until they passed through large red hills on both sides of the road. They were high, awesome red hills. They looked something like those he saw around Boulder.

A little further up the road, they were amazed how close the hills got to the road. A little further, and the creek was next to the road. They crossed a bridge, and the creek was now on the right side of the road.

Soft Feather

"That's the North St. Vrain Creek," he said. "It's pretty, isn't it?"

"It is beautiful," Mary said.

"It sure is," Jimmy agreed.

"Well, it is now. But when they have large rains up in the mountains, the water comes down the canyon, flooding everything. The creek gets big. In fact, it washes a lot of cabins away when that happens."

Mary and Jimmy looked at each other, then back at the creek.

"See up ahead where we start through the mountains? See how close together they are? That is where the beautiful 'Big Thompson Canyon' starts. It's a large canyon with lots of rock walls that go straight up hundreds of feet. It goes all the way up to the town of Estes Park. That is where we'll release my second pigeon, Celia."

"How come Celia and not Annie?" Jimmy asked.

"A good question, Jimmy. I've thought about it ever since I signed up for the three races," he said. "I believe Annie is the best for the last race. You see, we're going to release her on the other side of the Continental Divide near the small mountain town of Granby.

"Now, that's on the other side of the mountains, quite a ways from Boulder."

"The way I figure it is like this: Annie and I like each other a lot, and I give her more attention than my other pigeons. That's why I think she will have more drive to get home to be with me when she is far away, than any of the other pigeons I have. What do you two think?"

"I think she would," Jimmy answered. "I know that Lady Blue would be that way about me."

"Of course, she would," Mary said firmly. "The attachment she has for you is strong. If you were separated, she, too, would be anxious to get home."

Soft Feather

Jack rewarded her with a huge smile. That was a great answer. He couldn't have said it any better.

As they entered the canyon, the road began its upward climb through the mountains. The rock formations were both unusual and beautiful, with the creek running swiftly past them.

He pointed at some rocks that jutted upward along the canyon. "What do you see up there?" he asked.

Mary gasped and said, "It's four big-horn sheep. Look at them, Jimmy. How in the world do they climb up on rocks like that without falling?" she asked.

"How about that," Jimmy said, as they passed them.

"It's a normal instinct for them. They're just born knowing how to do that," Jack explained.

Mary looked through the window, continuing to stare at the sheep.

Jimmy did the same thing until they were out of sight.

"They are a few of many animals the Wild Life Bureau now released into the wild," he said. "A long time ago, they used to be all over these mountains."

"Talking about long ago, how long did it take for this creek to cut such a deep path through the solid rock we're passing through? How did it do it?" Jimmy asked.

"I guess by erosion," Mary said.

"Yes," Jack said.

Nothing else was said. They soon came to a wide place in the canyon. There was a grocery store and filling station. There were signs with pictures of ripe red cherries and the caption 'Good Cherry Cider Sold Here'.

A little further up the road, handsome cabins were built alongside the creek. It was amazing that wherever there was a small piece of flat rock, there was a cabin.

Up and up they drove, through the Big Thompson Canyon. Then they saw a dam across the canyon. Water ran

Soft Feather

over the top of the dam and down the spillway. Off to the side, there was a large hole in a rock on the bank below the dam, where a huge stream of water gushed out. It was a good twenty feet above the creek bed. The gravity caused this large stream of water to arc downward into the creek below.

Huge rainbows danced and played all along the canyon walls from the mist of the cascading water.

Jack pulled into the parking area above the dam. They got out and walked over to the edge of the dam and looked down at the awesome sight.

Water ran down the face of the sloping dam. It made a rippling washboard effect as it made its way to the creek below.

They watched it for a while. Mr. Starr walked back to the station wagon. Mary and Jimmy took their time, gazing at everything around them as they followed him.

"I sure am glad Mr. Starr asked us to come with him today," Mary said. "I wish I'd brought a camera."

"Having some pictures of this place, and other things we'll see today, would be nice," Jimmy agreed.

They got in the car and continued on up the road towards Estes Park. It wasn't long before they drove through the north side of town. It was a nice, small town and very clean. They passed a place that had rides for kids. Now that was something Jimmy and Mary wanted to do.

Mr. Starr drove into the main part of town. He pointed off to the right at a large white building. It looked like a big hotel. It seemed out of place in a small town like Estes Park.

"That's the Stanley Hotel over there. It was named after a famous man whose last name was Stanley. He was the man who built the Stanley Steamer Automobile."

"In fact, they have one of his steam-driven cars up there. They sometimes drive it down through town,

Soft Feather

carrying sightseers from the hotel. It's interesting, and lots of people gather around the car and take pictures."

"There is hardly any noise when it drives off, just a soft 'chug, chug, chug', and it's gone. I saw it one time when I was up here visiting friends."

He stopped at the red light, turned right, and drove up the road that led to the Stanley Hotel.

Mary and Jimmy sat on the edge of their seats, expecting to see the car he talked about.

He drove on past the hotel driveway and turned into a large parking lot where a crowd milled around. He drove along looking for a vacant space and waved at a few people they saw when they were in Loveland.

He found a space and parked. "This is where we will release Celia," he said. "Registration starts at 11:30 A.M., and it is 10:30 right now. That means we have about an hour to walk around and look in some of the shops.

"If we don't watch the time, we'll get caught up in looking at the things they have to sell in this town. So we have to remember why we are here.

"But first things first---let's look for a place where we can sit down and eat our lunch. I know it's a little early, but I've been up since six o'clock. You two were probably up at that time, also. So let's eat first, and then we'll go see what they have in the shops."

Mary & Jimmy reached behind the seat for their lunches and got out. Jack opened the back door and grabbed his lunch box and a blanket. He closed the door and looked around for a place to eat.

Mary spotted a place on the grass near some tables. They sat down, and opened their lunches. Mary had two ham sandwiches, and Jimmy had two chicken salad sandwiches.

A small thermos bottle of milk tasted good after Jimmy and Mary's sandwiches.

Soft Feather

Mr. Starr looked at his sandwich. He made it, and he would eat it. A thermos of coffee washed his down.

When they finished, Mary and Jimmy put their trash in a trashcan while Jack put his lunch box back in the station wagon. They looked at the people on the main street.

Mary looked at Mr. Starr and said, "We have some time now for you to explain how they figure out which pigeon is first. I would like to go look at all of those things on Main Street, but we can do that later. First things first."

"I'd like to know, too," Jimmy said.

A family at one of the nearby tables began to put things away. Mary went over and asked if she could have the table when they left. They said she could. She helped them put the last plates and cups in their basket and sat down.

Jimmy came and sat down next to her, while Jack went to the station wagon. He returned with a book and a spiral notebook. He sat down facing them.

"I'll try and keep this as simple as I can. I'll show you in this book the formula they use to figure it all out. It's really simple. It's just multiplication and division."

Jimmy looked at Mary, and they smiled. They were good in math.

"Briefly, the winner is the bird that covers the distance from the release point to its loft at home at the highest speed. The distance is calculated on what is known as the Great Circle System. It is an extremely complicated formula that allows for the curvature of the surface of the earth.

"The time of the birds release from the starting point is known. Each bird flies to its own loft where the time is registered on a special clock as it enters, and the average speed is calculated in yards per minute.

Soft Feather

"Your question is 'How do you know which pigeon arrived home first?' The answer is that, prior to the bird being dispatched, or before being set free, it has a rubber ring attached to its leg by means of a special ringing machine, which cannot harm the pigeon's foot.

"The rubber ring has the code numbers, one on the outside of the ring and one on the inside. The outside number is noted by the club committee and recorded on the competitor's entry form against the number of the metal identity ring that was placed on the pigeon's leg soon after hatching.

"The big problem that comes up is that not all of the clocks run the same: there will be some slow, and some that are fast. The slower would make it seem that the pigeon traveled faster than the clock that runs fast.

"All of the clocks are designed so they can only be opened by authorized members of the clock committee, or by the man who was appointed as the clock setter.

"The clocks are checked when they are turned in to determine how much too fast, or too slow, each of them are. This difference is then added into the formula to equal every pigeon's time.

"We find that the distance is given in miles and yards, then, reduced to sixtieths of a yard, and the flying time is reduced to seconds. By dividing the time taken into the distance flown, the speed is calculated in yards per minute."

He wrote some numbers on one of the pages of the spiral notebook. "Let's say that it took a pigeon until 8.00 A.M., and looking up where the loft is located on the Ordinance Survey map, we find it flew 198 miles, 282 yards. The flying time is, therefore, 6 hours, 15 minutes, and 58 seconds.

Soft Feather

"It can be calculated that the average speed is about thirty-one and one half miles per hour. This is not accurate enough, so we work it out as already mentioned.

"By converting it to yards we have:
198 miles reduced to 60th of a yard = 20908800
282 yards to 60th of a yard   =   16921
                                      20925720
Flying Time is 6 hours 15 minutes, 58 seconds =22558

To find the pigeons velocity, divide 20908800 by 22558.

Which makes the pigeons speed 927.64 yards per minute.

"There is always a small amount of error in this formula, but if everyone agrees to use this method, then no one argues. One must remember that it is a sport, and a good sportsman is in it for the sport. It's a love for their pigeons that they don't want to give up.

"I don't, Jimmy, do you?"

"No, sir. I like to win, but the judge has the final say."

"Well put, Jimmy," he said, as he folded his notebook and stood up. He looked at his watch.

"We have twenty minutes before sign-in begins. What do you two want to do?"

"Let's go see what they have down there on Main Street," Mary said.

As they walked back to the station wagon, they heard a funny sound behind them. They saw an old stagecoach coming down the driveway from the Stanley Hotel.

There were two people sitting up on top of it, and one drove the horses. As it passed, two people inside waved at them.

Soft Feather

They just enjoyed the sight. Then they realized they were waved at and waved back. People gathered along the sidewalk as the stagecoach passed and yelled greetings at those inside. It turned at the red light and drove off up the main street of town.

People yelled and clapped as it passed out of sight behind the buildings.

"How about that," Jack said. "Looks like we were at the right spot at the right time."

"Yeah," Jimmy said.

Mary grabbed his arm and grinned. "I agree," she said. "Let's follow along behind it and see all the sights along the way. I'm sure there is a lot more to see. In fact, I'm sure I could spend a whole day up here. I would love to go shopping if I had some money."

Jimmy looked at Mr. Starr and shook his head. They didn't say a word as they walked along, looking in the store windows.

"I'll have to see if I can get my parents to bring me back up here. I'm sure my mother would like to come and go through all these little shops. We could look at everything and maybe buy a few things."

Jimmy shook his head again. "Girls. They sure are different from boys," he thought.

Mary looked at them. "We only have fifteen minutes left today, so let's see all we can."

Up ahead, the stagecoach stopped in traffic. Everyone on the sidewalks stopped and took pictures. It wasn't long until the three of them were surrounded in a large group of people.

"There's an ice cream store over there," Jack said. "Let's go over there and get us an ice cream cone."

They didn't have to be asked twice. The stagecoach caused a lot of people to come out of the stores, which was

Soft Feather

great. There was no one in the ice cream store, and they soon walked along licking their double dips of ice cream.

The stores had all kinds of neat things. They seemed to be put together so they made you want to go into each one of them. There were all kinds of wonderful displays of beautiful paintings, carvings, clothes, food, books, furniture and even some Indian turquoise bracelets, necklaces and rings.

The time flew by, and when Mr. Starr looked at his watch, he grabbed their arms. "We only have five minutes to get back and register."

They turned and ran back towards the park. They soon found it hard to get down the sidewalk, with all of the people slowly walking along. Jack ran across the middle of the street, and Mary and Jimmy followed.

Instead of going back on the sidewalk, he turned and ran along the street next to the parked cars. They soon came to the corner of the park and headed up the street towards the registration area.

Jack stopped. He had to catch his breath. Mary looked up the hill.

"There's a line forming at the registration table. We don't have to hurry."

"That's great," he said, as they walked up the hill. He reached into his pocket and gave Jimmy his car keys. "I would like for you to go and get Celia for me, Jimmy."

Jimmy moved towards the station wagon as they walked to where a group of men stood in line. It was time to get serious and get this part of the triple pigeon races behind them.

Jimmy came up and handed Jack the keys and pigeon cage. Jack looked around for his friend, Mac, but he wasn't there. He remembered that the altitude bothered him. He even had to be careful in the town of Lafayette where he lived.

Soft Feather

Denver was known as the "Mile High City", and Lafayette was not far from Boulder. Boulder was higher, being at the edge of the mountains.

It wasn't long until he was registered. Another fifteen minutes, and Jack placed his pigeon, Celia, in a cage with a dozen other pigeons to be released with all the others.

As they walked towards the station wagon, Mary grabbed Jimmy's arm. "It sure would be nice if both of us could come up here and spend a whole day going through all of those shops."

Jimmy looked at Mr. Starr. Neither one said a word.

It took some time to get out of their parking place. They crept through the streets in town, having to wait for all the people crossing the streets at the traffic lights. It was slow going. Estes Park was not a place to drive through on a weekend.

The people liked to drive slowly so that they could enjoy peering at the items in the shop windows, and look at the people on the sidewalks. It was a little faster than walking, and Mary enjoyed it. She tried to remember where some of the places were. That way she would know where to go when her mother brought her back

Slowly, the crowds thinned out, and the streets were clear of people. Only cars moved now, picking up speed. They drove over the bridge that the Big Thompson Creek ran under. The road turned to the right, and they were soon out of town.

Jack pointed at a road that ran off to the left. "That's the road we'll take when we come back this way. It goes down to the small town of Lyons, then Longmont and finally Mercer. We only have one more release area to go to now."

Soft Feather

The car sped along as the road started to go up again. There were still patches of snow here and there. Up ahead, they saw cars winding up the side of the mountains ahead of them.

Jimmy looked at Mary and pointed. "Look at those cars up there. "It sure looks steep." Jimmy said.

"That's just the beginning of Trail Ridge Road," Jack said. "It goes up and over the Continental Divide. This is one of the most beautiful scenic routes one can take, especially in the summer. If you love the mountains in all their magnificent splendor, this way is the one to take."

"It's a different kind of beauty in the winter with the sparkling white snow blanketing the mountains. It's not often that this road is open during the winter. That's why there are so many cars on the road. I came over the pass only one time in the winter, and I still remember it."

They soon entered a large S curve. At the end of it, they started up a steep incline. As they drove up the switchbacks, they looked down on the road below. It was the road they just traveled on, and when they looked up, they saw cars above them. It was starting to get exciting.

Up and up they went. Jack had to shift into second gear. Slowly, they made it up the grade until the road leveled off. The highway was not as steep and was nice and wide.

Shifting back into high gear, they soon enjoyed the spectacular view. There was snow on everything in sight.

Large mountains rose up here and there, with deep valleys in between. Steep inclines ran almost up to the edge of the road. They soon drove through snow that was piled higher than the cars, on both sides of the road.

Mary looked down to the bottom of the valley and wondered aloud, "What would happen if someone drove off the road? Would those metal guards alongside the road keep a car from sliding off?"

Soft Feather

"Well, we sure hope they would, Mary." Jack answered.

"His answer was not too reassuring," she thought.

On and on, and up and up, they went. Then up ahead, they saw a large building sitting off on the right side of the highway.

The area was cleared of snow, and there were a lot of cars in the parking lot.

Jack slowed down a little as they drove by the entrance to the large building. "Well, you two, we're at the top of the pass. It's downhill most of the way now. All the way to Granby."

"Of course, we won't be going all the way into the town of Granby. We'll stop at the rest area at Grand Lake, which is a few miles closer."

It went downhill for a ways, then up again at the next mountain. The snow was so high alongside the road in places that it seemed they drove through a tunnel.

"I've never seen snow drifts that big," Jimmy said, and sat back.

"Neither have I," Mary replied. "I sure wish I had my camera."

Mary and Jimmy sat on the edge of their seats, not missing anything. Jimmy poked her and pointed at things he thought she might not notice.

Of course, she did the same thing to him.

Up and down the mountains they went for some time. Then, slowly, they got lower and lower. After fifteen minutes, they saw a sign that read, 'Grand Lake---5 Miles'.

"It won't be long now," Jack said.

He slowed down, and it wasn't long before they drove by a large lake off to their left. It was a brilliant blue. The shoreline ran around small mountains that jutted up out of the lake. Cabins were everywhere, and there were boats

Soft Feather

of varying sizes on the lake. They drove on, spotting a nice park up ahead.

"There is our third release area," Jack said. He watched for a place to park. Seeing an opening, he parallel-parked. A few people stood by a registering booth with their pigeons.

Jimmy got out and went around to the back door of the station wagon. He opened it and picked up the white cage for Jack and handed it to him. Jack closed the door and looked at Annie. He nodded his head at them, and they made their way over to the registration area.

A half dozen people sat at tables and waited for trainers.

Jack handed the man the papers for his pigeon, Annie.

"Hi, Jack," the man said as he took his registration form. "I'm Fred Wall. I met you at the rally in Boulder a couple of years ago."

Jack thought a minute. "Yes, I remember you now, Fred. You were with Jarvis. I believe you beat him that day. You won first place, didn't you?"

"That's right, Jack. That was one of my great days. How's your little Annie going to do today?"

"I have high hopes for her," he said. "High hopes."

"She's going to win first place," Mary said. "You'll see."

Fred looked at her, then back at Jack. "I certainly am glad I don't have a pigeon in this race today, Jack. It's hard to beat a determined woman, you know."

Jack nodded his head and grinned. He didn't say a word. He knew to be quiet when a woman spoke with determination in her voice.

"Take Annie over to the other table, Jack, and let him put her in with the other pigeons. We won't be

Soft Feather

releasing them until later this afternoon. That way you should be home by then to clock her in."

"Thanks, Fred," he said. The three of them went over and waited for another trainer to have his pigeon checked in. Then the number on Annie's leg was checked. It had to match the one on the checker's list. If it didn't, they would be disqualified.

It was, and the three of them were glad that was the last one. It was a lot of fun, and now it was time to head back over the mountain.

They walked back to the station wagon and looked around at the campground and surrounding area. It was nice, especially the big lake across the highway with the gorgeous, snow-capped mountains all around it. It made one feel good down deep inside.

They got into the station wagon. "I'm glad there wasn't a long line. We didn't have to wait until after 2:30 this afternoon to register, either," Jack said, looking at both of them.

"This way we can make it back over the Pass and be home before six o'clock".

He started the station wagon and backed out into the street. He drove back up the road they came in on.

They each gave a sigh of relief. A big weight was taken off their shoulders.

Up into the mountains they drove. This was not so bad, as the road was not steep at first. It did get steeper the farther they drove.

Everything looked different as they drove. Driving in the opposite direction surely made a big difference.

It took them some time to get to the top of Trail Ridge Road. When the road flattened out, they soon saw the sign 'Continental Divide---Elevation 11,796 feet'.

Up ahead they saw the large building they drove by earlier. Jack turned in and pulled up in front and parked.

Soft Feather

"You know what I'm thinking?" he asked, as he looked at the building. "I wonder if they have a hamburger and a nice cold bottle of pop in there for us."

"I sure hope they have a Nesbitt Orange," Jimmy said.

"I'd like one, too," Mary said.

"Let's go see if they do," he said.

With the three hamburgers, and three bottles of Nesbitt Orange, they went outside and sat at one of the tables. The view was something everyone should see close-up. There were patches of snow here and there around the parking lot. But the surrounding mountains were covered. One could tell without looking by the cool breeze that passed by.

"It's good to know that my Annie will be released later this afternoon," he said, sitting back in his chair. "I really enjoy working with homing pigeons."

Mary looked at him and frowned. "How long have they been racing pigeons?"

Jack looked at her and saw she was serious. "For a long time, Mary," he said.

"Why?" she asked. "Mr. Miller has a lot of pigeons that just fly around his barn. Jimmy takes some of his pigeons away, and they fly home when he turns them loose."

"I see what you mean, Mary," he said. "Why not just let them stay home and be content? I have just driven all over the place to let three of my pigeons fly home. That sure is a lot of work for nothing. Is that what you're saying?"

"Exactly," Mary said, nodding her head.

"I would agree with you, Mary, if that was all they did. But let's take a close look at what homing pigeons were used for when it was first discovered they could find their way back home after being released. No matter where

Soft Feather

they were taken, they found their way back to the place where they lived.

"In early years they were used, just like you said, to fly home from some place. The only difference was that they had a message tied to their legs. They were used to send messages back to headquarters during World War I.

"But the most famous of all of the homing pigeon stories involves a German banker, Meyer Rothschild. He became one of the richest men in the world. He was the founder of the international banking firm, 'House of Rothschild'.

"When Napoleon fought the great European war, he started a war with England. Meyer Rothschild set up his son, Nathan, as a banker in England. Everyone in England knew that Napoleon could not be defeated. The stocks and bonds were going down every day in England.

"Things got worse and worse, and the stocks went down even further. The British economy was collapsing. But Rothschild had people in the war area that kept sending messages back to England by homing pigeons. The messages told them that Napoleon had not won at Waterloo.

"With this news, Meyer Rothschild told his son to buy all he could, even if he had to mortgage everything they owned. He did, and it is said that he bought it all.

"The pigeons kept them informed, and when Napoleon lost the battle at Waterloo, England was saved. Which meant that the Rothschild family now owned almost everything that had to do with stocks and bonds in England.

"Overnight, they became the wealthiest family in all of England and most of the world. All because a few little homing pigeons did just what you said; they just flew home."

"Wow." Mary said. "That sure makes me think different about the homing pigeons."

Soft Feather

"Me, too," Jimmy said.

"Let's drink up, and like the pigeons, head for home," Jack said.

They left the empty pop bottles on the table and climbed back into the station wagon. This time they headed down the steep road they came up a few hours earlier. They got a little anxious as they went down.

Steeper and steeper, and again Jack had to shift down to second. Only this time it was to keep from going down the mountain too fast. He didn't want to burn the brakes out having to use them to slow down so much.

The large S curve, called a switchback, was finally in sight. They drove slowly down through the switchbacks until they were behind them. The road gradually leveled out, and he shifted back into high gear.

They were glad it was behind them. Even though it was exciting, it was also dangerous.

A few miles down the road, Jack turned off the highway onto a smaller road that bypassed Estes Park. Slowing down, they enjoyed the drive. They passed through an area where there were some fine-looking cabins. They were recently built in a newly developed area.

Men still worked on a couple of the homes, most of which were anything but small.

They soon came to the Longmont highway and turned onto it. They picked up speed and soon moved along at a fast clip, until suddenly the road started upward like some of the other steep roads. Jack slowed down as he drove around some really sharp curves. They finally reached the top.

As they rounded one of the curves on the top, they saw Estes Park way down below. It was located in a deep valley, surrounded by mountains. No wonder so many

Soft Feather

people wanted to live there. They marveled again that the town was so clean and picturesque.

They picked up speed again, passing by small places where people set up art exhibits, and other places where all kinds of crafts were sold. Then down a mountain they went, and soon they were in the town of Lyons.

They rode slowly through town and enjoyed looking at all the different types of businesses. The town was small but was enhanced by an abundance of window boxes on houses and businesses, filled with every color of flowers. They sped up again until they saw a town ahead of them.

"That's Longmont in front of us," Jack said. He looked at his watch. "I'm going to go around town on the east side. That way we can make better time and get you two home by five o'clock."

"That will be great," Jimmy said.

"My parents will be glad," Mary said. "They were kind of wondering when we would get back. I wasn't sure. They don't like for me to be out late."

"I agree," Jack said. "I want to get home early, too. That means I'll be home for supper. My housekeeper is at my house. She will be clocking in the time when my pigeons get there. She just might fix me something to eat before she leaves. Yep. I might be able to talk her into that."

It was five o'clock when Jack pulled up in front of the Wilson's house. Mary got out and said, "Thank you for a wonderful day, Mr. Starr. It has been one I'll remember for a long time.

"I'll see you tomorrow, Jimmy," she said. "Thanks for asking me to come along."

"You're welcome," he said. "Don't come over too early."

Soft Feather

They both laughed, and she walked towards her house.

Jack drove off, headed for Jimmy's house. "You have a nice friend, Jimmy."

"I know. We work well together."

Jack didn't say anything until he pulled up in his yard. "You got a good taste of what pigeon racers do today, Jimmy. What do you think about it?"

"I enjoyed it very much. I wondered exactly what you did and how it all worked. Now I know, and I think I'll be able to train my pigeons a lot better."

"Then I kept my word to your dad, Jimmy. I told him I would do my best to teach you what I know. Your dad taught me the same way."

Jimmy reached over and shook his hand. "Thank you very much."

"You're welcome. If you run into any problems, call me. You have my number now, so, don't hesitate to call. If I can't answer your question, I know people who can find the answer for us."

He reached into his shirt pocket and pulled out a folded piece of paper. "Here's your application for the 'Boulder Creek Pigeon Club'. You fill it out and send it to me. We'll get you registered into the club, and you'll be all set to enter some of your pigeons in the next race."

Jimmy unfolded the paper and looked at it, then at Jack."

"I'm the treasurer this year and your sponsor. I'll pay your dues for the first year."

"Thank you, Mr. Starr. I'll fill it out tonight and have it in the mail Monday."

"That will be fine, Jimmy," he said.

He opened the door and got out, shut the door and waved.

Soft Feather

Jack drove around the circle to the highway. He headed towards Boulder. He honked and was soon out of sight.

Jimmy ran up the steps. He opened the door and started to run into the house but stopped. He didn't want to slam the door as hard as he did yesterday. He remembered his grandpa got a bath in cold water.

He gently closed the door and walked into the kitchen where his grandparents were. Tom had his hands over his ears with his eyes closed, and Alice had an empty glass in her hand with her eyes closed. They slowly opened them and looked over at him.

"Do you want me to go back and close the door more softly?" Jimmy asked, and smiled at them.

"No," Tom said, smiling his best smile, "you did much better this time."

Alice looked at him, and filled the glass with water.

Tom looked at the glass of water in his wife's hand. "I tell you what. Let's forget all about the door and think about having supper. Would you like to have supper with us tonight, Jimmy?"

"I sure would, Grandpa," he said.

"You two are going to get more than supper," Alice said, raising her hand with the glass of water."

They both ducked. "I baked a cherry pie for you, so go clean up. Supper will be on the table when you get back."

Off they went down the hall, each trying to get in the bathroom first. Jimmy won. Alice set the table.

"Jimmy, don't take all night-- food's on the table!" Tom said.

"Okay." he answered.

She stopped and shook her head. "Nothing like having two men in the house who mind like those two."

Soft Feather

CHAPTER 15

Mr. Starr sent Jimmy a membership form from the 'Boulder Creek Pigeon Club'. With it was a note letting him know he was proud to have him in his club. There was also a surprise. There was going to be a race held in Longmont the first of the month. If Jimmy wanted to enter, he should let him know.

Jimmy wrote Mr. Starr immediately, telling him that he wanted to enter. He told him to let him know how much it would cost. He would have to start looking for things to do to make some money.

The training started, not so much for the pigeons, but for the trainers, Jimmy and Mary.

Mr. Miller bought some books, and they tried to do everything they read. It was hard, but they learned fast. All it took was time and determination on their part.

Mr. Miller couldn't enter this race because he had a lot of things to do on the farm. "Jimmy, you're welcome to use my clock. Your dad and I bought one when we were racing. He sold his, but I put mine in my room for a while. One day Jackie put it up in the attic. Boy, was it hard to find.

"We will have to take it over to Boulder and have it checked. They have to know if it runs fast, slow or on time. If one clock runs slow, then the owner would show his pigeon took less time than on the two other clocks."

Jimmy thought about what he said and nodded his head. "That's right."

"I'll call Jack Starr and set up a date we can have that done."

"I can go after school and on weekends, Mr. Miller."

"Don't worry about it. My wife goes over there a lot. She can do it if she has to. I'll let you know."

Soft Feather

"Okay," he said.

It wasn't long until they were taking the pigeons off on short-distance trial flights. They put the time down when they let them go.

Alice and Jackie wrote the time down when they heard the buzzer. They went out and checked to see which pigeon came in. Then they waited until it buzzed again and repeated the process.

At Jimmy's house, it buzzed three times in a row. It was some time later when it buzzed again. The last one in was Lady Blue. She was always last. It seemed that she liked to take the scenic route home.

It was a big disappointment for Jimmy. It shattered the big dreams he once had for her.

But it wasn't that way with Lady Snow White. She, too, watched his every move like her mother did. He talked to her, letting her know he liked her, and it wasn't long before she rode around on his shoulder. They both enjoyed their time together.

Jimmy began whistling low each time he fed her. She soon knew that when he whistled, he had food for her.

He picked her up one day and said, "You may be all white, and your mother all blue, but between the two of you, you have the softer feathers."

When the four pigeons returned from their exercise flight, Jimmy whistled softly when they landed. They soon learned to come into the pen for their meal when he whistled. By doing this, he knew it would help later when they raced.

In one of the new pigeon books, it said that a good homer trainer needed to train his pigeons to come into the pen quickly. Their tags had to be taken off their legs and put into the time clock as quickly as possible. It could mean winning or losing a race. It was just another part of their training.

Soft Feather

Soon, Lady Snow White was the fastest of his four pigeons. He checked the times of Mr. Miller's pigeons and was glad when he saw that she was the fastest. She would be the pigeon he would work with the most.

"Lady Snow White will be the Warrior Champion Racer," he said out loud one day. He liked that idea.

Jackie Miller checked the buzzer on their pen. Usually, the buzzer would buzz four times, one right after the other. Chuck's pigeons didn't bother flying anywhere else but home.

Alice started recording the time for Jimmy.

The time on Jimmy's pigeons was almost the same as Mr. Miller's. Each time, Alice told him that Lady Blue was last again. He talked to her more and more. She acted like she knew what he said, but it didn't help.

Then he started talking to her each day before he let her out, and to his amazement she started flying directly home. Her new actions made him feel better about her. He knew that what she needed was that extra encouragement, and she'd be a great homer.

His hopes were dashed the next time she flew. She was almost a half-hour late. Saddened, he stopped depending on her and turned to her daughter, Lady Snow White. She was dependable and fast. The books say that is what a trainer has to have to win races.

Mary went with them now and then and helped. After her adventure with Mr. Starr, releasing three of his pigeons, she got serious. She fell in love with Blue Boy and talked to him, wanting him to fly faster and beat his sister. He would sit on her finger and coo at her, but he wouldn't get on her shoulder like Lady Snow White did on Jimmy's shoulder.

She would put him on her shoulder, but he'd just fly off and land on the boardwalk, looking at her and cooing.

Soft Feather

She'd then put out her finger, and he'd hop up on it, cooing, then fly up onto the boardwalk and look at her.

Different feed and treats were tried, but no matter what she did, he just looked at her and cooed. She gave up.

Jimmy smiled and gently picked Lady Snow White up off his shoulder and put her on his finger. "Stick out your finger again, Mary."

Mary did and Lady Snow White cooed twice. Jimmy lifted his hand up, then quickly dropped it. She flapped her wings and flew over and landed on Mary's finger.

She lifted her finger up to her shoulder and she hopped off onto it. "That's what you're supposed to do Blue Boy," she said, looking at him.

They did it two more times, and were pleased with how quickly she learned.

There were many days when Mary came over after school and helped feed them. Then she sat with Jimmy when he let them out on their exercise flights. They talked and read about pigeons.

It was just like old times when they worked together. Jimmy soon found out that she knew as much, and sometimes more, than he did. They worked well together.

She liked pigeons, but she also liked being with Jimmy.

The next day Jimmy was in the pen feeding his pigeons when Mary came around the corner of the house and up to the pen. "You have a phone call from your dad."

He set the feed bucket down on the table and closed the gate behind him. Mary wanted to beat him back to her dad's garage. She didn't. Jimmy caught up, and ran along with her.

Into the office they ran. Her dad handed Jimmy the phone and sat down with Mr. Miller next to the pot-bellied

Soft Feather

stove. Mary went over and sat down with them. He put the phone up to his ear. "Hi Dad," he said.

He listened for a couple of minutes. "That would be great. Yes, sir."

Then there was silence again. Those listening leaned forward trying to hear what his dad said. Jimmy grunted a couple of times looking at them.

"Yes, sir. This weekend is Easter and there is no school Monday. I'll ask Coach Brown if I can get out of his class early Friday."

Silence again, then "Yes, sir. Bye." Hanging up the phone he said, "I guess I'll go home. I have to finish feeding my pigeons."

Mary jumped up walked over to him frowning. "Well," Mary said. "What did you father say?"

"Oh, not much. He just wants me to come see him in Big Spring, Texas this weekend. He's going to send the money by Western-Union for my bus fare. If I can get out of coach Brown's math class, I'll be able to catch the bus to Denver."

Mary's frown turned to a big smile, along with her daddy and Mr. Miller's. They all knew that Jimmy wanted to go see him, but something always came up. Now he is going to be able to spend some time with him, even if it is just a weekend.

Friday afternoon Jimmy was on the bus headed for Denver. Along with his luggage was an odd shaped box. It had a small rope tied around it with 'This Side Up' written on the top of each side of the box.

He had a four-hour layover in Denver, where he changed busses, and another two-hour delay in Amarillo, Texas, and three hours in Lubbock, Texas. It was four o'clock Saturday afternoon when he stepped off the bus in Big Spring. He made sure his box was okay.

Soft Feather

His dad gave him a big hug. "I'm double parked out front, son." He grabbed his suitcase and headed for the front door.

Jimmy picked up his box and followed. Outside was a pickup with 'Bud's Plumbing' on the door. Tommy put the suitcase in the truck bed as Jimmy got in the truck and put his box on the seat next to him.

"I have to make a service call," he said. A good customer has a leaky faucet. I'll take you by the VA Rehab building where I live. I changed beds with one of my friends who has an empty bed next to his.

Jimmy smiled as they drove off. It felt good being with his dad again. They pulled up in front of a large building and stopped. With luggage in hand they went into the building and up the stairs to the second floor. As they made their way down the large room, a big man started yelling at a man in front of him. He turned and ran out the back door with the big man chasing him.

Tommy shook his head as he put Jimmy's suitcase on one of the bunk beds. "Don't say anything to that man. He is the meanest man I have ever known. You can use this locker between our beds. I'll be back as soon as I can. You lie down and rest."

Jimmy nodded his head and his dad left. He put his cardboard box on the small card table next to the locker. Untying the rope, he opened the front of the box. There inside was a cage with Lady Snow White and her mother Lady Blue. Opening the cage door, he took out a small jar of food and water and filled their feeders and water pan. He closed the door.

It only took a couple of minutes to hang his clothes up. When he checked his pigeons, they finished eating and sat on the cage floor with their eyes closed. He smiled and lay down on the bunk bed. Before he knew it he was asleep.

Soft Feather

Tommy came in and walked up next to Jimmy. He stood and looked down at him. He was proud of him. He then heard a noise behind him. He saw the cage with the two pigeons in it. He looked closer and saw that they looked back at him. "Well, what do you know, it's Lady Blue, and you must be Lady Snow White."

Opening the cage door he took Lady Blue out and held her up. "You are a beautiful pigeon. "I can see why my son loves you." He put her back in the cage, closed the door, and shook his head. He knew that his son brought them just for him to see.

He reached down and shook Jimmy a couple of times.

Jimmy turned over and opened his eyes. His dad smiled at him. "It's time to wake up, Jimmy."

He rubbed his eyes, stretched, and yawned, and sat up.

"We'll go eat, then go downtown and see a movie. 'The Quiet Man' with John Wayne is playing tonight. I hear it's a good movie."

"A movie! Dad, that's great. I haven't seen a movie in a long time."

It was a great movie, but two big bags of popcorn and two big RC Colas made the movie even better.

Back at the Rehab Center, it wasn't long until the two of them were in bed. The next day was Easter. Jimmy fell asleep right away.

Someone shouting caused Jimmy to sit straight up and look around. It was getting light outside. Rubbing his eyes, he looked again. The large man across the aisle chased a man around the room, yelling loudly at him. The man ran out the door. He swung around and came stomping back to his bunk and sat down.

Soft Feather

He raised his arms and buried his face in them, and sat and talked to himself. Jimmy gasped. The man had no hands. They were off just above his wrists.

Tommy sat up in his bed. He heard his son gasp and he knew what caused it. "The man lost his hands when he crawled through a forest on one of the islands in the Pacific. There were land mines, and he pulled himself along with his hands, and touched one of them."

Jimmy watched him rocking back and forth saying something he couldn't understand. He got up and pulled on his pants, then opened the cage and took Lady Snow White out. Placing her on his finger, he made a cooing sound two times, lifted his hand, and lowered it quickly.

Lady Snow White flew across the aisle and landed on the stub of the man's arm. Startled, the man looked up and saw a white pigeon look back at him. The pigeon cooed a couple of times. Raising his right arm, he started to hit it, and it cooed softly again. His arm stopped in midair.

Instead of his squashing the pigeon, he slowly lowered his arm and stroked its head with his stub. Tears filled his eyes and ran down his face. The pigeon then flew up onto his left shoulder and sat there looking at him. She cooed again.

The man grinned a bit and the pigeon stopped moving. It just sat there, looking at his mouth. He had a gold tooth that sparkled from the light above him. Lady Snow White pecked at it and the man looked over at Jimmy.

Jimmy walked over and knelt down in front of him. "Her name is Lady Snow White, sir."

With tears running down his cheeks the man said, "She just kissed me. I can't believe what just happened. I asked for guidance on what to do. Here on Easter morning I get an answer. A white dove was sent my way and it kissed me. It loves me…me, a mean old man. If a little bird can

Soft Feather

love me then I need to love myself, and other people, too. I know that there is a plan for my life. I don't know right now what it is, but I know that very soon I'll know and when I do, I'm going to get on with it.

He dried his eyes on his right sleeve. "Yes sir, that little bird is an answer to my prayers.

Tommy walked up and said, "Jake, this is my son, Jimmy. He trains birds."

"Jimmy, this is Jake Bell. I believe you two are going to get along very well."

Jake patted Jimmy on his shoulder with his stub. "I want to thank you for bringing your pigeon with you. You'll never know how much I need the message she brought me."

"She helped change my life, sir," Jimmy said. I have her mother with me. She was my first love. Would you like to see her?"

"I surely would."

Jimmy went over to his cage and soon returned with Lady Blue. He placed her on Jake's other shoulder and stepped back.

Everyone in the room was now wide-awake. They gathered around and hardly believed what they saw, Jake sat, and didn't yell at anyone. He looked around at everyone and smiled. "I want to ask all of you to forgive me. I've been mean to you, but I'm going to change."

"Would you like to go to church with us, Mr. Bell?"

"Yes, I would," he said. "I need someone to help me get dressed."

Two guys stepped forward and he stood up. "I'll be with you and Jimmy in a few minutes," he said to Tommy.

With Jake all dressed up, everyone on the floor got dressed and went to church with Jimmy and Tommy. It was a great day for everyone.

Soft Feather

After lunch, Tommy took Jimmy back to the bus station. They were in high spirits. Jimmy made sure his box with 'This Side Up' was loaded right. With that done he grabbed his dad and hugged him very tightly.

"Thanks for making it possible for me to come see you, Dad."

"You are welcome, son. I want to thank you for bringing Lady Blue and her baby Lady Snow White. It did my heart good to see Lady Blue. She is beautiful."

"She's still last, Dad."

"She may be last in racing, but she's first with me in beauty."

Jimmy smiled. "Me, too. But you know that don't you."

I sure do. Well, I wish it could have been a longer visit. Maybe next time."

"Yes, sir. I'm sure it will be. They hugged again and Jimmy got on the bus. He found a window seat and sat down. He waved as the bus moved away from the station. Leaning back in his seat, he thought, "What would he do without Lady Snow White and Lady Blue?" Frowning, he shook his head. It sure would be a dull life.

Jimmy sat up late the next evening telling his grandparents and Mary what happened in Big Spring. It was a quick trip, but the bond between him and his dad was made stronger. It was a trip that he would never forget.

The next day, after school, Mr. Miller stopped by to see Jimmy. He was in the pen feeding and watering his birds.

"Mr. Starr called me this morning. He told me that the Longmont Club is checking all of the clocks for this race. I'm going over there in the morning, and I'll have my

Soft Feather

clock checked. I know you can't go, but I feel like we need to have it done as soon as possible."

"I'll stop by and let your grandma know if everything is alright. I've got it wound up and running. It seems to be keeping good time. But if it isn't, we need to know now so we can get it fixed."

"That's right, Mr. Miller. We sure don't want to wait until the last minute to find out we can't use it."

"I'll let your grandma know. Don't worry about it. If it's off a little they can adjust it right there. I've got to run."

"Okay," he said.

He left, leaving Jimmy looking at the bucket of water in his hand. He set it down and scooped some feed out of a sack and looked at it. "I sure don't need anything to happen right now," he told himself. He knew the clock was old and might not be fixable.

He'd know tomorrow, he thought, as he poured grain into all of the feeders.

The next day when he came in from school for lunch, his grandma met him at the door. She didn't usually do things like that, and he looked at her.

She smiled. "Mr. Miller came by and said the clock is working right on time. They were amazed that a clock that old was that good."

"One of the men there said, 'It's because it is an old clock. They made them a lot better then than they do now.'"

Jimmy grabbed his grandma and hugged her. "You kind of scared me, Grandma. I've been worrying about it ever since Mr. Miller told me yesterday."

"You've been worrying for nothing, Jimmy. Don't you know that worrying doesn't ever help anything? A lot of people worry themselves sick."

Soft Feather

"That's right. All they get for worrying is sick. Is that what you want to happen to you over a clock that might not be working right?"

"Well," he said. "If it didn't work right I… Well, it would…" He stopped and thought about what she asked him. It was a trick question. Or was it? He sure didn't want to be sick over a clock.

"I guess I wouldn't, Grandma. There are some things I surely wouldn't want to happen. It would stop me from doing what I've planned on for some time. But getting sick over them not happening… I sure don't like being sick. So, I wouldn't want to get sick over them not happening."

"Me, neither," she said. "I've got your dinner on the table. Everything worked out fine, so enjoy your meal. Oh yes, there's a piece of cherry pie in the refrigerator if you want it."

"Yes, ma'am, I do," he said, as he went into the kitchen and sat down.

The first of the month arrived on a Saturday. There was a lot of excitement around the Warrior house getting things ready. The exercise flights for Snow White were stopped so that she could rest.

Instead of flying, she had to listen to Jimmy talk. If she did everything he asked her to do, she would stay home.

Mr. Miller fixed everything like he wanted on the farm. That left him free to take Jimmy over to Longmont for the race. It was a long time since he attended one, and he, too, was excited.

Jimmy found one of his dad's old cages covered up in the garage. He sanded it down and painted it, and it

Soft Feather

looked like new. That was all he needed, as Lady Snow White was the only pigeon he would race.

As they pulled up at Roosevelt Park in Longmont, Jack Starr stood at the entrance, waving for them. Mr. Miller rolled his window down.

"Park over there by my station wagon, Chuck," he said.

"Okay," he answered, and drove over and parked. He got out and shook Jack's hand. "It's been quite a while," he said.

"More than I want to admit," Jack said, as Jimmy walked up to him with his cage.

"Who you got there, Jimmy?" he asked.

"This is Lady Blue's daughter, Lady Snow White," Mr. Starr. "You remember Lady Blue, don't you?"

Holding up the cage, he looked at her. "I sure do. She was the slowest pigeon I ever had. How good is her daughter?"

"She's faster than any of mine, Jack," Chuck said.

"That sounds good, but it doesn't mean much. I'm sure yours are not too great, living in a barn like they do. We'll see if she's faster than mine. She's got to be real good to beat my Annie, Jimmy."

"She won't have any problem beating her," Jimmy said. "Wait and see."

They all laughed. He was talking like a real trainer should. All of their pigeons are the fastest pigeons around, and they know it. If you don't believe it, just ask one of them.

"The registration tables are over there near the baseball field. Let's get them registered, and then we can check out all of the goodies they have here," Jack said.

They got in the shortest line and stood looking around to see if there was anyone they knew.

Soft Feather

Someone walked up behind Jack and grabbed him and started shaking him. Jack dropped his cage and tried to turn around but couldn't. When the shaking stopped, he turned around real fast; his face started to get red. Then he smiled. "Mac," he said. "What is the matter with you?"

"I saw that your Annie only got third place in the triple race," Mac said. "When are you going to get some pigeons that can race?"

"The only reason she didn't get first is because my housekeeper scared my Annie, causing a delay in her being clocked in. If that hadn't happened, she would have been number one, old buddy," Jack answered.

"That's the excuse I used to use when I first started. Don't you have anything new?" He looked at Jimmy, and then at the guy standing next to him.

"Is that you, Chuck?" he asked. "It is! How are you doing? No, that's not a good question. What are you doing with this loser?"

"I'm not with him, Mac."

The three of them stood there and looked at him, not smiling.

Mac thought about it, then looked at Jimmy holding a pigeon cage. "Oh, no. Jack's bringing kids along with him now," he said. "Chuck, doesn't he know this is a man's sport?"

He stopped and looked at Jimmy again. "You were with Jack at the triple race. He had you with him, didn't he, young man?"

"Yes, sir."

"And you were holding one of his birds, weren't you?"

"Yes, sir."

"He didn't win then, and he isn't going to win now. Right?"

"Yes, sir."

Soft Feather

"You know who is?"

"Yes, sir. I am!"

"You? Is that your bird?" Mac asked, looking sideways at him.

"Yes, sir," he answered.

"You need to know something, young man. I've never had a kid beat me. Do you hear me? Never!"

"The way everyone is looking at you, I believe everyone around heard you, sir."

Mac looked around and smiled. "I sure do know how to get everyone's attention, don't I? Tell me about your bird's lineage."

"She's from Lady Blue," Jack said. "Remember her? You're the one who sold her to me."

Mac turned around and looked at Jack. "Sorry about that, Jack. You know, she's got the best lineage around. You've got to admit that."

"You're right, Mac. How come you're right when you do what you did to me? Please tell me. I can hardly wait. I'm sure everyone around here would like to hear it, now that you have our attention. Please tell us."

"The best lineage around," Mac said. "The most beautiful blue pigeon I've ever seen. Kind of shy, but other than that she's got the best lineage of any I've ever had."

"That's right, everybody. The only thing he didn't say was she's a homing pigeon that stays home. She does fly. Alone. Loves the scenery everywhere she flies. Flies around it a couple of times, making sure she doesn't miss anything."

Everyone laughed, knowing what he was talking about. Most of them had at least one like that.

Mac looked at Chuck. "It's sure good to see you again. What have you been doing since I last saw you?"

"I've been farming," he said, smiling at him. "I see that you haven't changed since I saw you last."

Soft Feather

Mac looked at Jack, then back at Chuck. "I've changed a lot, Chuck. I make all of this noise to try and forget a lot of things that happened to me."

Chuck looked at Jack. "The war," he said.

"Where are your birds, Chuck?" Mac asked. "You and Tommy used to have all of those winners. We had a lot of good times those days."

"We both got out of racing pigeons; Tommy went his way, and I went mine," Chuck answered. "He had some problems in the war."

"Jack told me about it. Looks like we both ran the same race. I just got out first, and he's still running."

They moved up the line and were now first. Jimmy told the registrar his name and that he was a new member of the Boulder Creek Pigeon Club.

The man found his name and filled out some papers and handed them to him to sign.

He set his cage down and read them, signed them, and handed them back to him.

The registrar handed him the numbered tag for his pigeon and smiled at him. "You're the first one today who read what they signed. I could have put a blank check in front of most of them, and they'd have signed it."

Jack took out a blank check and handed it to him.

The man took it and wrote on it, then handed it back to him.

In big letters it said, "YOU OWE ME $1000."

"If that's true, you better call the sheriff. I haven't seen $1000 in a long time. You were supposed to sign it and give it back."

"Sorry, the only thing I have for you is this form," he laughed.

Jack signed his form without looking at it.

Soft Feather

The man handed him the numbered tag for his pigeon. Everyone laughed, including the man at the registration table.

They stood and waited for Mac to register his pigeon. When the registrar gave him the paper to sign, he picked it up and pretended to read it. The man behind him poked him in the ribs. He jumped, and signed it and grabbed his numbered tag, turning to tell everybody "goodbye."

They all said "goodbye," and laughed, as he walked off with his friends, headed for the long line of booths. They knew that in one of those booths were things they couldn't get along without. Of course, their wives would let them know quickly where all the other things they couldn't get along without that were never used, were located.

It wasn't long before they found a table, and Jack bought Jimmy a Nesbitt Orange soft drink and three Royal Crown soft drinks for himself and his friends.

When their bottles were empty, Mr. Miller looked at Jimmy. "We need to head for the house," he said. "They will be turning all the pigeons loose pretty soon. If we want to get home before they do, we'd better leave."

"Yes, sir," Jimmy said, getting up. "I sure don't want to miss that. I've got to learn how to get Lady Snow White into the pen quickly and clock her in."

"Lady Snow White?" Mac said, looking at Jimmy.

"Yes, sir. She sure is a lady, and she's snow white. She's my fastest pigeon, and she loves me. She stays on my shoulder all the time I'm in the pen. I talk to her, and she listens. When I want her to come, I whistle low. When she comes back from her exercise flights, I whistle and she comes in real fast to be on my shoulder."

Mac looked at Chuck, then Jack. "Don't tell anybody, but I just learned something from a kid. I can't believe it. I've been racing pigeons for so many years I

Soft Feather

can't count them, but never have I thought about whistling at a pigeon."

"If you knew his background, you probably wouldn't have said what you did when you first met him," Chuck said. "He caught a large hawk and trained it to hunt, along with two of its babies. He won first place prizes all over Colorado with them. When he found out he couldn't hunt with them for food for his grandparents, he gave them to the Air Force Academy in Colorado Springs."

"Hawks," Mac said, turning up his lip.

"He had Lady Blue eating out of his hands and resting on his shoulder. She came out of her dark hiding place the first day he saw her, Mac," Chuck said. "The first day."

"But hawks," he said. "They're the birds we hate."

"You wouldn't have hated these. They were just like Lady Blue," Chuck said. "He and birds get along real well. He has a gift for working with birds," Chuck said, standing up.

"It's good seeing you, Jimmy," Mac said. "I can see that you've got what your daddy had, only more of it. I'm proud to know you."

"Thank you, sir. I think you're a nice man, and I like you."

Mac looked shocked. He didn't say a word as tears filled his eyes. It was a long time since someone said that to him, and really meant it. He tried to say something but couldn't, so he saluted him.

Jimmy's dad taught him how to salute after he was discharged from the army. He came to attention and saluted.

Mac looked at Jimmy, trying to hide the tears that ran down his cheeks. Jimmy walked to where he sat, put his arms around his neck, and gave him a big hug. He stepped back, and they looked at each other.

Soft Feather

"It's an honor to know you, Mr. Mac. Just knowing that you were one of my daddy's best friends makes me proud to know you."

Mac reached up and hugged him. His face registered a mixture of emotions.

Jimmy stepped back and smiled. He walked over to where Mr. Miller stood.

Chuck waved at Mac, and they walked towards his car.

Mac pulled a large red handkerchief out of his back pocket and wiped his eyes and smiled.

Jimmy stopped when they got to the car and looked back at Mac.

Mac still stood and looked at him. He saluted Jimmy and held it.

Jimmy came to attention again and saluted. He opened the car door and got in. He wiped his eyes and looked at Mr. Miller. He, too, wiped his eyes.

Jimmy felt good about saluting Mac. He was sure that he was a good man with a lot of problems that he didn't bring upon himself. Just like his dad. Jimmy didn't think he would ever understand why there had to be wars. "Why couldn't people live in peace?" he wondered.

It wasn't long until they headed down the road towards home. It was good visiting with pigeon lovers.

He sat back in his seat. He now wondered how good his pigeon was. This was all new for him, and he got excited as they headed home.

When he walked into the house, Mary sat on the couch in the front room. She was reading one of the pigeon books Mr. Miller gave them. Jimmy asked, "What are you doing here?"

Soft Feather

"You're not going to do this all alone, Jimmy Warrior. I want to be in on all of the things we have to do to clock Lady Snow White." Mary said.

He looked at her. "OK. But you'll have to wait outside the pen until she is inside. I don't want anything disturbing her. I've got her trained to come in to me alone."

"I know that. I just want to be in on how it's done. In fact, I believe I can help you do it faster than you can do it by yourself."

Jimmy thought about what she said. "That sounds like a good idea. Let's go out to the pen and practice. Mr. Starr got a third place with Annie. That's great, but he said she would have won first place, but she wouldn't come to his housekeeper like she should have. It took longer than it should have. I don't know about that, but it's something to think about."

"We sure don't want that to happen to Lady Snow White. You stay out until she's in the coop, and I have control of her. Then you come in with the clock, and we'll get the tag off her leg and into the clock as fast as we can. Not too fast, though. We don't want to mess up."

Mary nodded her head in agreement. "This reminds me of things we did when we caught those baby hawks down by the creek. Remember, you climbed up the ladder to the top of that cottonwood tree. I waited below. The three babies' fuzzy down disappeared, and new feathers started taking its place. You picked up one of the largest chicks and handed it to me, and I put it in the basket, then the next largest chick. You left the smallest one for the daddy hawk. "

"Yeah," Jimmy said. "I remember that. After I got the second one and put it in the basket, the daddy dived at me. I had to swing around the ladder to get away from his claws. His claws hit the ladder, and splinters flew everywhere. That was close."

Soft Feather

"It sure was. But our teamwork worked. That's what counts."

They practiced a couple of times with the clock, then sat down outside the pen. They didn't want to be inside the pen when she arrived.

Jimmy was about to say something when Mary put her finger up to her lips and said, "Ssssh! I think I see something," she said, looking up in the sky.

Sure enough, Jimmy saw it, also, closer and closer, then almost overhead. It was Lady Snow White. He got up and went inside the pen and watched her. She was coming home.

She landed on the top board next to the entrance opening and hopped down into the pen and onto the walk board. Jimmy whistled a couple of times, and she flew over and lit on his shoulder.

He reached up and gently grabbed her and brought her around to where he could see her. He spotted the tag. Mary handed him the pliers. He took them and removed the tag and handed it to her.

She placed the tag in the clock and pushed the lever. It made a funny noise, and the time was recorded.

They looked at each other. "That was great," Mary said. "I'd say it was close to five seconds. No more than ten."

Jimmy thought about it. "Maybe in between," he said. "Whatever it was, we got it done as fast as anyone else could have done it."

He placed her back on his shoulder and went over and filled her feed and water bowls. He placed her up next to her nest, and she drank some water and ate.

Mary carried the clock out of the pen. He followed and closed the gate. As they walked towards the front of the house, they heard a car pull up. They hurried around the house, and there sat Jack Starr.

Soft Feather

"What's he doing here, Jimmy?" she asked.

"I don't know. Maybe he wants to... I believe I know what he wants to do. Let's go over and find out. This could be great."

They walked up to his car. "Hello, Mr. Starr," Mary said. "What are you doing here?"

"I was driving by, and a thought came to me," he said, rubbing his chin. "Why don't I stop and see if his pigeon arrived? If it hasn't, I'll wait until it does.' But seeing you with the clock in your hand, I believe she arrived. Am I right?"

"Yes, sir," Jimmy said. "She just came in, and we clocked her in."

"Great. I'll take the clock with me, so you won't have to ask Chuck to make a special trip over to Boulder."

"That's a great idea," Jimmy said. "I wondered how I was going to get it over to you. Mr. Miller does so much for me. It bothers me sometimes not being able to do anything for him."

"From what I heard him say about you over in Longmont, I think he is proud of you and likes to do things for you. I feel that way, too."

Jimmy didn't say anything, and Mary stood there smiling. "Our three families are close, Mr. Starr," she said. "We try to do things for each other all the time. It's just natural for us to help each other."

"You better watch out, or I'll join your family," Jack said. "I felt close to the Warrior family when Tommy helped me out many years ago. If he hadn't got me interested in homing pigeons, I don't know what would have happened to me.

"I guess you're right, Mary. It's good to have friends like your family and the Millers and Warriors have. It's hard to find that anymore.

Soft Feather

"I've got to head for home and see how my Annie did. I'll let you know the results as soon as I know."

"Mr. Starr, thank you for being our friend," Jimmy said. He and Mary stepped back. Jack nodded. He drove to the highway and was soon out of sight.

"Things are working out real well," Jimmy thought.

"I've got to go home, Jimmy. I'll see you tomorrow."

"Okay," he said, as she squeezed his hand. "Thanks for your help."

"It worked out great." She turned and headed home.

When school was out Monday afternoon, Jimmy went home quickly. Mary told him she had to stay after school and practice with the cheerleaders. Instead of going downtown, he went straight home. As he neared the house, he saw a car parked in the front yard. It looked like Mr. Starr's car. When he arrived home, he opened the front door.

"Hi, Jimmy," Mr. Starr said, as he came into the kitchen. "How are you doing?"

"I'm doing fine, sir," he said, with anticipation. He saw the clock sat on the table next to his grandma. "I didn't know you were going to bring the clock back."

"Well, I wouldn't have except I felt like I had to. I just started to tell your grandma why I had to bring it back when you came in. Would you like to know why?"

He looked at his grandma, and she nodded her head.

"Yes, sir," he answered.

"Your Lady Snow White won first place. It's the first time that I know of that a first-time trainer's entry has ever won first place.

"First place!" Jimmy said, looking at his grandma. "WOW! How about that, Grandma? Lady Snow White won

Soft Feather

first place. I'm so proud of her. She's not just beautiful and loving, she's fast."

He looked back at Mr. Starr. "She deserved to win," he said. "She did it all by herself. Can you believe it? I'm so proud of her, Mr. Starr."

Jack reached down beside his chair and picked up his brief case. He put it on the table and opened it and took out a trophy. There was a pigeon proudly standing sideways looking to the front. "Here's your trophy with you and your pigeon's names on it, Jimmy. They usually send it, but I called and asked if I could deliver it. They said they are proud of you for your achievement."

He handed it to Jimmy and shook his hand. "I'm proud of you Jimmy, just like you are proud of Lady Snow White. I believe that the love you have for that pigeon is what made her do her best for you."

"Mr. Starr, thank you for all you've done for me, and thank you for believing in Lady Snow White. I, also, want to tell you I had some help from my friend, Mary Wilson. She has inspired me to keep on the right track, and my grandparents have helped me with that, too."

"I'm proud of you, Jimmy," his grandma said. She got up and gave him a hug. "Your dad is going to be proud of you, too."

"I've got to run," Jack said. "I won second place with my Annie. I told Mac she was faster than any of his pigeons. She was. I'm sure he's not laughing about it right now," he said, chuckling.

"Mac got third place with his pigeon, Sergeant York. We can be proud of our pigeons, Jimmy. Sergeant York has been the winner around here for a long time. We messed up his little game, didn't we? He has to get busy and raise some pigeons faster than ours."

Soft Feather

Jimmy ran over and hugged him. "Thanks for Lady Blue. Without her, this would not have happened. Everything worked out for the best."

Jack closed his briefcase and walked over to the door. "You're right, Jimmy," he said. "It all worked out for the best for all of us."

"I called Mr. Miller and let him know what we've done. He's sure proud of you."

Alice stepped up and hugged him. "Jack, I want to thank you for all you've done for my grandson. From now on, you're an honorary member of our family."

"Thank you, Alice," he said, "I am honored."

They went out on the porch. Jack walked out to his station wagon and drove out of the yard and up to the highway.

As he headed towards Boulder, he honked his horn. They waved, then went back inside and sat down at the kitchen table.

Alice picked up the trophy. "Yes, your dad is going to be one proud daddy, Jimmy. I'm going to sit down and write him a letter right now."

As she got out the paper, they heard a car pull up in the yard. Jimmy looked out the window and saw it was Mr. Miller. He motioned for him to come outside. He hurried outside and to the car. "Go tell your grandma that your dad is on the phone down at Mr. Wilson's garage."

Jimmy ran back inside and told his grandma. She started her letter to him, but put the pencil down, and they hurried out and got in the car.

"This is a wonderful surprise, Chuck," she said. "Mr. Starr delivered Jimmy's trophy, and he hasn't been gone long. I just started a letter to Tommy."

"I know," he said. "We planned it this way."

Soft Feather

Alice gave him a mean kind of look (almost), then smiled. "I sure do like surprises. You know that, don't you?"

"Yes, ma'am," he said, as they pulled up in front of the filling station.

Alice beat Jimmy in and picked up the phone before he got to it. "Hi, Tommy. How are you doing?"

"I'm fine, Mom. Jack called me this morning and told me that Jimmy won first place with his pigeon, Snow White. He said that she is out of Lady Blue's lineage. How about that? He sure knows how to pick them, doesn't he?"

"Yes, he does. Just like you used to pick them. How are things going for you down there in Texas?"

"Fine. I'm still working for a heating and air conditioning company. Not much air conditioning this time of the year. But they're keeping me busy."

"I'm glad to hear that. Here's Jimmy."

Jimmy took the phone. "Hi, Dad," he said. "I guess you heard what happened before I did."

"I sure did. You can't keep a good word like that a secret, you know. Especially when it's Jack Starr, and it was one of his bird's offspring that did it. I knew that Lady Blue had a good breeding line, but her first fledgling to win first place in her first race is unheard of. I'm real proud of you, son."

"Thanks. She deserves all the credit. All I did was take her over there; she did the rest."

"That's right, son. But I'm proud you took her. Jack told me that she is like her mother. He also said that my good friend, Mac, is proud of you, even though you beat him. Now that is something that never happened before. He's very competitive."

"I really like Mr. Mac," Jimmy said. "He had a problem with shell shock, just like you did, Dad. He got

Soft Feather

over his just like you're doing. I told him that I really liked him."

There was silence on the phone. "You know what, son, you could have done nothing nicer than that for Mac. You don't know how much we long to hear someone tell us that they like us and really mean it."

"Well, I really like you, Dad, and I love you, too. You know that, don't you?"

"Of course, I know it, Jimmy. I'm so proud of you. I'm working as hard as I can to do all the right things, so I can be able to someday be with you and my mom and dad. I wish I could feel that I have a chance to also be back with your mom someday. It's hard, but I'm going to win."

"Grandma and Grandpa pray for you all the time. I do, too."

"Thank you." There was silence for a few moments. "You'd better watch out, Jimmy."

"Why, Dad?"

"Well, when Mac likes someone, he sometimes becomes a pest. He did with me. I had to tell him to let me try to do things that I needed to learn how to do, but he would come over and take things away from me and do them."

Jimmy laughed. "He is funny, Dad. Mr. Mac yelled at me, and then asked me if I heard him. I told him I believed everyone around there heard him."

Tommy laughed, along with those in the filling station. "He may not be that bad with you then, especially since your bird beat his 'Sergeant York.' Maybe you'll be lucky, Jimmy. We'll see."

"Yes, sir,"

"Let me say goodbye to your grandma. Remember I love you."

Soft Feather

"Grandma started to write you a letter when Mr. Miller drove up. I love you, too. Goodbye, Dad." He handed the phone to his grandma.

Alice talked to Tommy as Jimmy went outside and sat down on the bench. Then he jumped up and went back inside. His grandma looked at him. "Tell him we talked to Mom, Grandma. He mentioned her, but I didn't tell him."

She nodded her head, and he went back outside and sat down. The sound of her talking faded away as he thought about all that happened to him. Things were working out. Maybe some day his parents would get back together.

Soft Feather

CHAPTER 16

One day Jimmy and Mr. Miller took their pigeons over to a nearby town. They drove on one of the county dirt roads. It snowed the day before, but melted. The only thing that remained was some large water-puddles, along with some sizable ruts in the road.

They drove by a fairly large lake. A group of people skated back and forth on the lake near the shore. Mr. Miller pulled the truck over to the side of the road, and they watched for a while.

"Maybe we could bring our skates the next time we come this way, Mr. Miller," Jimmy said.

"That's not a bad idea, Jimmy," he said. "I used to come over here to Fisher's Lake and skate a lot when I was younger. I forgot all about this place. I'm glad we came this way."

They sat and watched. Mr. Miller pointed to a guy a few feet from them. "That guy skates real good," he said, "but the girl with him seems to be just learning." Just then a car drove up near the edge of the lake, and a man got out.

He walked over to a group of people who stood near the edge of the lake, and talked to them. Soon everyone skated over to the edge of the lake and took off their skates.

Mr. Miller made a motion towards the man and said, "That's Andy Fisher, Jimmy. He owns the farmland the lake is on. I wonder why they're leaving so fast. He can be kind of grumpy now and then. Especially, when he thinks someone might get hurt. I can't blame him for that."

They watched as people got into their cars and left. Mr. Miller started the truck and drove to the next town. They planned to release their pigeons at two different places today. That way they wouldn't fly back together to

Soft Feather

Mercer. Jimmy brought only Snow White this time. He wanted to see what she could do on her own.

As they rode, they realized they stayed at the lake longer than they should have, and evening was coming on. They came close to the city limits of the small town up ahead and stopped.

There were some houses, and a few people were out in their yards. Mr. Miller and Jimmy got out of the truck and opened the tailgate.

Mr. Miller pulled his pigeon's cage out of the truck bed onto the tailgate. He opened the cage door, reached in and brought out his two pigeons. One at a time, he released them.

He looked at his watch, took his notebook out of his shirt pocket and wrote down the time.

He put it back in his shirt pocket and looked up at the sky. His pigeons circled. Then, suddenly, they headed in the direction of Mercer. As he looked up, Mr. Miller noticed that the clouds looked dark and threatening.

As the birds flew off, there was a cold gust of wind that blew past them out of the north. Mr. Miller looked toward the north and shivered. "It's going to get cold real soon, Jimmy, and I don't like the way those clouds look," he said.

"I tell you what we can do. Let's just drive a little further to the next town, and release Lady Snow White. I know we planned to go further, but I think we need to head for home."

Jimmy agreed, and they quickly climbed back into the truck. They drove through the small town, and on to the city limits of the next town. The wind gusted so bad that the truck swayed back and forth.

Mr. Miller stopped the truck and looked at Jimmy. "Get out and get your pigeon, Jimmy, and put her up here

Soft Feather

in the front seat with us. We're heading home. I hope mine makes it all right."

Jimmy jumped out and ran around the truck and opened the tailgate. He grabbed the cage and closed the tailgate.

He fought the wind and made his way back and placed it on the front seat. He climbed into the truck and struggled with closing the door behind him.

Mr. Miller slowly turned the truck around and headed back down the road towards home. The temperature dropped fast as dust, and large snowflakes blew around them.

He had to stop a few times because he couldn't see the road. Chuck realized that the puddles of water quickly froze, as the road was extremely slippery in places. He put the truck in second gear and slowed down. Snow and dirt now stuck to the windshield. He turned on the windshield wipers, but they just streaked the windshield to the point that he couldn't see to drive.

He stopped again and let enough snow fall that the windshield wipers cleared off the windshield enough to see the road.

They slowly moved along. The shoulder of the road was only seen now and then.

The windshield cleared for a moment, and Mr. Miller saw Mr. Fisher's lake up ahead. They made it back to where they were an hour ago. It was hard to believe the weather changed so quickly and so drastically.

"It's a good thing Mr. Fisher came by when he did and got everyone off the lake," Jimmy said.

Mr. Miller nodded his head in agreement. "Yes," he said. "Andy's a nice person. I'm sure he warned the people that this storm was coming." Just then a large puddle of ice appeared on the road up ahead.

Soft Feather

Before he slowed enough, the front tires were on the ice, and the left tire broke through, causing the truck to spin around. There was a loud scratching noise as the truck slid off the road and into the barbed wire fence stretched alongside the road.

One after another, the strands of barbed wire broke, until only one strand kept the truck from going down the embankment and onto the lake.

"Wow, that was close, Jimmy," Mr. Miller said. The engine still ran, and the truck was in gear. He pushed the clutch pedal in, and the truck slipped a little more. He reached over and grabbed the door handle and opened the door.

Mr. Miller wanted to see what the ground looked like underneath the back tire. But when he leaned over, his foot slipped off the clutch pedal. The truck jumped forward, and the last strand of barbed wire broke.

Over the road embankment the truck lurched. It turned over one complete turn before it landed on its wheels. Both of them were thrown from one side of the front seat to the other.

The door closed when the truck turned over, and Mr. Miller struck his head against the door as it closed. He was knocked unconscious.

When the truck landed on its wheels, it rolled down the rest of the embankment and out onto the lake. The ice under the tires made a loud popping noise like gunfire as it cracked under the weight of the truck.

The cracking slowly stopped, and the truck sat there. There was no movement inside. So far, the ice was thick enough to hold the truck's weight.

Jimmy hit his head on the dashboard, which cut his forehead and broke his nose. His forehead bled a little, but his nose gushed blood. He took his handkerchief out of his

Soft Feather

back pocket, rolled up one corner and stuck it up his right nostril.

He rolled up the far corner and stuck it up his left nostril. It stopped the large flow of blood, but it soon soaked through.

He folded the rest of the handkerchief and pressed it up against his nose with his left hand. He felt a small place get wet, but the pressure he applied stopped the flow of blood.

Jimmy leaned his head against the dashboard and sat still. His head slowly cleared. He sat up and looked around. Lady Snow White's cage was on the floorboard, and she cooed up at him.

She didn't know what happened, but she seemed to want Jimmy to know she was all right. He slowly reached down, picked up her cage, and put it back on the seat.

He opened the glove box and found two rags. He took one of them and wiped the blood from his forehead and out of his right eye. He turned the mirror around so he could see his forehead. There was a fairly large cut above his eyes, and it was bleeding. He put pressure on the cut with the rag. It stopped bleeding. He tied the rag around his forehead.

He reached over and shook Mr. Miller. Slowly, he regained consciousness. Jimmy told him what happened and where they were. When he finally realized where they were, he looked at Jimmy. All he saw was the bloody handkerchief up his nose, the rag around his forehead, and all the blood on his face and clothes.

"Wow!" he said. "I'll get out and see if I can get to the bank, Jimmy. You stay here and don't move."

"Andy Fisher lives in the first house down the road, and I'll go see if he can bring his tractor back and pull us off this ice."

Soft Feather

Mr. Miller opened the door and stepped out onto the running board. There was another loud crack under the truck. His extra weight on that side of the truck caused the left front tire to break through the ice, and the running board dropped out from under his feet.

He fell forward, catching hold of the steering wheel with his right hand. He tried to pull himself back into the truck with one hand while he reached for the door with his other hand. The door flew wide open, and then swung back with a great force and hit him on the shoulder.

The pain caused him to let go with his right hand, and it dropped into the center of the steering wheel. The momentum of his body was now backwards toward Jimmy. Jimmy heard a snap, and Mr. Miller moaned loudly, passing out again.

Jimmy was now really scared. Again, Mr. Miller lay next to him unconscious. Shaking him did not wake him. He didn't know what to do.

The truck now sat at a funny angle with the front left tire in the lake. The undercarriage of the truck had to be sitting on top of the ice. There continued to be all kinds of funny little noises coming from the front of the truck.

Jimmy wondered if anyone would miss them and come looking, but decided they probably wouldn't have any idea where to look. Lady Snow White looked up at him and cooed.

The wind died down, but it was cold and would soon be dark. Lady Snow White cooed again. He knew now, what he would do. He opened the glove compartment and rummaged through it until he found a pencil and some paper.

Jimmy slowly printed a note telling his grandma what happened and where they were. He rolled it up and looked at Lady Snow White. "How am I going to tie this to your leg?" he wondered.

Soft Feather

He looked in the glove compartment again but found nothing. He sat and thought for a few minutes and thought of the bloody rag that was around his forehead. He took it off and tore a small strip.

He took Lady Snow White out of the cage and rolled the note around her leg. He took the strip of cloth and put it around the note on her leg. Then he made a knot, being careful to not tie it so tightly that it would hurt her.

"I want you to go home," he said softly to her. "I want you to go straight home as fast as you can. I know you understand what I'm telling you. You have gone home every time I've sent you."

Jimmy opened the side window slowly and pushed Lady Snow White through the opening. He released her and watched her rise above the truck. She made two large circles, then, flew toward home.

"That's a good girl," he said softly, as he watched her fly off. He rolled the window back up. It was cold in the truck, but colder outside.

Now came the waiting. "How long will it take?" he wondered. "Will Grandma go out and check her when she comes in? She has to. She just has to," he thought. Jimmy stopped and bowed his head.

"Lord, let my grandma go out and check Lady Snow White when she gets there. Please. That's not too much to ask, is it?"

Darkness approached fast. Mr. Miller groaned, and Jimmy reached over and slowly took his arm out of the steering wheel center. He knew that his arm was broken by the way it looked.

He wiped the blood out of his eyes. Gently, he lay him back against the seat and watched his face as the pain came and went.

There were more funny noises up at the front of the truck. Jimmy was going to have to do something soon.

Soft Feather

They might sink into the lake and drown if someone didn't come by to help them.

Jimmy slowly rolled the window down again and stuck his head out. He looked at the ice on his side of the truck. It looked solid to him. He rolled the window back up and turned the door handle. The door creaked open. He put his right foot onto the ice, instead of the running board of the truck, and put his weight on his foot.

The ice was very slippery. Gingerly, he put his other foot on the ice and eased himself out of the truck.

He bent over and got down on his hands and knees. Slowly, he crawled on the ice and headed for the shoreline. He could just barely see it through the blood running into his eyes.

He wiped his eyes with his coat sleeve until his vision cleared.

He crawled toward the shoreline up ahead. It would soon be too dark to do anything. As he neared the shore, he moved faster until he was on the water's edge.

He stood up and stepped off the ice and onto the frozen ground along the shore. It felt good. His handkerchief came out of his nose when he crawled, and he forgot to put the rag back around his head.

He looked back and barely made out the outline of the truck. It still sat at a strange angle with its left front side in the lake. It looked like it had a broken leg.

Jimmy remembered Mr. Miller's broken arm. He turned and staggered toward the road. By the time he reached the road, the blood ran into his eyes and down his face again.

Jimmy wiped his eyes on his coat sleeve again and held it against his head until it stopped bleeding. He looked around too quickly, and his head spun. He wasn't feeling too well. He walked over and leaned up against a fence post to catch his breath.

Soft Feather

He rested for a few minutes, and his head stopped spinning. "Which way did Mr. Miller say the house was?" he wondered.

"Mr. Miller said 'down the road,' but which way is down the road?" he asked himself.

Jimmy looked both ways, and off to his left he saw some lights. He headed toward the lights. Slowly, they came closer and closer, as he got weaker and weaker. Then he stopped and looked around. He stood in the middle of the road in front of the house.

He was dizzy and had a hard time making his legs do what he wanted them to do.

He stumbled down the lane toward the house and fell. He struggled to his feet and trudged on toward the lights ahead of him. When he reached the porch to the house, he tried to step up onto the porch. He didn't step high enough, and he fell flat on his face.

It made a loud noise as he hit the wooden porch with his head. He moaned. His nose bled again.

He lay there and groaned. His head really hurt now, and he slowly rolled over and tried to get up, but couldn't. There was a small pool of blood around his head.

There was the sound of footsteps in the house. Suddenly the front door opened, and light streamed all around him.

Then someone screamed.

Soft Feather

CHAPTER 17

Alice stood at the kitchen window and looked out at the darkening sky. "It's going to get bad," she thought to herself. She hoped Chuck and her grandson were all right. "They should have been home by now," she murmured as she went to another window and looked out.

She went to her chores, but now and then she went back to the window and looked out. Each time she went back to her work, something seemed to draw her back to the window. Something was wrong. She felt it in her bones.

Tom worked late that night, and she was alone. She didn't know what to do. Again, she went to the window and looked down the lane. Someone was coming. She ran to the front door and opened it.

Mary came up the steps. She knocked on the door, then opened it. "Hello," she said."

"Come in, Mary," Alice said.

Mary walked into the kitchen and stopped. Her smile disappeared when she looked at Alice. "What's the matter, Alice?" she asked.

"I don't know, Mary," she said. "Maybe it's nothing. But I have a feeling that something happened. I don't know what it could be. Chuck and Jimmy went off this afternoon to release their pigeons like they've done before.

"I have a feeling inside something went wrong. I don't know what. I just don't feel good about it."

Mary walked over to the table, and they both sat down. "Have the pigeons come back?" Mary asked.

"Jimmy only took Snow White this time," Alice said. "He wanted to see what she could do by herself. I thought something might be wrong with the buzzer, so I went out and checked the pen a while ago. The other three pigeons are in the pen, but no Lady Snow White."

Soft Feather

Mary thought and said,. "Did Mr. Miller take any pigeons with him?"

"Yes, he did," she answered. "He had his two pigeons in a cage in the truck when they left here."

"I'll run over and check with Mrs. Miller," Mary said. "If his pigeons haven't come back, maybe they stopped off somewhere to see someone. Probably stopped somewhere to talk about pigeons. That's all Jimmy talks about nowadays."

"I know what you mean. I listen to him, too, you know. But he loves them, doesn't he?" Alice added.

"Yes, ma'am," Mary said. "Guess I'll have to get some pigeons if I want him to pay any attention to me again."

They both laughed as Mary got up and left. Alice watched as she ran down the lane and up to the highway.

She was tired when she got there, and stopped to catch her breath. It grew colder, and she pulled her coat up around her ears and walked the rest of the way. The Miller farm was outside of Mercer a couple of blocks.

She walked up onto their porch and knocked. Mrs. Miller came to the door. When she saw it was Mary, she asked her to come inside.

"It sure is getting cold out there," Mary said, stepping inside.

"It looks like we're in for a bad storm, Mary," Jackie said. "Come in and sit down. Let me get you something warm."

"I can't stay, Mrs. Miller," Mary said. "Mrs. Warrior is worried about Jimmy, and she sent me over here to check on Mr. Miller's pigeons. She wondered if they came in yet."

"Yes, Mary," Jackie replied, with a smile. "Nothing to worry about. They came in a little while ago. I logged their time in his book when I heard the bell ring. So everything is okay, I guess."

Soft Feather

Mary looked at her and didn't say anything. Then, slowly, she said, "I think we do have something to worry about, Mrs. Miller. Jimmy's pigeon hasn't come in yet."

"Well, I still don't think there's any reason to worry," Jackie answered. "They were going to release the pigeons at different locations today. That way they would know they flew on their own and not as a group. Jimmy's pigeon is probably there by now."

Mary felt better hearing that, then started to open the door and leave, but Jackie stopped her.

"I'll take you back, she said. "I want to see Alice anyway. She has a pattern for a dress that I want. Just wait a minute until I get my things, and we'll go back together. It's too cold for you to be out walking."

Mary agreed that she would rather ride than walk in the cold. Jackie got her things, and they went out to the garage and got into the car. She started it, and they drove over to the Warrior house.

She parked in front, and they jumped out and headed for the front door. Just then they heard a bell ring in the house. Mary knew what it was and turned and ran toward the garage, with Jackie not far behind.

Alice heard a car pull up in front, and car doors slam. Then the bell rang. She rushed to the window and saw Mary and Mrs. Miller head for the pigeon coop.

"I told you his pigeon would probably be here," Jackie said, as she rounded the corner of the garage."

Mary was inside the pen trying to catch Lady Snow White. Jimmy didn't have any trouble catching her, but Mary had problems. Finally, she got her cornered and caught her.

She picked her up and looked at her foot. "I thought I saw something on your leg, Lady Snow White," Mary said.

Soft Feather

She carefully untied the strip of cloth that was around her leg, and threw it to one side. She unwound the rolled up paper, then put Lady Snow White back on the wooden walkway and ran out of the pen.

Jackie latched the door to the pen and ran after her.

She entered the house and hurried into the kitchen where she found Alice and Mary reading the note.

"They've had an accident, Jackie," Alice said, looking up at her. "Chuck has a broken arm, and Jimmy has a broken nose and a cut on his head. The car is sitting on Lake Fisher, and the right front tire has broken through the ice."

Alice looked at the note. Jackie grabbed the note and read it. "Let's go, girls," she said. "We've got to get there before that car goes through the ice. We'll need your dad's tow truck, Mary."

Jackie's words brought Alice out of her shock. She ran and grabbed a coat and cap from the closet and her bag with herbs and salve. "Wait just a minute," Alice said. "I have to leave a note for Tom so he will know where we are if he happens to get home before we do." She wrote a quick message and left it on the table. The three of them ran out of the house and headed for Jackie's car. They jumped in the front seat and drove off.

"Daddy is at home working on his books," Mary said.

They sped over to the Wilsons' house. The car slid to a stop, and they jumped out and ran into the house.

Mary ran into Mr. Wilson's room and told him what happened. Jackie and Alice were right behind her.

Mr. Wilson got up and got his wrecker keys off the hook by the back door. He grabbed a heavy coat, gloves and cap. "Let's go, ladies," he said. "We're wasting time."

They all piled into the front seat of the wrecker and drove off. Mr. Wilson drove slower than usual. He knew

Soft Feather

that time was very important, but he drove a wrecker long enough to know that it was also important to get there safely.

Alice and Jackie took turns asking Bill if he couldn't drive a little faster.

He always came back with the same answer. "We don't want to have an accident, do we?"

They agreed, but they still wanted him to go faster.

Mary was with her daddy before on trips like this, and she didn't say anything. Not because she didn't want him to drive faster, but because she knew he wouldn't.

It quit snowing, but the roads were slick, so he had to go slowly.

As they drove along, the four of them prayed the truck would not fall into the lake. Soon Mr. Wilson turned on his headlights. "It sure is a bad night for anyone to be out," he said, shaking his head. "The temperature is still dropping, and it looks like it might start snowing again."

"The Fisher Lake is on the right, past his house up ahead," Bill said, pointing through the windshield. As they neared the Fisher's house, they noticed that all of their lights were on. Bill slowed down and turned into the driveway and drove down the lane. He stopped in front of the house.

The headlights brought Andy out onto his front porch. He couldn't see who it was, so he hurried down the porch steps and ran over to the truck.

"Oh, I thought you were the doctor," Andy said. Then he stopped and looked closer. "Is that you, Bill? What are you doing out on a night like this?"

"I believe I'm doing the same thing you're doing, Andy," Bill said, opening his door. "Who needs a doctor?"

"A boy came up on the porch a while ago with blood all over him," Andy said. "We heard him as he fell

Soft Feather

and hit the porch. He's in pretty bad shape and hasn't come to yet. We called the doctor, and I thought you were him."

Alice got out of the truck and went into the house as fast as she could go. She knew who it was. She looked around and hurried into the bedroom where they put him on the bed.

She went over to him and placed her hand on his forehead. She looked up as the rest of them came into the room. "He has lost a lot of blood, but he is going to be all right," she said.

"I'll give him some of the herbs I brought. It will take time, but that will help him rebuild his blood supply." She took a deep breath and opened her purse. "My grandson is going to be all right."

A lady came into the room with a hot pan of water and some rags. "This is my wife, Beth," Andy said.

"Where is my husband?" Jackie cried. "Didn't he come in with Jimmy?"

"No one was with him," Andy said.

Alice grabbed Jackie's arm. "Chuck is still out there on the lake, Jackie. You take the men and go get him before he freezes, or that truck sinks through the ice, or both. Go on. Mary and I will take care of Jimmy."

Jackie spun around as if someone slapped her. "Chuck," she said, and ran out the door and into the front yard. She jumped into the truck and yelled at Mr. Wilson. "Let's go! Chuck is still in the truck out on the lake."

Bill told Andy about the pigeon bringing the message. He stopped and looked at Andy.

"I'll get my tractor, Bill, and follow you," Andy said. "You go on ahead and see how things are. If you can pull him out, you do it, but if you can't, I'll be there in a few minutes."

Bill ran out the door and got into his truck. It was pitch-dark now. He backed up, turned around, and headed

Soft Feather

back out the driveway. He drove down the road to the entrance of the lake.

He turned onto the lane that ran over to the lake. He slowed down and drove along until he came up to the edge of the lake.

The lights of Bill's truck now shone across the lake, but they couldn't see Chuck's truck.

Then Jackie pointed. "There he is, Bill." Then, softly, she said, "Please, Lord. Let Chuck be all right."

Bill backed up, turning the steering wheel to the left. The lights moved across the lake until he had the truck in his headlight beams. It was not too far from the edge of the lake. "He's still on top of the ice, Jackie," he said. "He's going to be all right."

"All we have to do now is get him out of his truck."

Bill shifted the truck into low gear and drove up onto the shoreline of the lake. He stopped when he heard the ice begin to crack under the weight of the heavy truck.

"I'm sorry, Jackie. "We'll have to wait until Andy gets here with his tractor," he said, sadly. "My truck is just too heavy."

Off in the distance they heard the popping of a John Deere tractor coming up the road. Soon they saw the headlights as the tractor rolled down the lane and up to the shoreline of the lake where they sat. The tractor rolled on past them and headed for the truck in Mr. Wilson's headlight beams.

Bill and Jackie jumped out of the truck and ran after the tractor. They hoped they were not too late.

They heard the ice crunch under the big wide tires of the tractor as they ran along behind. There was more cracking, but the tractor kept on moving. It was a beautiful sight in Jackie's eyes.

Andy swung the tractor to the left and up the embankment where the truck rolled down. He stopped the

Soft Feather

tractor, then, let it roll back down until it was just on the edge of the ice. Andy jumped off and unwrapped a long rope he'd put on the tractor.

"Here, Bill. You take this end of the rope and tie it onto the bumper of Chuck's truck," he said, and handed the end of the rope to him. "Be careful."

Bill took the end of the rope and headed toward the truck. "Slowly, Bill," Andy yelled. "Slowly. We don't want you and the truck in the lake!"

Bill stopped and gained control of his emotions. He took short steps, as he got nearer and nearer the truck. Suddenly, there was a loud crack, and the front right tire dropped through the ice. Bill froze.

"I'm so close," he thought. "Don't you fall into the lake now." He started to take another step, but his weight caused the ice under his feet to crack. He put his foot down and stopped his forward movement, and the cracking stopped. He retraced his steps back towards the shoreline, and then stopped, and walked back to where Jackie and Andy stood.

She grabbed the rope out of his hand and headed out across the ice. She didn't weigh as much as Bill. When she was about ten feet from the truck, the ice started cracking.

The cracking didn't stop her; she continued until she reached the truck. She quickly tied the rope onto the back bumper and pulled it tight. She made sure it was a good knot.

She turned around and slowly walked back toward the two men. "Okay!" she yelled. "Please hurry, Mr. Fisher."

Andy pulled the slack out of the rope and tied it to the tractor. He climbed up into the tractor seat and put it in low gear. He gave the tractor a little gas and tightened the

Soft Feather

rope. The truck creaked and groaned as the tractor put a strain on the rope.

The big tires started to spin a little on the frozen ground, then bit in the dirt firmly.

Slowly, the truck moved backwards and upwards. Ice broke under the front of the truck as the axle was dragged along.

Oh, so slowly, the truck moved backwards. The ice kept breaking under the front tires, and the front of the truck started to sink. But the tractor wouldn't let go of its catch. One tire finally came up out of the ice, and then the other.

Mr. Fisher knew what he was doing.

Jackie jumped up and down on the shoreline. She could hardly wait until she could get Chuck in her arms. Then she remembered Jimmy wrote in his note that Mr. Miller's arm was broken. She knew that he could go into shock.

She started to panic. "Get him over here quickly," she shouted. "Hurry, Mr. Fisher! Hurry!"

Andy didn't know what caused her to panic now; they rescued him and the truck, but he gave the tractor a little more gas and turned the steering wheel. He drove down the shoreline, and the truck followed.

It wasn't long until he got it where he thought it was safe enough for them to go out to the truck.

He stopped, and Jackie ran over to the truck and opened the door. Chuck sat and smiled weakly at her. "I watched you in the side mirror, when you came out and put the rope on the truck, honey," he said, softly. "Sorry I couldn't help you. Every time I tried to get out of the truck, I'd faint."

"I'm too weak to get out by myself. I'll need your help, honey."

Soft Feather

Jackie looked at Chuck. He was covered with blood from a wide cut along the side of his forehead where he'd hit the steering wheel. His right arm hung limply on the seat beside him.

"Don't you worry about needing help, my love," she said. "You're the bravest man I've ever known. Come on, let me help you out of the truck."

"Don't do that, Jackie," Mr. Fisher, said. "The doctor will be at my place any time now, if he's not there right now. Let's let him look at your husband first. We don't want to do something we'll be sorry for later."

Jackie looked at Chuck. "He's right, Chuck. Just hang in there a little longer, my love."

It wasn't long before two lights came up the road and turned onto the road leading to the lake. Dr. Bixler soon pulled up beside the truck and stopped. He got out and looked at Chuck. He then went around to the other side of the truck and got in. After he checked his arm, he looked up at him and said, "I'm sure you know it's broken, Chuck. I'll have to set it," he said, as he got out and went to his car.

He returned with splints and bandages and got back into the truck. There was a cry of pain, and Chuck passed out again. Dr. Bixler smiled at Jackie.

"I'm sure glad he passed out," he said. "It makes my job a lot easier this way, for him and for me."

Jackie gave a slight smile. She knew he was right, but still she hurt inside for her husband.

Dr. Bixler placed the splint over the break and wrapped it tightly. Then he bandaged Chuck's forehead. Chuck moaned as he lay there, then, slowly opened his eyes.

"He'll be okay now," he said to Jackie. "Let's get him over to the Fisher's farmhouse."

Dr. Bixler got out of the truck, and Bill got in. He tried to start it, but it wouldn't crank. After a couple more

Soft Feather

tries, it started. "Some truck you have here, Chuck," Bill said, laughing. "I'll drive it to Andy's house, and Jackie, you follow in my truck."

Jackie agreed as Bill slowly drove the truck off the lake and up to the road. "It's good to be back on solid ground," he thought.

They helped Chuck out of his truck when they got to the Fisher's house. Jackie drove up and jumped out and helped Chuck go toward the house. Mr. Fisher drove the tractor on past them and into the back yard. Dr. Bixler pulled up and parked behind Bill's truck.

Jackie put her arm around Chuck and gave him a hug. He flinched and gave a slight grin.

They walked into the house and found Jimmy sitting in the front room eating a piece of cherry pie. "What's this?" Mr. Miller whispered, looking at Jimmy. "Where's my cherry pie?"

Jimmy got up and came over to Mr. Miller. "Here," he said. "You can have mine."

Mr. Miller smiled as he looked at him. "No, Jimmy," he said. "I want a whole piece, but thanks, anyway." Everyone laughed.

Beth Fisher came into the room with a large piece of cherry pie on a plate. "Who said they wanted some of my great cherry pie?" she asked, looking at Chuck.

He tried to reach for it with his right hand but couldn't. "Sorry," he said. "I'm so used to using my right hand. I guess I'll just have to get someone to feed me."

He turned and looked at Jackie. "Gladly," she said, "but right now you need to be in bed. I'll feed you when you wake up, my love."

His eyes reflected his pain as they led him into the bedroom. Jackie covered him with quilts, and he was asleep as soon as his head touched the pillow.

Soft Feather

CHAPTER 18

Jimmy and Mr. Miller were the two most pampered people around Mercer, Colorado, for the next week. The only problem was, they were kept apart during that time. Chuck told Jackie that he wanted to go over to the Warrior house the first chance they got.

He heard what happened from everyone except Jimmy, and he wanted to hear it from him.

Even though Chuck's right arm was broken, his left arm was in good shape. The doctor put a cast on his arm, but that didn't slow him down much. He was up and around the next day. Jackie found him out in his workshop puttering around, every spare minute he could find.

She scolded him about it, but soon gave up. She knew he had to be doing something, and it might as well be something constructive. She wondered now and then what he was making, but she knew he'd tell her when he got ready.

When the weekend arrived, he told Jackie he wanted to go over to the Warriors' house and talk to Jimmy. Jackie finally gave in, so they went out and got into their car. Chuck put something he wrapped up on the back seat of the car. He gave his wife a little smile.

She put her hands on her hips and shook her head. She threw her hands up into the air and smiled back. His head was still bandaged, and his right arm was in a sling. Jackie shook her head again at him as she started the car.

Jimmy rested most of the time for a couple of days, but he gave the pigeons their food and water and visited with them some every day. Today wasn't any different from most days. He came in from outside, and Alice asked, "Are they all right?"

Soft Feather

"Yes, ma'am," he replied. "Lady Blue has two new eggs under her. I'm going to separate her and Big Boy. I don't need a big bunch of pigeons right now."

"I agree," Alice said. She looked at Jimmy. "Come here. I want to look at that cut on your head."

Jimmy sat down at the table, and Alice unwrapped the bandage. "It's looking good, Jimmy." She opened a cupboard door and took out some gauze and adhesive tape and scissors. She cut a small piece of gauze and two strips of adhesive tape. Gently, she put the gauze over the cut, then put the tape on each side of the gauze.

"I'm glad that large bandage is finally off, Grandma," Jimmy said.

Jimmy got up and went into the front room. He looked out the window and saw a car pull up out front. "The Millers are here, Grandma," he shouted, as he opened the door.

Alice came into the front room as Chuck and Jackie Miller came up the steps and into the house. Jimmy closed the door and listened. They all seemed to talk at the same time. Tom came out of the bedroom where he was resting.

"What's going on out here?" he asked, looking at everyone. "A working man doesn't have a chance around here to get his needed rest."

They laughed and joked with Tom about his sleeping all day.

They sat down around the kitchen table. It was good to be together like this, especially, after all that happened.

Chuck sat next to Jimmy. He put his hand on his shoulder and looked at him. "I just want to go over everything I've been told and see if that's really what happened, Jimmy," he said.

"Oh," Jimmy said, looking at him. "Go ahead. Tell me everything you remember."

Soft Feather

"Well," he said. "I hadn't thought too much about how everyone got out there to the lake that night, and helped us out like they did. I assumed you'd gone to Andy's house, and he called everyone.

"But then I found out that you put a note on Lady Snow White's leg, and she flew back home. Alice, Mary and my wife just happened to be here when she flew in."

He stopped for a couple of seconds and then continued. "I never thought I'd owe my life to a bird. The way things turned out, I believe I do. I've always loved homing pigeons, but not like I do now. They will always have a special place in my heart, Jimmy."

"I understand," Jimmy said, looking down at the floor. "I knew that Lady Snow White was a special homer. One I could count on when I had to. She's what my dad told me about. He told me, '"Jimmy, the first babies you raise will always be special to you."' I agree, don't you?"

"I sure do, Jimmy," Mr. Miller replied.

Jimmy thought for a moment. "Well, everything happened just like everyone told you it did."

"You know, Mr. Miller, Lady Snow White is so different from her mother in so many ways," Jimmy said, "but so much like her in others. I love Lady Blue for giving me Lady Snow White. It's great to have both of them."

Chuck agreed. He then looked over at Jackie and nodded. Jackie got up and opened the front door. As she started to go out, Alice asked where she was going.

"Oh, I'm just going out to the car, Alice," she said. "I'll be right back. It's too cold out there for me to stay very long."

Jackie went out to the car, and when she returned she had a package under her arm. She went over and gave it to Chuck. "It's even colder than I thought it would be," she said, and shivered.

Soft Feather

"Have you two checked your pigeon's water like Tommy told you to do, since it got real cold?" Tom asked, laughing."

"I checked mine before we came over here," Chuck said.

"I checked mine right before they got here, Grandpa," Jimmy replied.

They all laughed this time. They knew that Chuck and Jimmy would check to make sure their pigeons were in fine shape, before they did anything else.

Mr. Miller laid the package on the cast on his right arm. He looked at Jimmy and said, "I have something for you, Jimmy. It looks like I've made a habit of giving you these things, so I see no need to stop now."

Mr. Miller pulled the paper off and held up a beautiful blue plaque he made for Jimmy. On the plaque was a white pigeon with the words `Soft Feather' across the bottom. He handed it to Jimmy. "Hope you like it, Jimmy."

Jimmy looked at the plaque for a long time. "It looks just like Lady Snow White," he said, not taking his eyes off the plaque. "I like it very much, Mr. Miller."

Jimmy turned to his grandma and handed the plaque to her. Tom came over and looked at it with her. "It's beautiful," he said.

"She's a lot like her mother, you know," Jimmy said. "I thought her mother had the softest feathers I ever felt, but when Lady Snow White feathered out, I held her one day and discovered that she had even softer feathers than her mother."

Mr. Miller looked at Jimmy. "I know what you mean," he said. "But the plaque is also you. Your love for the pigeons Tommy gave you softened your heart. It shows when anyone talks to you these days."

"That's what I call a compliment," Alice said, and looked at Jimmy.

Soft Feather

"Yes, Grandma," Jimmy said. "I know."

Jimmy turned to Mr. Miller. "We both owe a lot to Soft Feather Lady Snow White, don't we, Mr. Miller?"

"We sure do," he replied.

"We, also, owe a lot to someone who kept his head and did the right thing when he had to," Jackie Miller said. That someone is you, Soft Feather Jimmy Warrior."

Everyone agreed, as Jimmy didn't know what to say. Alice walked back into the kitchen. "Anyone around here want some cherry pie?" she asked.

"I do," Jimmy said, laughing. He wasn't at a loss for words when it came to eating his favorite pie.

"Then come and get it, Soft Feather Jimmy Warrior," she said.

They all followed Jimmy into the kitchen and sat down around the table, happy to be together.

Alice put the pie on the table in front of Jimmy. There was a note stuck into the pie on a toothpick. Jimmy pulled the toothpick out of the pie and read the note. He smiled and got up and hugged his grandma. Jackie opened the note so the rest could see what it said.

It read, `Made especially for Jimmy Warrior'.

Jimmy sat back down and looked at the pie, then, at the plaque Mr. Miller gave him. He read the words across the plaque and smiled. "Thanks, Soft Feather Lady Snow White," he said, real low.

There wasn't one crumb of Grandma's pie left when they all said goodnight.

Jimmy took the plaque to his room and set it on top of his dresser. He would have to rearrange all of his plaques tomorrow. He was glad they were not real big ones.

He took a couple of steps towards his desk, then, stopped. There on the desk was the feather holder that his

Soft Feather

grandpa made for him. It held a third feather, a beautiful soft white, with a black tip.

His grandpa honored him again. Tears came to his eyes as he stood and looked at the three feathers. "All I did was what anyone else would do," he thought. That was all he did.

Printed in the United States
113189LV00005B/14/P